PENGUIN BOOKS

The INVINCIBLE SUMMER of JUNIPER JONES

The INVINCIBLE SUMMER of JUNIPER JONES

BY Daven McQueen

PENGUIN BOOKS

To my younger self and all the kids like her, wishing for
books they could see themselves in. This is for you.

PENGUIN BOOKS

UK | USA | Canada | Ireland | Australia
India | New Zealand | South Africa

Penguin Books is part of the Penguin Random House group of companies
whose addresses can be found at global.penguinrandomhouse.com.

www.penguin.co.uk   www.puffin.co.uk   www.ladybird.co.uk

Published in Great Britain by Penguin Books in association
with Wattpad Books, a division of Wattpad Corp., 2020

001

Text copyright © Daven McQueen, 2020

Cover illustration by Chelsea Charles
Typesetting by Sarah Salomon

Wattpad, Wattpad Books, and associated logos are trademarks
and/or registered trademarks of Wattpad Corp.
All rights reserved

wattpad **W**

FSC
www.fsc.org   FSC® C018179   Stewardship Council® certified paper.

Author's Note

The Invincible Summer of Juniper Jones is a story about friendship, family, and growing up. It is also, first and foremost, a story about race. It's a story about the struggle that it was and is to be black in America. And because that is a hard thing, this story deals heavily with racism in the attitudes and languages of certain characters.

In this book, white characters use racial epithets such as *nigger* to refer to black characters; this was not a language choice that I made lightly, but one meant to show the historical (and continuing) use of the word as a slur. If you are not black, please be thoughtful about the harm this language causes when used by non-black people, and use abbreviations like *the n-word* instead.

Sometimes, content like this is kept away from teens and younger readers because it might be hard to handle. It is hard to handle. But even though this book is fiction, anti-blackness is an undeniable reality. These characters have lived it; I've lived it, and maybe you have too. That's why it was important to me to tell this story as honestly as I knew how—in hopes that one person might read it and empathize with someone different from them, and that another might read it and feel seen.

June 2015

As seems to be the custom, bad news comes with the afternoon mail: the news that his granddaughter was rejected from her top-choice college, then a call to jury duty. Today, though, it is much worse. The death of someone he knew many years ago, accompanied by an invitation to the funeral in Ellison, Alabama. When he reads the name, typed in curled script, he knows that he will be attending.

It has been sixty years.

Frozen on the front stoop with the door wide open, Ethan leaves the rest of the mail discarded on the doormat. His fingers, gnarled and spotted with age, shake as they cling to the ornamented piece of paper. Slowly, he stumbles back into the house. He stops when he knocks into the kitchen table but doesn't feel the pain.

A mug tips over and spirals to the floor. The blue porcelain shatters with a sickening series of cracks, sending sharp fragments skidding about Ethan's feet. His wife comes down the stairs.

"Honey?" she calls, appearing in the doorway in her slippers. She sees the mess and *tsk*s quietly, shaking her head as she tiptoes over the pieces and retrieves a brush and dustpan from the cupboard.

"What happened?" She groans with the effort of crouching down. Her hair is pulled into a wrap, but a few stray curls slip out and fall around her face. Ethan watches as she sweeps up the mess, leaving the checkered tiles clean, but he doesn't know where to start. As she tips the dustpan into the trash and returns to his side, he holds out the letter to her without a word.

She takes it from him gently as one thin hand pushes her glasses up her nose. He watches her lips move as they always do when she's reading something to herself; he watches her face change, her lips droop, and her eyes widen as she continues down the page.

"Oh," she murmurs, finishing the letter and letting it drift from her hand and onto the kitchen table. "I see." That is Eleanor—always matter of fact. It's how she has always been. It's how she was, all those years ago, when he first told her about what had happened to him in Ellison, Alabama. But she is compassionate too, and just like that, she is holding him, shielding him from that town thousands of miles away.

When she pulls away, he is surprised to find that her eyes are damp. Ethan touches his own cheek and feels no tears. He is numb.

"I have to go," he says hoarsely. They both stare down at the piece of paper as if it might catch fire at any moment.

"You don't." Eleanor's voice is sharp. "You don't owe that place anything."

Ethan shakes his head. "It's not for them. It's for me."

She places her hands on his arms, squeezing tightly.

When she looks at him, he knows she understands. "Closure," she says, and he nods.

"After all these years."

Eleanor sighs. "Fine. But you don't need to do this alone."

"I know." He squeezes her hand. "And I'm so grateful to you for that. But I think it's better if I do."

Eleanor strokes his cheek. She looks just as beautiful now—gray hair, wrinkles, and all—as she had in college, when he was just a wide-eyed freshman and she was only a sophomore. She had been president of the Black Student Union, and he had fallen in love with her at that very first meeting. Nearly fifty years of marriage and she still challenged him every day—but right now, she takes a step back. She looks at him with a sad, understanding half smile and nods—because she knows what he can handle. And so does he. After everything, this is nothing.

"Okay," she says. "But if you change your mind . . ."

He nods. "I know." He smiles at her and picks up the letter, tucking it into his pocket. He remembers, then, the pile of mail that fell from his fingers, and goes out to pick it up. As he opens the front door and looks out into the summer afternoon, he can't help but think of Ellison.

He never thought he would find himself going back there again, after what happened. Sometimes, when he closes his eyes at night, he still sees them in his mind, taunting, teasing, screaming. From conversations with his cousin, Henry, he knows that things have gotten better, but there's still work to be done. Ethan knows that when he steps back into Ellison, he won't be witnessing a complete transformation. He will be grateful for what has changed, but nevertheless, it will be a painful return.

But it wasn't the town that hurt, not really. That summer

almost sixty years ago was just a blink; one of many summers spent in many towns. It will be painful because of her. The girl who breezed into his life with confidence and wonder, who took one look at him and knew he was the friend she needed. The girl who changed everything. He closes his eyes and, even now, so far removed, he sees her smile.

She had forest-fire hair and hurricane eyes, and when he met her it was as if his world had been set aflame. She hit him in the best way, like a rainstorm after five years of drought, healing the parched earth with a gentle touch; and in the worst way, like an unexpected earthquake, leaving dust and debris in her wake. She was, in equal parts, a gift and a natural disaster.

Her name was Juniper Jones.

June 1955

ONE

The dust here never settled. When Ethan thrust his suitcase onto Aunt Cara's driveway, a lazy cloud of dirt meandered into the humid air and lingered, lapping gently about his ankles. Like everything else in this town, even the ground seemed half immersed in slumber.

Ethan stood still with his thumb on his brow, squinting at the afternoon sun and the white-paneled house below it. His muscles, tight and tired from a long drive spent crunched into the passenger side of his dad's Mercury as his younger twin siblings kicked at his seat, seemed to breathe a sigh of relief. His stomach, on the other hand, was twisting with pent-up adrenaline. He fought the urge to run.

"Give me a hand with this, would you?" Ethan turned to see his dad, knees braced against the bumper, drops of sweat inching down his forehead as he struggled to haul a box of records from the trunk.

"Were these really necessary?" he asked, dropping the box onto the sleepy earth.

Ethan winced, but stepped over his suitcase and lifted the records with ease. He looked down at his dad in annoyance. "You're shipping me off to Nowheresville for three whole months," he reminded him, an edge in his voice. "I need these or I'll go crazy."

His dad exhaled loudly. "If you didn't want to be here, you shouldn't have punched that boy in the face. It's that simple, Ethan."

Ethan felt his face grow hot with rage. It wasn't the first time on this trip or in these past few months that his dad had said something to that effect. In his mind, no amount of explaining could justify Ethan's behavior. Ethan quickly learned that the best response was a deep breath and a change of subject. They stared at each other for a long moment, green eyes meeting brown. Then Ethan let out a sigh.

"Anyway," he muttered, hefting his record collection in his arms. "I'll go ahead and bring this inside, make sure they're home or whatever." No sooner had the words left his lips than the front door was flung open. A woman with blond hair and wide eyes stepped onto the porch with a wave and an unsteady grin. Her stomach made a wide curve beneath her flowy top, revealing the final months of her pregnancy. The baby was due at the end of the summer.

From behind him came a sudden chorus of "*Aunt Cara!*" and then Anthony and Sadie leapt from the car, their tornado legs kicking up a storm of dust. The last time the twins had seen their aunt was nearly seven years ago, when they were still in diapers, but they clung to her legs as if they had missed her all this time. Ethan, who had been eight back then, had all but forgotten her face.

"Hey, hey." Aunt Cara laughed, her eyes softening. Her

voice rolled out in that smooth southern accent that her brother had lost after two decades on the West Coast. She pressed Sadie's mousy hair back from her forehead and detached herself from their grips. "Hey, Andy."

"Cara." Ethan's father had made his way onto the porch and leaned over to pull his sister into an embrace. "Great to see you again."

"Hi, Aunt Cara," Ethan murmured but stayed where he was.

His aunt's smile slipped as she cleared her throat, pausing for too long with her fingers on her stomach before saying, "Come in, come in, and bring all that, Ethan."

The kids immediately dove toward the house, but their father's warning tone reined them back. "Anthony, Sadie, back in the car," he said firmly, pointing to the blue sedan. "I told you we wouldn't be long." They peered up at him with rosy cheeks so like his own, their bottom lips already beginning to tremble. He silenced a chorus of protests with a kind but pointed look, and the twins moped their way back to the driveway.

"Trust me," Ethan muttered as they passed him, "I'd trade places with you in a second." Then he shook his head, repositioned the box, and forced himself onto the front porch.

"Oh, but don't you want to stay for dinner?" Aunt Cara asked. "I made enough casserole for everyone."

"Thanks, but we really shouldn't," his dad replied. "It's a long drive back. Besides, the twins start summer camp in a few days and . . ." He trailed off, a frown coming to his lips as a pickup truck came bouncing down the road, slowing in front of Aunt Cara's driveway before continuing out of sight. Ethan briefly locked eyes with the driver, a man about his dad's age with a scowl on his lips. "Anyway, I want to get back as soon as possible."

Ethan frowned, noting his father's suddenly shifty eyes. Aunt Cara tilted her head.

"If you insist," she said, holding open the screen door. "Go ahead and bring that inside, Ethan." Sticking her head back into the house, she called, "Rob, the Harpers are here! Show Ethan to his room, would you?" A grunt sounded from somewhere inside. Aunt Cara's smile grew painfully wide as she turned to Ethan. "Go on in," she said.

Ethan silently obliged, kicking his sneakers against the doormat before stepping inside. He found himself standing in a small, neat living room with a TV near the window, running a game show on low volume. The powder-blue love seat was empty. He glanced back over his shoulder only to find that his aunt had already vacated the porch and was waddling over to help his dad unload Ethan's record player and luggage.

"Um," he said to the silent room.

"Ethan," muttered a deep, accented voice. A tall man emerged from a doorway to Ethan's left with the Sunday paper in one hand and a glass of beer in the other. He slouched in a casual button-up shirt, the barest beginnings of a potbelly stretching forward over the edge of his pants. There was no expression on his unshaven face and no shine in his blue eyes as he looked his nephew up and down.

"Uncle Robert?" Ethan asked, hesitantly.

"That's me," the man replied. "Come on."

Ethan had never met his uncle. When Aunt Cara had announced her engagement two years prior, only his father had made the trip from Washington to Alabama for the wedding. He was expecting someone at least mildly cheerful—not this grunting, stoic man. Nonetheless, Ethan followed his uncle through a bright kitchen and into a hallway, where a door stood open in front of him.

"Your room," Uncle Robert said, gesturing inside. He disappeared into the kitchen once Ethan was through the doorway.

Lowering the record box carefully onto the carpet, Ethan surveyed the room that would be his until September. It was simple: twin-sized bed, window seat, desk, dresser. Not quite as much space as his room back home, but he figured he could lock himself up with some records for hours on end and survive.

Back in the living room, there were sounds of conversation as his dad greeted Rob. Moments later, the two of them, along with Aunt Cara, appeared in Ethan's doorway. His dad held the turntable in both arms, and Uncle Rob carried the suitcase behind him.

"Hope this is all right," Aunt Cara said, poking her head into the room. "Not too big or anything, but I'll tell you, it's comfy as can be."

"It'll be fine," Ethan and his father assured her in unison.

Ethan took the record player from his dad's quivering arms and set it gently on the desk as Uncle Rob placed his suitcase next to the bed. Aunt Cara surveyed the space with satisfaction. "Now, I know y'all can't stay long," she said, turning to her brother, "but do you want something to drink before you hit the road again? We've got some Cokes in the fridge if you want 'em."

"Well, I might just have to take you up on that." He followed his sister out of the room, leaving Ethan and his uncle alone. For a long moment, they just stood still, neither willing to meet the other's eyes.

Finally, Uncle Robert cleared his throat. "So," he said. "Hear you got in a little trouble back home, got yourself sent down here."

"I don't want to talk about it," Ethan muttered, examining the floor.

"Right. Well, this town's got a history of trouble with . . . with your folk, and we don't want to see any more of that."

Ethan frowned, eyeing his uncle in confusion. "Sorry?"

"All I'm saying is, we expect you to behave. The rest of the folks in town should barely know you're here."

Ethan remembered the sign they'd passed on the way in: ELLISON, ALABAMA. POPULATION 734. From Aunt Cara's driveway, Ethan had had to squint to see the next house, which was about half a mile down the road. Ellison seemed like the kind of town you only stopped in if you were desperately low on gas. He almost scoffed and said, "What folks?" but forced himself to nod instead. "Yes, sir."

Uncle Robert jerked his head in approval. "And another thing." He cleared his throat. "You'll be working for me this summer. Monday through Friday, nine a.m. to one at the malt shop downtown. Earning your keep, and all."

Ethan groaned, the anger in his stomach set suddenly ablaze as he cursed his bad luck, his overreacting father, and stupid, nasty Samuel Hill. Ellison, Alabama, could rot in hell for all he cared; all he wanted was to be back in Arcadia, catching a movie with that cute girl from down the block or running at the park to train for track. Back home, the sun didn't try quite so hard, and when the dust was disturbed, it always found its way back to the ground. He didn't want to spend his summer in Ellison going stir crazy and bussing tables at some job that wouldn't even land him a paycheck. He wanted to run and run and run until the worn soles of his sneakers found their way back home.

But he managed a weary smile and repeated, "Yes, sir."

"Good," Uncle Robert said. There was still something hard about the look in his eyes.

Just then, Aunt Cara stuck her head back in with a smile on her lips and a frosty bottle of Coca Cola in her hand. "Are you boys bonding?" she asked loudly. "That's great. Well, sorry to interrupt, but Ethan, your dad's just about to head out. Here, want a Coke?"

Ethan accepted the fizzing brown drink and followed her out the door. His father was waiting on the porch, clutching his own drink tightly in one fist. He stared at Ethan for a long moment before holding out his free hand.

"Be good, Son," he said. Ethan's eyes begged to go home, but his father kept his troubled gaze firmly fixed on the ground.

Ethan settled for a sigh and a quiet, "Bye, Dad."

As his dad said good-bye to Aunt Cara and Uncle Robert, Ethan set his drink on the porch railing and made his way back to the car, where the twins sat waiting. He said good-bye to Anthony and Sadie, leaning through the open window to wave. They responded distractedly, too absorbed in a fierce game of Crazy Eights in the back seat.

"See you later," he mumbled as he backed away from the car. His dad edged past him on his way to the driver's side. He paused with his hand on the door handle before turning and wrapping Ethan in a stiff hug.

"This is the right decision." The last word curved itself into question. He pulled away and stepped into the car without another word. Starting the engine, he looked up and gave his son a conflicted glance. The look hit Ethan like a jab to the gut. This was the look his dad would give his mom when Ethan misbehaved as a child. Ethan hadn't seen the expression cross his father's face in years, and when he blinked, it was gone. Ethan was left weak kneed on the driveway, blinking against the sun.

His father was already putting the car into gear. The twins scrambled over each other to stick their tanned faces out the window and shriek their good-byes to Aunt Cara. They ignored their brother, who was inching back toward the house.

"See you in September!" Aunt Cara called, and Ethan waved. His father stared ahead, hands tight on the steering wheel, as they rolled out of the driveway and back onto the road. With a rev of the engine, they were gone, and Ethan was struck suddenly by all the days he had to clamber through before they returned. The dust, disturbed by the tires, rose into his mouth and clawed at his eyes. It stayed there, suspended. So did he.

TWO

Ellison was silent at eight o'clock in the morning. Not even the wind could rouse itself to combat the thick summer air. Ethan trailed his uncle down the lane toward downtown. The wide dusty path curved through the trees, jutting off every now and then to reveal a driveway to another little house. Far off in the forest, bugs kept up a constant buzz. Ethan squirmed away from the bulbous flies, feeling like little insect legs were crawling up and down his body. Uncle Robert was unfazed.

It took about fifteen minutes to reach downtown—if the area could really be called that. Back in Arcadia, downtown meant six city blocks, twelve streets, two movie theaters, twenty restaurants, a hotel, and countless stores. In Ellison it was a single intersection, though the road was paved here, at least. There was a general store, a gas station, a mechanic's shop, a post office, two small restaurants that both claimed to have the best burgers in town, and Uncle Robert's malt shop. A little way down the road was the town hall, but according to

Uncle Robert, the mayor had so little to do that the building sat empty most of the year. And that was all. Other amenities had to be brought in from the next town over, about a twenty-minute drive away.

Ethan was horrified.

He kept his head down and watched his sneakers scuff the pavement as he followed Uncle Robert. It wasn't until they reached a small grassy area next to the post office that he finally looked up—and jarred to a halt.

In this clearing, two benches faced each other across a bubbling fountain. Next to one of them was a flagpole, its three flags hanging limp in the absence of wind. On the top, the American flag, its forty-eight stars lost in the folds. Below it, the simple, diagonal red cross of Alabama's state flag. And at the bottom—its edges lifting in a sudden light breeze—was a pattern Ethan had seen only in history books: a red background with a dark blue X across the center that was filled with bright white stars.

Uncle Robert, a few paces ahead, noticed that Ethan was no longer following and glanced over his shoulder in annoyance. "Come on," he snapped, but he paused when he saw the path of Ethan's eyes.

"Uncle Robert," Ethan said, swallowing hard. "Why is that here?"

His uncle straightened, a defensive look coming across his features. "Well, it's an important part of our history. It'd do you well not to disrespect a cultural symbol. Now, come on."

Ethan ducked his head, feeling his cheeks burn. He forced his gaze away from the flagpole and trailed after his uncle, the sweat on his arms feeling suddenly like crawling ants. The realization was forming in the pit of his stomach that this was where his father had grown up—that he had walked these dusty streets, passed beneath that flag probably thousands of times. And still, he had sent him here.

That hot rush of anger, which had subsided overnight, boiled up again in Ethan's chest. He clenched his fists as Uncle Robert stopped in front of a pale-green storefront and pulled a ring of keys out of his pocket.

"Here we are," he said, pushing open the door. Ethan ducked in after him, taking a long, shaky breath. The malt shop, at least, looked like the one he and his friends frequented back home. Ethan saw the black and white checkered floors, the cold metal counter with the red spinning chairs, the jukebox against the wall. A wave of familiarity washed over him, and with it, a tide of homesickness. One day into his summer exile, and he was already nauseated with dread.

Uncle Robert went behind the counter of the small shop and flicked a switch, flooding the place with light. "So, this is it," he said, sweeping a hand to cover the five tables complete with sweetheart chairs, a soda fountain, and the counter. "The Malt. The life of the town."

Ethan scoffed—then realized a moment too late that his uncle was serious. "Cool," he amended, shoving his hands into the pockets of his chinos. Uncle Robert eyed him carefully.

"Nothing fancy here," he went on. "Menu's only got a few items, and since you have the morning shift, you don't need to worry about closing down. You'll be okay?"

"Yes, sir." Ethan nodded. It seemed that conversations with his uncle shrank his vocabulary down to just those two words. He didn't have the voice to mention that back home he had worked at the local Steak 'n Shake for half a year. He wasn't sure if anyone in this town had ever even seen a Steak 'n Shake.

"Listen, I wasn't planning on this." Uncle Robert looked uncomfortable as he ran a hand over his stiff hair. "But your dad didn't want you lazing around all summer, and the boy who worked here last summer, ah—well, he's gone now."

Of course, Ethan thought, seething. As if being sent to this place wasn't enough.

"Anyway," Uncle Robert went on. "Let me give you a tour of the place."

As it turned out, the place wasn't much—just the main shop plus a small kitchen in the back, behind a set of metal doors. Tuesday was burger day, Ethan learned, and the only time the rusting old stove ever got put to use. The rest of the time, sodas and milk shakes were the only items on the list.

"Real variety," Ethan muttered, glancing over the laminated menu. Uncle Robert, thankfully, didn't hear.

Ethan learned how to operate the soda machine—how to blend ice cream into a milk shake the *right* way—and where, exactly, to kick the jukebox in case it stopped in the middle of a song. All of this instruction was given in Uncle Robert's curt tone, and all without a single heartbeat of eye contact. Ethan gave his understanding in halfhearted nods, all the while eagerly awaiting the moment when Uncle Robert would leave, and he would finally be alone.

At a quarter to nine, Uncle Robert completed his tour back in the main area. Ethan looked out of the rectangle of glass on the door and didn't see a single soul on the street.

"Well, then," Uncle Robert said, fixing the collar of his shirt. He coughed into his fist. "Do you understand?"

Ethan nodded. "Yes, sir."

"Are you sure? I don't want any slipups."

Hollowly, Ethan recited the same response.

"Good. Good." Uncle Robert adjusted his pants and

looked at the mirror above the counter, then at the song list next to the jukebox—anywhere but at his nephew. "In that case," Uncle Robert continued. "I'll leave you to it. There's a telephone in the back if there's an emergency. Try not to call."

"Yeah," Ethan mumbled. "No sweat."

Uncle Robert nodded quickly, his receding hairline catching the light. "I'll be back in a few hours," he said, leaving as if he couldn't get out quickly enough.

Once his uncle had disappeared down the lone cross street of downtown, Ethan stood in the center of the malt shop, taking everything in. It was slightly cooler in here than it was outside, but every move Ethan made still felt like he was swimming through the air. It hung; it lingered; it sat on his shoulders and buried his feet in the checkered linoleum. He felt heavier in this place.

Sighing, he forced his leaden feet to march behind the counter, snagging a squeaky vinyl stool on the way. Once he was situated, positioned conveniently behind the cash register, he looked both ways, licked his lips, and lifted up his shirt.

Tucked into the waistband of his pants were the two latest issues of *Strange Suspense Stories*. He had read them about a dozen times each already, of course, but they had been the first of the stack he had smuggled into his suitcase.

Pulling the comics carefully out, Ethan placed them on his lap. He flipped the top one carefully to the first panel, so as not to wrinkle the pages. His uncle probably would not have approved of this, reading comics while on duty. If he noticed, of course. Which he hadn't that morning, when, at the breakfast table, Ethan made it through the first edition of *Outlaw Kid*—twice. He'd absently stirred his oatmeal as his aunt spoke loudly about their neighbor down the road, her voice expanding as if she wanted it to crawl up the walls and nestle into every corner of the woodwork. He wondered if she knew how terrified she sounded.

The minutes ticked by like years, and not a single customer walked through the door. For four hours Ethan read and reread the comics, stared at the wall, and dug some spare change from his pockets to play a few songs on the jukebox. Most of the options were Elvis. He hated Elvis.

By the time one o'clock rolled around, Ethan was thinking that in all his fourteen years of life, he had never been so incredibly bored. "This is such a drag," he announced to no one. He felt energy building up inside of him, trapped between these four white walls, and he had to bite down on the inside of his cheek to keep himself from leaping to his feet and bolting out the door.

Instead, in a grueling display of self-control, he ran a hand over the soft curls of his cropped, dark hair and swiveled back and forth on the stool, knocking his knees against the counter.

Uncle Robert strolled in just past one o'clock, and Ethan heaved a sigh of relief.

"How was it?" he asked as Ethan rushed to shove the comics back up his shirt.

"All right. Empty."

"Usually is, in the morning." Uncle Robert grunted as he circled around the counter, a guttural sound that made Ethan shudder. "Summer, so most kids are sleeping late. They'll be streaming in about half an hour from now."

Ethan frowned. As much as he abhorred the idea of spending his already abysmal summer stuck in a crowded busboy job, he wondered why his uncle wouldn't stick him in the busier shift for the extra hands. "You sure you don't want me to stay through the crowds?" he asked. "I could help out, if you need it."

Uncle Robert paused with his hand on the back door, his head perking up in what seemed to be genuine surprise. "No," he assured Ethan, shaking his head slowly. "That's all right, I can handle it. In fact, you should probably head on home. Cara's got lunch waiting for you, and it'll get cold if you don't hurry."

Relief and confusion mingled in Ethan's mind as he stood, brushing invisible dust from his slacks. "All right," he mumbled awkwardly. "See you back home, Uncle Robert."

From the corner of his eye, Ethan saw the man flinch at the title. He lowered his head and quickened his pace out the door.

Outside, it seemed that the town had finally come alive. Or at least, as alive as was humanly possible in a town with barely more than a few hundred people. Unlike the morning, there were a few people milling about in the streets: two women in floppy sun hats arched out of their seats at the restaurant down the street, their rosy lips in full sprint; across the street, in front of the general store, two little boys turned a jump rope for a little girl in a pink dress; inside, a few slow-moving figures pulled items from sagging wooden shelves.

Ethan met the scorching sun with his face turned skyward, and for a long moment, he simply stood on the sidewalk in front of the malt shop, taking dusty breaths. The skipping rope and scratching feet coaxed up the dirt from somewhere beneath the pavement to coat the skyline gray and brown. With a sharp kick to the concrete and a dry cough, Ethan turned and headed home.

Something strange happened as he paused at the intersection, looked both ways, and crossed the street toward the general store. A man, a woman, and a sweet-faced little boy stepped through the ringing door just as Ethan's feet touched the curb. It seemed as if their necks had been tugged by the same string, three fair-haired marionettes with piercing green eyes that met his gaze head-on. Something electric and frosty passed between them, a chill in the summer heat. The woman moved suddenly, one hand gripping her husband's arm, the other flying to her purse; her son melted into the rustling folds of her dress. The man seemed to grow four inches in fear. He whispered something into his wife's ear, then turned his frigid glare back to Ethan.

"Keep walking, boy," he barked. "There's nothing to see here."

Ethan swallowed hard, sweat breaking out on the back of his neck. He hunched his shoulders, buried his chin in his chest, and took sweeping steps past the family. It wasn't until he had put a store between them that he dared look back. They were in the same place, frozen, all three staring at his receding figure, wishing him away.

Ethan whipped back around, and for the first time, but certainly not the last, he ran through the town of Ellison. His feet pounded the pavement and startled the dust as the family's blank gazes lurched to life and chased him all the way home.

*

That was the first encounter of many. Over the next few days, Ethan's life fell into a routine. Wake up, exchange a few sleepy words with his aunt and uncle, eat breakfast, escape to the malt shop. Sit for four hours reading comics without seeing a single customer, wait for Uncle Robert to come and take his place. Walk home, run home, try to decipher the whispers and the stares.

"—you remember Andrew Harper?"

"What is that boy doing here?"

"That's his son, I heard—"

"—last time one of 'em was here, it was all trouble."

"Married that Negro woman, God knows why."

"—too many colored folks moving into these parts—"

"—doesn't belong in our town."

He caught words here and there as he walked home, arranging and rearranging them in the back of his mind. With each passing day, he was becoming more aware that there was no one here who looked like him. The stares of the people here, their curiosity wrapped in disgust, was familiar in a deep, ugly way. It was as if some part of him had expected it. It reminded him of the way Samuel Hill and those other boys had looked at him after his parents split up, and his mom left town—the same way they had looked at him ever since. Even still, Ethan longed for Arcadia; for his next-door neighbor and the cute girl down the road and the malt shop that was packed with people all day long. He missed walking down the street and getting lost in the crowd, being passed without a second glance. He missed being outside without feeling fear and anger wrestling for control of his emotions, leaving him exhausted and drenched in sweat.

At dinner, he fended off Aunt Cara's attempts at conversation and shoveled food robotically into his mouth. Her voice was still too loud.

*

It was on the second Thursday of June, a few days since he'd first set foot in Ellison, that Ethan Harper first met Juniper Jones. He was polishing the already spotless countertop, his eyes trained on the glossy pages of last month's *Crimefighters* issue, when the bell above the door let out a jingle. It took a moment for his mind, lost in the action, to register the arrival of a customer. By the time he realized that someone had come inside, she was already at the counter and sticking a freckled hand in front of his face.

"Hello," she said, her voice like wind chimes.

Ethan looked up quickly, his mouth hanging open and his arm still reaching out to wipe at an invisible smudge. He dropped his rag, cleared his throat, and stared at the girl who was now sitting calmly on the stool across from him, spinning herself in a slow circle. A volcano of bright orange hair erupted from her head and spilled down her back in loose, messy curls. Beneath the harsh malt shop lights, she was luminescent.

"I—" He licked his lips and tried again. "Hi."

She swung back to face him, a wide, crooked-toothed grin splitting the galaxy of freckles on her cheeks. "Hi, there," she said, extending her hand again. Ethan shook it gently. "My name is Juniper Jones, but you can call me June, Junie, or Starfish. Or Juniper, I guess. Or JJ. But really, I prefer Starfish."

Her accent was just a quiet hint lingering on the edges of her words, and her sky-blue eyes never once strayed from his face. He fought the urge to take a step back.

"By gosh, you're sure quiet." She snorted. "What's your name? Don't make me pry it out of you."

"Uh, I'm Ethan Harper," he mumbled.

"That's it?" Juniper cried. "No nicknames, no exciting alias?"

"I—my middle name is Charlie?" Ethan shook his head. "Listen, Juniper, it's nice to meet you. Can I get you something?"

"Juniper again." She shook her head. "I've been trying to convince someone to call me Starfish. It's catchy, don't you think? Anyway, Ethan Charlie Harper, I'll have a root beer float, please."

"Fifteen cents," Ethan said, but her coins were already sliding across the counter. As he put them in the register, he felt her watching him.

"You're new," she said, slightly frowning as he moved toward the soda fountain. "I don't think I've ever seen you before. And you know, that's pretty rare in Ellison. I probably know everyone in this whole town. We could walk down the street, and I could tell you, 'That's Betty, that's Stu and Laura, those are the Shaefer twins.' Guess you're not from here, huh?"

By the time Juniper finished her speech, Ethan had spent so much energy listening that he could hardly manage a response. He forced himself to nod. "My uncle owns this shop," he murmured. "I'm here for the summer."

"Mr. Shay is *your* uncle? I never would've guessed. Y'all just don't look the same, is all."

Ethan studied the dark skin of his hands but said nothing.

"Not that I mean anything by that, you know," Juniper went on. "Some folks here think everyone should stick to their sides, you know, white folks and colored folks, so of course they were real frosted last year when that school in Topeka got all mixed up again, the way it shoulda been in the first place. Anyway, I thought it was ridiculous that they were so rattled because there isn't a single Negro within twenty miles of this town. And Lord knows if they tried to force that here, half this town would be lined up in front of the school-house to stop it. Whoa, careful there!"

Without realizing it, Ethan had knocked an elbow against Juniper's root beer float, sending dark soda sloshing over the edge of the glass. His eyes had been fixed on her face, and his heart was hammering. The cold stares of the townspeople resurfaced in his memory. He imagined them all lining up in front of the malt shop during his shift, murmuring about how he didn't belong, forcing their way inside, and smothering him with their furious gazes.

"Shoot, sorry." Ethan shook his head to clear the image and reached for the rag.

"No worries." Juniper flashed another smile. "You know, one time when I got a float here —"

Ethan tuned her out as he cleaned up the spill, letting her rattle on uninterrupted. Thoughts of being cornered by the townspeople still lingered in his mind, but Juniper clearly didn't notice. She only paused her chatting to take sips of her drink.

"So, why are you here in Ellison? Is Mr. Shay your only uncle? Are your parents on vacation? Do you like it here? Are you going to stay for the fall? It's real beautiful in the fall."

She watched him with doe-like eyes, grinning expectantly. Ethan sighed. "My dad sent me here for the summer, but I can't wait to split. No offense, Juniper, or Starfish, or whatever, but this place is a killjoy."

Juniper gasped loudly and suddenly, startling Ethan into a stumble. When he righted himself, her hand was slapped across her mouth in disbelief. "Ethan Harper!" she scolded. "Clearly, you have not experienced the wonders Ellison has to offer. It may be small, but it's a real gem if you dig deep enough."

"Gonna take a hell of a lot of digging." He didn't have the heart to tell her that he'd already figured he'd never find anything to like about this place. Not with the way he felt whenever he stepped outside.

"Then it's just your lucky day!" Juniper grinned. "I've been looking for a summer sidekick for Lord knows how long, and, well, here you are."

"Summer sidekick?" Ethan echoed, blinking at her.

"Yes," she said. "I want to have the most fantastic summer ever. The summer to end all summers." She spun slowly in her chair, spreading her hands in front of her face as if conjuring an image in the air. "I want this summer to be—to be invincible. But obviously, you know, I need a little help. Everything is better with a friend. So far I haven't found anyone fit for the job, but you're perfect. You got a bike? No? Well, we'll get you one, you'll definitely need it. My adventures are not for the weak or the bikeless."

Ethan blinked, staring in disbelief at Juniper as she calmly sipped her float, and tried to decide whether this girl was actually being serious. Her smile was disarming and genuine, but what if she was just teasing him? What if this was the next level of those whispers on the sidewalk? After all, no one in their right mind would actually ask to be called Starfish.

"How long are you gonna stare at me like that before you say yes?" Juniper asked, tilting her head. "Boy, you really don't talk much."

"I—" Ethan attempted a response, but his words turned to sludge on his tongue. The surprise, the confusion—the sudden contact with another person after a week of near silence—it was too much to handle.

"Great!" Juniper Jones bounced in her seat, clapping her hands. "Consider us friends, Ethan Charlie Harper. Ethan

Charlie Harper," she repeated to herself. "E-C-H. Ech! Like that sound you make when you try to eat a whole lemon! Have you ever tried to eat a whole lemon? Let me tell you, when they say lemons are sour, they *mean* it."

This time Ethan didn't even bother trying to respond. When Uncle Robert waltzed through the door at two minutes after one, Juniper was still there, swinging her legs against the counter and twirling the straw of her now-empty drink. He smiled at her with a warmth that Ethan hadn't thought the man was capable of.

"Mr. Shay!" Juniper exclaimed. "How are you?"

"Great, Juniper. Glad to see you." He crossed behind the counter with a nod to Ethan and disappeared into the back. Ethan, who had returned to reading his comics as Juniper went on a tirade about the injustice of bug torture, glanced up warily.

"How's your aunt doing, June?" Uncle Robert asked, returning into the main room.

Juniper's grin wavered for a split second before she replied, "Oh, you know. She's all right. Speaking of her" — she squinted at the clock on the wall above Ethan's head — "I'm late for making her lunch! Thank goodness you reminded me." She leapt off the stool, her gangly limbs askew, and smoothed her yellow dress down the front. "Bye, Mr. Shay. Bye, Ethan Charlie Harper. I'll see you soon!"

Her final word became a single-note melody as she swept out the door, a tumbling breeze in the stagnant heat. Ethan stared after her, blinking in confusion. He looked at his uncle, who shrugged as he watched the redhead disappear around the corner of the building.

"What can I tell you?" he said. "That's Juniper Jones."

THREE

It only took a week for the stillness of Aunt Cara's house—punctuated by the radio shows always playing softly in the background—to become oppressive. Ethan spent hours lying on his bed, staring at the ceiling. He played record after record, but soon even Ella Fitzgerald's gentle voice felt like sharp nails on the inside of his skull.

After breakfast on his first Sunday in Ellison, Ethan stood in the center of his room and dreaded the empty day to come. Aunt Cara knocked gently on the door and leaned in.

"Hey, Ethan," she said. "Your uncle and I are heading out to church."

Church, of course—however little Ethan knew about his dad's hometown, he knew how devoutly Christian it was. His dad complained about it occasionally, and now only took the family to Mass on Christmas and Easter. Ethan stared at Aunt Cara blankly, fearing an invitation and yet knowing, somehow, that it wouldn't come.

"You'll be okay here by yourself for an hour?"

Ethan nodded, resisting the urge to groan. As Aunt Cara smiled and edged out of his room, he flopped facedown onto his bed, arms spread wide. A few seconds later, he heard two sets of footsteps walking through the living room, then the front door slammed shut.

Ethan rolled onto his side, staring at the stack of comics on his desk. He'd already gone through all of them at least ten times, and even his favorites had begun to bore him. If this was how he felt after a week, he could hardly imagine the state he'd be in at the end of the summer. His dad would pull up in his Mercury on September 1 to find Ethan catatonic in his tiny twin bed, comic books and records strewn about the room. That would show him, Ethan thought, almost managing a laugh.

After half an hour spent knee deep in self-pity, Ethan finally pushed himself to his feet. "I gotta get out of here," he muttered. So far he'd only been between the malt shop and Aunt Cara's house, but there were other things to see in town—few enough that he could count them on one hand, but things nonetheless. And besides, the general store might even have a comic or two.

Ethan slipped on his shoes and hurried out the front door, making his way down the dusty road toward town. Trees towered on either side of him, branches swaying gently in a breeze Ethan couldn't feel. When he reached the edge of town, he found the main street empty—everyone, he guessed, was at the church service. He felt the tension that always gathered on his shoulders when he was in town dissipate, and he was almost relaxed by the time he pushed open the door of the general store.

The bell tinkled brokenly as he pushed into the shop. Ethan crammed his hands into the pockets of his jeans and tried to duck behind the ceiling-high shelves before he could be noticed, but he had hardly made it across the threshold before a voice called out, "I wondered when I would see you here."

Ethan looked up meekly, swallowing the sudden urge to bolt from the store. Around a shelf of various snacks, he met eyes with a bearded man standing behind the counter. His dark eyes were wide and close set, and his brown hair stuck out in thick waves from the yarmulke pinned to the back of his head. "Sir?" Ethan mumbled.

The man scratched his beard, smiled tightly, and stared at Ethan with a cool gaze. "I've heard all about you," he announced, setting his newspaper on the counter. "If people in this town are good at anything, it's running their mouths. I certainly consider it a privilege to meet the boy who has singlehandedly sent them into an uproar."

Sarcasm dripped from his words like molasses. Ethan nodded and said awkwardly, "I'm Ethan."

"Oh, son—I know." The man laughed. "My name's Abrams, and I'm the only Jew around for miles. In case you were wondering. So we're not so different, you and I, in a place like this."

Ethan felt small under the man's piercing stare, though he towered over Abrams by several inches. While Abrams's gaze was intense, it was not unkind. He had none of the other townspeople's disgust in his eyes—just something that seemed like confusion and perhaps, if Ethan was reading it right, a little bit of sadness. Unnerved, Ethan turned away.

"Well, I welcome you to my store," Abrams said after a moment, sweeping his arm to encompass the small but tightly packed space. "I hope you find what you're looking for."

There was no discernible order to the store, so Ethan wound his way through the aisles, occasionally picking up a box of crackers or can of paint and staring at it for a moment with feigned interest before returning it to the shelf. He was flipping through one of the five outdated and off-brand comics the store had when the bell above the door dinged. Ethan froze, two fingers pinched around a page mid flip.

"—and it's just real tragic," a woman was saying. As she swept into the store, Ethan recognized her as the woman from the family he'd seen on his first day in town. She had a white hat on her head and was dressed in her Sunday best. Ethan dropped the comic and hunched his shoulders, wishing he could dive between the fishing poles and sewing kits and disappear before she could notice him. Thankfully, it seemed she was making a beeline for the other end of the store.

"It really is," another woman agreed, her voice affected and nasal. "That boy shouldn't be in this town."

Horror sank deep into Ethan's gut as he realized they were talking about him. Sweat collected on his upper lip as he glanced around in a panic, searching for a way out. He couldn't let them see him here—he didn't know what he'd do if they did. The door was blocked as more women filed inside.

"If only he wasn't Cara's nephew," another woman inserted. "Then we could get him taken care of just like the last one." She laughed, and though Ethan had ducked behind a row of beans and soup, he could read the smugness on her face. The others murmured their agreement. Ethan slouched down an aisle away from the women, catching a glimpse of Abrams from between the cans. The man was staring at the group of women with dark disdain.

Taking a deep breath, Ethan waited until the women's voices had drifted to the other end of the store, then stepped away from the cans, ready to make a quick getaway. His heart was in his throat as he edged toward the door.

He made it halfway there. Then the first woman said, "Cara, you poor thing," and the familiar voice that responded stopped Ethan in his tracks.

"Yes, well." Aunt Cara laughed nervously, her voice growing closer as they turned into the next aisle over. When Ethan squatted a little bit and squinted through the cereal boxes, he could just see them walking in a colorful huddle. "Some things can't be helped," Aunt Cara continued, her voice artificially bright. Through the gap in the shelves, he saw her wring her hands in front of her stomach.

"Well, it could have," the second woman soothed, wrapping her arm around Aunt Cara's shoulders. "If your brother hadn't"—she tilted her head with a knowing look—"you know."

Another nervous laugh. "Oh, Elizabeth," Aunt Cara murmured, "you know my brother. He was always the reckless one. Even when we were kids. Does it really surprise you?"

"Of course it surprises me," Elizabeth said, shaking her head. "I knew your brother was a troublemaker, but to marry a Negro woman—to bring mixed-breed children into the world—no offense of course, but when he left Ellison, he must have lost his mind."

Aunt Cara said nothing—she didn't have to. Ethan had heard enough. Blood rushed hot through his head and pounded in his ears, turning the rest of their conversation to waves. He had just enough sense to hold his tongue against the anger, to wait until they had walked into another aisle before bolting out the door. He didn't wait to see if the ringing bell had alerted them to his presence. He didn't care. His feet hit the sidewalk and he kept running until his legs had carried him all the way home.

*

Ethan was red faced and panting by the time he made it back to the house. He burst through the front door with a force that shocked Uncle Robert, who was sitting on the couch with a beer in his hand.

"Jesus, Ethan," Uncle Robert said, jumping in his seat.

"Sorry," Ethan muttered. He could barely hear his own voice.

His uncle frowned at him. "Didn't realize you were out. Where did you go?"

"On a run," Ethan snapped, and stalked into his room. Once there, he sat on the bed and tried to dissolve the wall with his gaze. The radio was on in the living room, playing the latest episode of *Our Miss Brooks*. Eve Arden's voice grated today, so he tuned out the sound, sat still, and stared.

He didn't know how long he sat there; it was as if time had stopped moving, becoming an indiscernible cloud. Ethan couldn't think clearly. His eyes, his head, his heart—they pounded together in a painful symphony. He realized that he was still panting. His T-shirt and slacks clung uncomfortably to his sweaty skin, and his hair, beginning to grow out in its tight curls, felt like a burning helmet on top of his head.

Sure, he knew he made Aunt Cara uncomfortable. He could see it every time she looked at him—or rather, all the times she didn't. But this past week, she'd been nice. She filled his plates with heaping portions and always asked how his day was, even though he hadn't once had any interest in telling her. And she was his *aunt*, his blood relative. Didn't that have to count for something?

Apparently not, Ethan thought, remembering the pained smile on her face as her friends had comforted her. She didn't want him here at all.

Aunt Cara came home a few minutes later, or maybe a few hours—he couldn't tell. But at some point, through his fury, he heard the front door creak open, the radio volume go down, and his aunt murmur something to his uncle in a hushed voice. He saw her through his cracked bedroom door, grocery bags in arm, and felt her betrayal like a fist to the stomach.

Sensing his gaze, Aunt Cara turned sharply and met his eyes through the sliver of space between the door and the wall. Ethan shifted his glare to the floor with such intensity that he didn't even hear her approach until she was already at his door.

"Ethan," she pleaded. "Can I come in?"

Ethan nodded tightly, unable to keep his emotions from appearing in the furrow of his brows and set of his jaw. Aunt Cara slipped inside, leaving the door slightly ajar behind her. With one hand on her stomach, she lowered herself onto the desk chair.

"I saw you leaving the general store," she said after a moment, her eyes on the floor. "I suppose—I suppose you heard what the ladies and I were saying."

Ethan nodded again. He opened his mouth, ready to shout, but surprised himself when tears welled up instead. "Do you hate me, Aunt Cara?" he asked, voice wavering. "Does everyone here hate me?"

Aunt Cara's face crumbled as Ethan turned away and swiped angrily at his eyes. She pressed her lips together and stared at the wall for a long moment before replying. When she did, her voice was shaky and almost imperceptible.

"I don't hate you, Ethan," she said. "Of course I don't. But this—this is a complicated place. These are complicated times. The people here don't know what to make of someone like you."

Someone like you. Ethan looked up, meeting his own eyes in the mirror on his closet door. He took it all in: the curls on his head, the brown of his skin, the fullness of his lips, the wideness of his eyes. It seemed impossible that Aunt Cara, with her fair skin and golden hair, could be related to him in any way. He wished, suddenly and vehemently, that she wasn't.

"If you don't hate me," he said slowly, "then why didn't you say anything to them?"

Aunt Cara stared at the floor. "That's complicated too."

Ethan didn't understand what was so complicated about telling those women off; he was no stranger to dealing with bullies. But he didn't press his aunt. Instead, he hunched his shoulders and stared down at his knees. He still felt angry and sad, but tired most of all. Exhausted.

"I don't like it here," he said after a moment. "I don't understand why I have to be here."

"I know, sweetie." Aunt Cara shook her head. "I know. And I'm so sorry. I wish I could make it different for you."

You could have, Ethan thought, *if you'd just told your friends that they were wrong.* He said, "Wishing doesn't change things."

Aunt Cara looked him in the eyes for once, her eyebrows knit. "You're right, I suppose. And I am sorry. For everything you heard. Sad to say, that's just the way it is around here."

Ethan was taken aback by her easy complicity but didn't

voice it. Instead, he shrugged. He didn't speak again until Aunt Cara stood and asked if he'd like a chicken sandwich for lunch. Then he said, "Sure."

As she left the room, Ethan called after her, "Aunt Cara? I'm sorry you're stuck with me."

She looked quickly over her shoulder, her expression so sorrowful that Ethan had to look away. "Oh, sweetie, no," she murmured, fingers rising to her lips. Then she released the door handle, letting it swing quietly shut.

FOUR

True to her word from that first day in the Malt, Juniper Jones did, in fact, see Ethan soon. She strolled into the shop that Monday morning in a flourish of checkered fabric that startled Ethan from his sleepy reverie. He hadn't slept well the night before, tossing and turning as he ran Aunt Cara's words over and over in his head. *That's just the way it is around here.* And yet this, here, was where his dad sent him to learn the consequences of his actions. This, in his father's eyes, was what he deserved.

Shame and fear had weighed heavy on him all night, and now as Juniper approached, he could hardly manage a smile. She didn't notice—she seemingly started talking before she even walked through the door. By the time she reached the counter, she had finished her sentence. She stared expectantly at Ethan.

"Come on, Ethan Charlie Harper," she said, after a second passed without his response. "Don't tell me you've forgotten me already."

This, despite everything, drew a laugh out of him. Ethan already knew that Juniper Jones would be impossible to forget. He shook his head. "You were talking too fast. What'd you ask?"

Juniper sighed theatrically. "I *asked*," she said, "what the special of the day is."

Ethan blinked at her. "Special of the day?"

"Yeah, you know—the hot new flavor, one day only, get it before it's gone." She shaped her voice into that of a radio-commercial broadcaster, throwing out her arms for emphasis.

"We don't really do that here." He pointed up at the menu on the wall behind him. "Those are your options."

He was sure that she, a loyal customer, knew this well. Still, she was unfazed. "Sure you do that here," she insisted. "Look at all these ingredients you've got. You could make the best special of the day the world has ever seen."

"I don't really know how I would—"

Juniper reached across the counter, cutting him off with a hand to his arm. "Try. Please?"

She looked at him so kindly, so imploringly, that Ethan wondered if she saw through his tired gaze, and knew, somehow, what he had heard in the general store the day before. It was this gentleness that compelled him to nod and murmur, "Yeah, sure."

Juniper spun away from him, grinning. "I can't *wait* to see what you come up with," she said.

Ethan turned to the ingredients behind the counter—the ice cream in frozen tubs, the sprinkles and candy toppings, the soda fountain with its sugary flavors. He glanced once at Juniper, who had moved to examine the jukebox, and shook his head.

If he was being honest, this request, while ridiculous, was a welcome distraction. As Ethan added all three flavors of ice cream to the blender and topped it off with a splash of Pepsi, then root beer, then 7 Up, he forgot, for a moment, about everything. He watched the blender churn the ingredients together into a muddy grayish brown and thought about which toppings would best complement this concoction.

Juniper had returned to the counter and now leaned against its metal surface, watching Ethan's progress. She oohed as he poured the float into a tall glass and spooned two, then three more, scoops of rainbow sprinkles on top. He finished it off with a leaning pile of whipped cream that had already begun to spill over the side of the glass by the time he pushed it toward her across the counter.

"It looks," Juniper began, then burst into laughter. Ethan frowned as she leaned close to the drink, squinting at a cluster of sprinkles.

"It'll taste better than it looks," he muttered.

"We'll see about that." Ignoring the straw that Ethan handed her across the counter, Juniper perched in one of the spinning seats and lifted the glass to her lips with both hands. Whipped cream spilled across her nose as she took a long, loud gulp.

Ethan watched as she set the glass back down on the counter, licking her lips. She nodded thoughtfully for a moment, then turned to him and said, "Ethan Charlie Harper, I've gotta say—that is absolutely disgusting." But even as she pushed the drink back across the counter, she was smiling.

"It can't be that bad."

"Really? Try it, I dare you."

Rolling his eyes, Ethan stabbed a straw into the drink and took a big gulp—too big, he realized almost instantly, because as soon as the drink touched his tongue, he couldn't help but spit it back out, straight onto the counter. Juniper leaned away from the splatter, cackling.

"What did I tell you!" she cried.

"Yeah, well"—Ethan wrinkled his nose—"at least I don't have whipped cream all over my face."

And Juniper did have whipped cream all over her face: on her cheeks, across her nose, and somehow on her forehead. As she squinted at the countertop, trying to see her reflection in the polished metal, Ethan smirked and passed her a handful of napkins.

"Thanks," she said, scrubbing her face clean. Ethan watched as she balled up the damp napkins, amazed by how, even in her gracelessness, she moved with such confidence. He was suddenly aware of how small this town made him feel, so tightly wound, and so he straightened his shoulders.

"I think I'll just have a root beer float." Juniper pushed a quarter across the counter, her eyes bright with laughter.

"That I can handle," Ethan said.

Juniper chatted to him as he made the drink, telling him about her weekend—how she'd tried to read an old book from her aunt's library, but it was so dusty she couldn't stop sneezing. Somehow, with her waving hands and impassioned drawl, she made the most mundane incident into a spectacular story. Ethan found himself transfixed even as he scooped ice cream into her float.

"And what about you?" she asked as he replaced his botched daily special with the new glass. She had concluded her tale by explaining how she had thrown the book across the room and nearly broke a vase that had been passed down from her grandmother. "How was your weekend?"

Ethan was caught off guard, blinking at her for a moment

before answering. "Fine." He wiped away the milk shake he'd spat out onto the counter.

Juniper took a long, loud slurp of her float, and Ethan could feel her eyeing him carefully. "Fine?"

"Fine."

She was silent for a moment as Ethan moved to wipe another part of the counter, then said, "And what's the real answer?" Ethan looked up. Juniper sat with both hands on the glass, the condensation making her palms damp, and gazed at him seriously. "I'm good at a bunch of things, Ethan, and one of them is knowing when people are trying to bamboozle me. So 'fess up, what happened this weekend?"

Since the day before, Ethan hadn't felt like thinking, much less talking, about the incident. But something in Juniper's face, wide eyed and kind, made him feel like he had to say something. In fact, her stare made him feel like he could say anything.

"My aunt," he began, "said some things." He recounted the whole story, still running the cloth back and forth across the counter. Juniper listened quietly, her float melting beside her, untouched.

"It doesn't really matter," Ethan finished. "Anyway, nothing I can do about it."

Juniper reached across the counter to put a hand on Ethan's arm, coaxing his gaze up to her face. "Sure it matters," she said. "It made you sad." When Ethan said nothing, she went on, "I'm sorry it happened. People *are* like that— I've seen it around this town before—but that doesn't make it right."

Ethan shrugged. Juniper studied him for a moment, her nose wrinkled in concern. Under the malt shop lights she was bursting with color, too bright for this little room and,

Ethan thought, for this whole town. He wondered, as he had since meeting her, how she'd managed to turn out so different from everyone else he'd met in Ellison, and why, of all people, she saw a friend in him.

"Hey," Juniper said, brightening suddenly. "I think I know something that'll cheer you up."

"You really don't have to do that, I'm—"

She held up a hand, leaning across the counter. She said, "I want to tell you about my invincible summer."

Ethan remembered the words she'd gushed at him when they first met, about having the perfect summer with him as her sidekick, about the adventures they'd have. She was smiling at him now, wide eyed. Ethan shrugged.

"Go for it," he said.

She took a deep breath. "Summer is my favorite season," she began. "It's when school is out and the sunflowers are high and the lake is good for boating. There's so much to do in Ellison that you wouldn't even guess, especially when it's so beautiful out. For all my fourteen-almost-fifteen years of life, I've wanted to spend a summer exploring it all with someone. But the thing is, I've never really had any friends here, except Gus the dock manager, who is old and has a bad knee. And he's great, but I've always wanted a friend my own age.

"I love this town. I love it with every little bit of me. But people here aren't always so kind. I guess you've noticed." She smiled ruefully. "When I first saw you here the other day, well, I thought the town probably wouldn't be so nice to you. And they aren't so nice to me either. Folks around here think I'm weird. So I figured, you know, it never hurts to have a friend when things are hard. And there's nothing like an adventure to take your mind off all the bad stuff."

She studied her drink. "Anyway," she said, her voice softer now. "I just wanted you to know that you have someone here on your side. If you want it."

For a long moment, Ethan didn't respond; he simply stared at Juniper Jones with something akin to wonder. She was right: it never hurt to have a friend. In fact, after everything that had happened since he'd arrived in Ellison, a friend felt like an incredible relief. He looked at her in the spinning chair, cheeks flushed and smile small, and saw an earnestness in her eyes that was almost overwhelming. Even if he couldn't understand why or how, Juniper meant what she'd said.

Ethan smiled, shyly. "I think that would be nice," he said.

"Do you really?" Juniper beamed. "That's great news. Well, we'll have to start right away, of course. I have *so* much to show you. We'll have to make a list of all my ideas—oh, and your ideas too, if you have any, but I figured you wouldn't since you're new here. This is going to be wonderful, Ethan, absolutely wonderful." She grabbed her float and took a hearty gulp. "Come on, what are you waiting for?"

Ethan laughed as she leapt from her chair and stumbled gracelessly into a table. He pointed to his apron. "Still on shift, remember?"

"Oh." Juniper righted herself, smoothing out the front of her gingham skirt. "Fair point. Well, that doesn't mean I can't start brainstorming." She came back to the counter and reached for her float, finishing it in one long swig.

"Impressive," Ethan said, raising an eyebrow.

"I know." She slid the glass back across the counter, and Ethan caught it before it tumbled off the edge. "Well, then," Juniper said. "I'll start thinking, and I'll see you soon for day one. Deal?"

When Juniper grinned, it seemed as if rays of sunlight were escaping from between her teeth. She held out her hand and shook Ethan's with gusto. He smiled, feeling in the curve of his lips the thrill of starting over.

"Deal."

FIVE

For the next several days, Ethan ignored Aunt Cara as best he could. She tried to push past it at first, giving him extra servings of food at every meal and trying to make conversation with him about his records.

"I like Louis Armstrong too," she told him at one point. "Great on the trumpet."

"Cool," Ethan replied, all the while wondering what made Louis Armstrong, with the brown skin of his cheeks puffed out as he blew into his trumpet, easier to handle' than her own nephew.

He tried to focus, instead, on Juniper Jones. Every day at the malt shop he waited in the morning silence, looking up at every sound as if she might come bursting through the door. When Aunt Cara spoke to him and he didn't respond, it was in part because of his lingering anger but just as much because of his growing excitement for the adventures that lay ahead.

After a few days of one-word responses and uninterested

stares from Ethan, Aunt Cara eased back. And by then, Ethan's anger had begun to subside. It was exhausting, he realized, to put energy into hating his aunt on top of everyone else in this town. He only had so much to go around. So he eased back too, allowing their relationship to return to civility.

If Uncle Robert noticed the tension turned truce, he didn't mention it. At the end of the week he showed up at the Malt to relieve Ethan from work with an uncomfortable look on his face. After a moment, he cleared his throat. Ethan, who had been watching the door for any sign of Juniper, jumped at the sight of his uncle.

"So," Uncle Robert said, coming around the counter to join Ethan, "Cara told me what happened. At the store."

"I don't want to talk about it."

"She didn't mean anything by it. Those women are nasty gossips. What Cara said—it's just about keeping up appearances."

This didn't satisfy Ethan, but he was tired of thinking about the incident. So as Uncle Robert looked at him imploringly, Ethan just nodded. Then, with an awkward frown, Uncle Robert reached into his wallet and pulled out two stained, wrinkled dollar bills.

"Here," he said, thrusting the bills in Ethan's direction. In the cramped quarters behind the counter, he couldn't do much but gingerly take the money from his uncle's grip. "Just, you know," Uncle Robert went on. "To apologize. I see you reading those comics all the time. Maybe you could get some more."

The older man looked so uncomfortable that Ethan softened. "All right, Uncle Robert," he said. He took off his apron and hung it on the peg next to the blender. "Thanks. I'll see you."

It took a long moment of standing at the threshold before Ethan was able to coax himself into the general store. When the bell rang and the door closed behind him, Abrams looked up from the counter in surprise.

"Cara's nephew," he said. "Didn't think I'd see you here again, after last time."

Ethan shrugged. "Yeah, well."

Thankfully, Abrams didn't pry any further as Ethan wandered the aisles—and thankfully, the store really was empty this time. No one else came in as Ethan pulled his items from the shelves, though he still felt tense as he approached the register.

"Quite the meal," Abrams noted with a smirk as he rang up the items: a bag of chips, a box of Oreos, and a bottle of Coke, still frosty from the cooler. "And quite the read." He nodded his approval at Ethan's choice of a *Captain America* comic.

"All right, son, that will be one dollar and sixty-four cents." Abrams stuck the bills that Ethan handed him into the drawer and passed back a quarter, a dime, a penny, and a paper bag of his items.

"Thank you." Ethan nodded at the man, happy to be making it out of the store unscathed. "Have a nice day."

"And you as well," Abrams replied. He waited until Ethan's hand was on the door before adding, "Glad to have you in the store, of course. But for your own sake, I'd try to avoid this place if you can."

"Right," Ethan said. He wasn't planning to frequent the six-aisle general store. "Thanks for the tip."

Outside, the humidity was stifling. Ethan felt sweat seeping into the handle of the bag as it swung in his grip.

Dust stormed around his ankles in small tornadoes, and he coughed when the occasional stray speck tickled his nose. As usual, the dirty clouds remained unsettled.

The sun was relentless, but when he made it out of town, the trees provided some relief. The leaves left crisscrossed shadows on the road, and somewhere in the distance birds called back and forth. Perhaps for the first time since arriving in Ellison, Ethan felt his muscles relax. In moments like this, just him and the trees, he could almost forget where he was.

He was about halfway back to Aunt Cara's house, lost in thought, when he heard the sudden rustle of branches and nearly jumped out of his skin. A moment later, three kids who were a little older than him emerged from one of the forest paths. The girl, a brunet, lifted her skirt to step over a bush. She linked arms with one of the boys, a tall, stocky blond. The other boy was dark haired and lanky, and he followed the couple with crossed arms and a sharklike grin.

They were evidently in the middle of a conversation, but when they noticed Ethan standing quite conspicuously in the center of the road, they all halted in their tracks. Surprise crossed their faces, but almost immediately, the blond boy's lips twisted into a sharp leer.

"Well, would you look who it is," he drawled, dropping the girl's arm. "The new kid. I've heard about you."

Ethan's feet itched to sprint away, but he held his ground, gripping the bag tighter in his hand. The boy came closer and looked Ethan up and down. "Anyone ever tell you we don't like your kind coming round here? Alex, look at this kid." He beckoned to the other boy, who sauntered over with that predatory smile. Only the girl stood off to the side, staring pointedly away from Ethan, her arms crossed over her chest.

"Hey, blackie," the blond boy jeered, leaning in toward

Ethan's face. "Why aren't you saying anything, huh? You scared?"

Ethan swallowed but did not respond. "He's terrified!" Alex shrieked, and rammed his shoulder into Ethan's. Shocked, Ethan stumbled back, his heart beating relentlessly against the butterfly bones of his rib cage. He couldn't respond now even if he wanted to; his anger had stunned him to silence.

When he didn't react, the blond boy's face seemed to catch on fire, his cheeks turning red and his eyes flashing. "Say something," he ordered, shoving both of Ethan's shoulders with the heels of his hands. "Come on!"

Ethan gritted his teeth. His free hand was a fist at his side, but he thought of Samuel Hill and took a deep breath. He couldn't lose his cool. Especially not here.

"All right," the blond said. "All right. Seems like you don't care about anything, so I guess it won't rattle your cage if I, say, do this." His arm shot out, ripping the bag from its handles and out of Ethan's grip.

"What do we have here?" He pulled out the Oreos as Alex looked on, snickering. "Babe, you want this?" He didn't wait for the girl to respond before tossing the box over his shoulder. She had to dive forward to catch it before it hit the ground. Ethan glared at her, but she cradled the cookies to her chest with an almost helpless shrug.

Next, the boy's hand found the potato chips, which he looked at for a long moment before dropping them unceremoniously to the ground and planting his boot in the center of the bag. It exploded, letting out a loud pop and sending shards of chips scattering across the dirt.

Ethan couldn't help it as he cried out, "Hey!" and reached an arm uselessly toward the ground.

"He speaks!" the blond cried, pulling out the bottle of

Coke and handing it to Alex. Alex somehow managed to remove the sealed cap with a gnash of his teeth. He spat it onto the ground and took a long swig.

Finally, the boy pulled out the comic and tossed the empty bag behind him. "*Captain America*, huh?" He nodded slowly. "Yeah, all right. I'll take that." He folded the comic down the middle and shoved it into his back pocket.

Fury clouded Ethan's vision until the three kids were just a blur in front of him. He thought—wished—that molten lava might stream from his ears and pour down his shoulders and onto the road to consume his tormentors.

"Give that back," he said, barely hearing his own voice.

"What's that?" one of them taunted. "What do you want, blackie?"

"Give that back," Ethan repeated, taking a step toward them. The boys, clearly unbothered, laughed.

"Give that back!" Alex taunted, the Coke sloshing onto his hand.

That was it—Ethan couldn't let this slide. He made a fist so tight that his nails dug into his palm and pulled back his arm. It was then that a pair of tires squealed to a stop just a few feet from where Ethan stood. When the dust cleared, he saw Juniper Jones, her fiery head framed by the midmorning sun and a hard frown on her thin lips.

"What's going on here?" she demanded, stepping off her bike and letting it fall to the ground. "Ethan?" She looked at him with his fist pulled back, then back at the others. "Noah O'Neil, what is this?"

"Well, if it isn't Little Miss Juniper Jones," the blond boy, Noah, replied. "Or should I say *Starfish*."

Alex barked a laugh. The girl, still holding the Oreos, had backed up almost to the tree line.

Juniper crossed her arms over her chest, but her voice remained surprisingly calm. "Don't be like that, Noah. Come on. Give Ethan back his stuff."

"Hm." Noah pretended to think for a moment, rubbing his chin theatrically. "I'm gonna go with . . . no. And of course you're buddies with the Negro. You make a perfect pair: two people who shoulda never been born."

Juniper blinked as though she'd been slapped. "Hey," Ethan said roughly. "Keep the stuff. Whatever. I don't need it. But get the hell away from us."

Something in Ethan's tone must have conveyed his seriousness, because Noah glanced at Alex and the girl. "Whatever," he snapped. "They aren't worth it anyway. See you around, blackie. And *Starfish*. Come on, Courtney." He grabbed the girl roughly by the arm and seemed not to notice when she stumbled into his side. He pulled her after him as Alex trotted behind.

"And by the way," Noah added, stopping inches away from Ethan. "I heard about why you were sent down here. What you did to that boy. And maybe up where you're from folks just get a little mad, but down here we handle things differently." He smiled darkly, making sure to graze Ethan's shoulder with his own as he pushed past.

Ethan took in a shaky breath, only exhaling when Juniper said, "They're gone." Then he let his shoulders slump, letting himself feel not just anger but also the fear that pulsed beneath it. In Noah O'Neil's eyes he hadn't seen a shred of compassion. He felt cold thinking about what those boys might have tried if Juniper hadn't pulled up just then.

Juniper approached him now, standing a few feet away with her hands wrung together, looking lost. When Ethan turned to her, she forced a wan smile.

"You okay, Ethan Charlie Harper?" she asked.

Ethan licked his lips and mumbled, "Yeah, I guess. Thanks."

"Sure thing. And I'm sorry about them." She jerked a thumb over her shoulder. "Those guys talk big, but really they're just big dummies. They're just saying what they hear other people say."

"I don't know." Ethan shrugged. "Sure seems like they believed it." To this Juniper said nothing. "Anyway, it's good to see you," he said, and meant it. "And not just 'cause you distracted those jerks."

"Good to see you too," she said. After a pause, she asked, "And hey, what was Noah saying just then? About why you were sent here? Guess you haven't told me that yet."

Ethan could hear the strain in her voice, lingering just behind her usual brightness. He couldn't look at her.

"I got in a fight," he said tightly. "With a boy at school. Broke his nose. My dad was real mad."

Juniper laughed suddenly. "Is that all? Well, boys get into fights all the time. Noah's been in his fair share."

Ethan said nothing, remembering the feeling of Samuel Hill's nose under his fist—and of his cruel words just moments before. The memory froze his tongue, and he could only nod. Juniper, unfazed, smiled brightly again.

"Well, anyway, don't think I forgot about our adventure, Ethan Charlie Harper! Just you wait, I'll fix everything. There's a lot more to this town than Noah O'Neil, and I'll prove it." Her energy renewed, she lifted her bike from the ground and climbed onto the seat with a small grin, her skirt draping over the frame. "I have to go make lunch for my aunt, but I'll see you soon, okay?"

She pedaled off in a cloud of dust, but somehow, it settled

in her wake. Ethan watched her go, and just before she disappeared around the bend, he murmured, "See ya, Starfish."

Then he took a deep breath and trudged on down the path toward home, leaving a pile of crushed potato chips in the dust behind him.

SIX

Ethan had never liked NBC's nightly newscast. John Cameron Swayze had a funny way of talking where he pursed his lips but never properly opened his mouth and ended up sounding incurably congested. He'd always sort of reminded Ethan of an unhappy fish. Back home, his family always watched *See It Now* on CBS, even though Edward R. Murrow's ratings had been dropping since '54. The Harper household was very anti-Swayze.

Uncle Robert, on the other hand, was NBC's biggest fan. He reclined on the couch every evening with a pack of Camel cigarettes and smiled in self-satisfaction as the logo flashed on the screen and the white letters spelling out *Camel News Caravan* switched to John Cameron Swayze's fishy face. Ethan and Aunt Cara would sit dutifully in the living room, each staring at different points on the wall and pretending to care about the monotonous news report as cigarette smoke strutted boisterously about the room and invaded their noses and eyes.

After dinner at the beginning of Ethan's third week in Ellison, the three eased into their seats and watched the broadcast begin. The prerecorded intro came on as usual, reminding households across the nation to sit back, relax, and watch the news that had unfolded over the past day. Uncle Robert muttered the show's tagline in time with the recording, a cigarette tucked into the corner of his mouth. He rearranged himself in his chair.

The image on the screen became one of Swayze leaning against his desk with a map of the world as his backdrop. *"Ladies and gentlemen, good evening to you,"* he began in his nasally voice. Ethan suppressed a groan. *"Controversy has risen in the city of Montgomery, Alabama, after a fifteen-year-old Negro schoolgirl from Hope Hull was arrested this afternoon on the Q7 bus route. The Negro girl refused to give up her seat for a white woman, becoming hostile when asked by the driver. This story is reported for us now by David Brinkley, NBC News, Montgomery."*

Ethan frowned, leaning forward in his seat as Brinkley, the other, less frequently aired anchor of *Camel News Caravan*, appeared on the screen. He opened with a short greeting, then the picture cut to a slightly blurry school photograph of a smiling, dark-skinned girl. Footage of Montgomery buses rolled across the screen, and Brinkley spoke.

"In Montgomery, colored passengers must sit at the back of the vehicle, leaving the front seats open for white passengers. Today, a child defied this law. When asked by the driver to relinquish her seat to a white woman who had just boarded, she refused, insisting that the woman could stand. Law enforcement was called to the scene, and the girl was taken into custody."

Swayze returned, his lips pursed. *"This incident follows in the wake of the Supreme Court decision in the Brown v. Board of Education case last year . . ."*

Ethan had stopped listening, gripped by another image of the girl on the screen, this one of her in handcuffs. She was dwarfed by the heavyset white policeman as he pulled her toward the squad car, but her eyes were narrow, defiant. She stared directly into the camera with a resolve that seemed too expansive for her small frame.

Colored passengers must sit at the back of the vehicle. Brinkley's words spiraled through Ethan's mind. He thought of Arcadia, where no one would think twice about where he sat, and imagined a bus split cleanly in half by a color line. And Montgomery wasn't far away—how easily could it have been him instead of this girl, his same age, with skin not so different from his own?

As Ethan gaped at the screen, Aunt Cara cleared her throat. "Robert," she said, "maybe we could watch something else."

At this, Ethan tuned back into the program just in time to see the Montgomery police chief appear on the screen. But before the officer could speak, Uncle Robert had pushed himself out of his seat and turned the dial to another channel. Now it was on CBS, where Murrow was conducting an interview with Groucho Marx. Usually, the *Person to Person* program was Ethan's favorite; tonight, for once, he just wanted Swayze to come back on and tell him more.

"Uncle Robert," he ventured, "would you change it back?"

"Quiet," his uncle snapped. "I'm listening." He stared at the set so hard that sweat broke out on his forehead. His cigarette laid forgotten in an ashtray on the coffee table.

*

The sky was falling.

At least, that's how it sounded. Something was exploding outside Ethan's window like a million tiny shards of broken glass crashing against the pavement. He rolled over in bed with a groan, pulling a pillow over his face.

"Go away!" he growled.

The thundering stopped for a moment, as if considering his command. When it started up again, it was accompanied by a wind-chime voice.

"Wake up, Ethan Charlie Harper! It's Saturday morning, so I *know* you don't have work. Our invincible summer isn't gonna wait!"

Ethan opened one eye at a time and drew the pillow under his chin. He knew who would be standing outside his window, grinning a grin of lopsided pearly whites. Still, when he gathered the strength to turn over onto his side, the sight of Juniper Jones, her freckled nose pressed against the glass, gave him a start.

"Are you awake?" she asked, her voice muffled. "Come on, hurry!"

Squinting against the morning sunlight, Ethan stretched an arm toward the window. When he opened it, Juniper stuck her head through immediately. "Come on, Ethan! Come on, come on, come on!"

"Juniper, what are you doing outside my window at seven o'clock in the morning?"

She rolled her eyes. "I said I'd see you soon, remember? For our first adventure? So would you *please* hurry up?"

"Some warning would have been nice." Ethan yawned. "I'm still in my pajamas, so can you cool it for a minute while I go get dressed?"

Juniper blew out an exaggerated sigh. "Fi-*ine*," she grumbled, leaning dutifully against the windowsill.

Ethan ruffled through the closet for a T-shirt and a pair of jeans as Juniper began to sing to herself outside. He could still hear her—"*Someone's in the kitchen with Di-NAH!*"—when he stepped into the pink-tiled bathroom and closed the door behind him. There, he dressed quickly and splashed water on his face, then stared into the mirror as he smoothed back his hair with one hand.

He was really doing this, it seemed—going on an adventure with Juniper Jones. He was skeptical, even a little suspicious, but at least on the surface she seemed to be friendly. If she was like the others in town, he doubted she could have hidden it so well.

When he figured he had left Juniper waiting long enough, Ethan returned to his room with his pajamas rolled under his arm. He opened the door slowly and nearly fell to the floor in surprise—Juniper Jones had climbed through his window and was now lying on his unmade bed as if she owned it, her nose buried in a recent issue of *Adventure Comics*.

"There you are!" she cried when he stepped inside, sitting up and tossing the comic onto the bedside table. "I was worried you'd drowned in the toilet."

Ethan rolled his eyes. "Keep it down, wouldya? My aunt and uncle are still asleep, and I don't think they'd be too cool with finding a girl in my bed."

Juniper blinked innocently. "Why not?"

"Because—are you really—never mind."

"*O*-kay, Ethan," Juniper said, getting to her feet. Today, she had traded her usual skirt for a cuffed pair of jeans, and the colorful plaid print of her collared blouse matched the ribbon that was looped through her ponytail. As Ethan dropped his pajamas on the foot of his bed, she held out her hand.

"Come on, city boy," she teased, tugging him toward the

window. "I'm gonna show you just how great this town can be."

✳

Juniper had parked her baby-blue bike a little ways down a path behind Aunt Cara's house that Ethan hadn't even known existed. "There are forest paths all over town," Juniper explained as they walked. "We're outdoorsy folk, here in Ellison."

Her bike was leaned against a tree, a picnic basket swinging from its handlebars. She righted it, then bit her lip and studied Ethan through squinted eyes.

"Well, seeing as you don't have a bike, you can just stand on my pegs. The ride's not too far."

Ethan eyed the metal pegs skeptically. "Where are we going, anyway?"

"The lake," was all she said, her smile furtive.

Right. His dad had told him stories about growing up on the lake, swimming and fishing and boating in the summer months, and trying unsuccessfully to ice skate after the odd winter snowstorm, but since arriving in Ellison, no one had so much as mentioned it to him. He'd begun to wonder if it had just dried up years ago.

"This path loops around through the trees and ends up by the water," Juniper was saying, mounting the bike and placing one foot against a pedal. "Come on, Ethan. Hop on."

Frowning dubiously, Ethan stepped forward and placed one foot, then the other, on the pegs, wrapping his fingers gently around Juniper's bony shoulders. The bike tilted a little bit.

"All right," June said, a mischievous smile stretching across her face. "Let's hightail it."

She lifted her other foot to its pedal and took off down the road.

Ethan had intended to keep his grip light, but as Juniper took off at a breakneck pace, he found himself holding on for dear life. Hot air blew her hair into his face and brought tears to his eyes. When he looked up, the trees were bent into natural mosaics and he thought that he must not be in Ellison anymore. Juniper laughed that wind-chime laugh, and it brought up a carbonated happiness in his stomach until he was laughing too. The sound spewed out of him hesitantly at first, then grew until his entire body shook.

When Juniper screeched to a halt at the edge of the lake, Ethan tumbled from the bike and rolled, cackling, into the grass. Juniper stood over him, looking childishly pleased.

"Glad you're having fun," she said. "But you've got to get off the ground. That was only the beginning."

Ethan climbed to his feet and brushed loose dirt from the seat of his pants, taking in the scene around him. The lake stretched out ahead of them in a bean-like shape, so large he could hardly see the other end. They were on a small beach, but the rest of the lake seemed to be surrounded by trees.

"Nice, huh?" Juniper asked. Ethan nodded, trailing her alongside the glittering water and toward a shingled gray boathouse at the edge of the trees. At the door, she handed him the picnic basket and rapped lightly against the wood.

"That you, June?" a gruff voice asked from within.

"Who else?" Juniper rocked onto her toes, and a moment later, the door swung open to reveal an aging but clearly athletic man. His teeth sliced through his salt and pepper beard as he stepped through the doorway and offered the energetic redhead a crooked smile.

"This the boy you were telling me about?" he asked. "The Harper boy?"

"That's me." Ethan stepped forward and shook the man's outstretched hand.

"I'm Gus," he said, nodding briskly. "Knew your dad growing up. Good guy." He grunted. "Anyway, bet you kids want to go out on the lake. Come with me."

They followed him into the dimly lit boathouse, where a line of rowboats were tied up along the dock.

"This one!" Juniper cried, stopping in front of a wooden boat that looked exactly like all the others. She all but leapt into it, sending the boat rocking. "Welcome aboard the SS *Juniper*," she said, holding out a hand to help Ethan climb in after her. "It's named after me."

"That's right," Gus affirmed, unhooking the SS *Juniper*'s rope and tossing it into the boat. "And she's a real star out on the lake." He leaned off the dock and pushed aside the wooden doors, revealing the lake in all its cerulean glory, then handed Juniper a pair of oars.

As she positioned them above the water, Ethan reached out tentatively. "Do you want me to—?"

Juniper snorted. "Please. Leave the real work to the girls who can handle it." And with a surreptitious wink, she cut the oars through the water and sent them gliding out into the glassy blue.

The air smelled different out here. Ethan took a breath and thought he must be inhaling the entire forest, that saplings must be sprouting between the bones of his rib cage. Juniper chatted up a storm as she rowed, and though he tried to listen, he found himself mesmerized by the rhythm of his lungs. Trees surrounded them, casting their long shadows across the water. It was a dance of the senses, touch and smell and taste, and another sense: the feeling of calm.

"And, we've arrived," Juniper announced, snapping Ethan from his reverie. He looked around to find that they were in the middle of the lake, floating on the open water. Juniper laid the oars across the bow and reached for the picnic basket. "From here, we drift."

Ethan craned his neck, taking in the sunlight, the tumbling leaves, and the mist of the water as it carried them along on timid waves. "Wow," he said.

"Wow is right." Juniper paused for a moment to glance around the lake and smile. "This is my second favorite place in the whole entire town."

Ethan raised an eyebrow. "Second? What's your first?"

"Oh, no, you don't." She wagged a finger in his face. "That's for another day. For now, take one before they get cold." She pushed the basket toward him and, looking in, he saw that it was filled to the brim with misshapen biscuits that all seemed a little bit burned. Juniper gave them a sheepish glance. "My baking skills could use some work," she said. "But I also have jam, and jam fixes *everything*."

Ethan stared at her, with her wild red hair and big blue eyes, hunching over a basket of botched biscuits, and maybe the absurdity of their makeshift friendship hit him all at once, or maybe there was something left over from the bike ride, but suddenly he found himself laughing relentlessly. He doubled over until his face was nearly pressed against the damp wooden hull, until he was coughing and nearly crying, until Juniper had joined in and their combined glee made the little rowboat quake.

When the guffaws had subsided into spurts of loud chuckles, Ethan clutched his aching stomach and took a shivering breath. "I don't know," he gasped, "what's actually so funny."

"Neither do I," Juniper replied, brushing tears from her eyes. "But by gosh, isn't that just the best way to laugh?"

It took another short eternity for them to catch their breath enough to handle Juniper's breakfast. They sat on the lake and ate the smoky, but surprisingly soft, biscuits dipped straight into jars of strawberry jam, and even Juniper was silent. They ate until their happy sore stomachs were filled to the brim, then sat there as the boat drifted in lazy spirals across the lake, watching the clouds go by.

*

"That one looks like a rabbit."

"No way, it's definitely a platypus."

"Juniper, not every cloud can look like a platypus."

"Says who, the cloud police?"

Ethan elbowed Juniper in the side, a gesture she returned with a smack to the chin. They were each lying on one of the two center benches, their shoes discarded and their toes grazing the water. The clouds took a stroll overhead, slow and gentle.

Sighing, Ethan lifted himself into a sitting position, twisting once in each direction to snap the cricks out of his back. Juniper remained where she was, her eyes closed and her hands folded across her stomach. A peaceful smile tugged at her lips.

In the past hour, in between cloud watching and biscuit eating, Juniper Jones had laid bare her invincible summer, piece by piece. She'd been thinking about it, she said, since that day at the malt shop. Ethan wasn't sure how she remembered it all. She wanted to have a race through the entire town, but holding kites. She wanted to organize a sock hop night at the Malt. To plant sunflowers on every front lawn in Ellison. To paint a mural on the empty wall outside the general store. To climb to the top of Big Red, allegedly the tallest tree in all of Alabama. She wanted to go to the movies in Montgomery, learn how to use a record player, read twenty-one books in a week, put on a puppet show. And the list went on. She'd scatter her ideas through their conversation like she was coming up with them on the spot.

"And that's why Mrs. Westbury has warts on her feet," she'd say. "Also, I want to knit scarves for all five of Mr. Callahan's new puppies. I don't know how to knit, though. Oh, that too! I want to learn how to knit."

Ethan wasn't sure how, but something about the upside down and sideways way she spoke made sense to him. He mentally made a note of all her summer plans that were plausible—when she suggested holding her breath for two hours, he carefully dissuaded her—and did not once wonder if they would actually follow through on all of them. She made it all seem effortlessly possible.

At one point he had said, "You know what we should do? We should get a really long piece of paper, like a scroll out of an adventure flick, and we should write everything down. We can hang it up somewhere, and every time we finish something we can check it off."

Juniper had grabbed his arm and shook it, squealing, "Yes! Ethan Charlie Harper, you are an absolute *genius*!"

Now, Ethan crossed his legs on the bench and glanced over at her, lying there with her eyes still feigning sleep. On a whim, he passed a hand over her face. No response. He poked her in the side. Only the slightest twitch. "Hey, Juniper," he said loudly, "I think you're dead. Hope you don't mind, I'm gonna toss your body into the lake now."

He reached toward her with both hands and was mere inches away when she leapt to her feet and then dropped heavily onto her butt, rocking the boat so hard that water splashed them both from over the side.

"No, I can't swim!" she shrieked, then snapped her fingers. "That's another thing! I want to learn how to swim."

Ethan snorted, shaking his head incredulously. "You're telling me," he said slowly, "that you've lived in a lake town your entire life and you've never learned how to swim?"

"Well, no one ever taught me!" Juniper crossed her arms and huffed, then muttered, "Also, the lake water is really cold."

"Ha! Maybe we should call you Chicken instead of Starfish."

"How dare you!"

"Relax," Ethan said playfully. "Look, I'll teach you to swim, all right? That'll be an easy one."

She shoved his shoulder again, but this time with a hint of a smile. "Fine. Chameleon." Ethan raised an eyebrow. "Chameleon," she repeated. "I'm Starfish, and you're Chameleon."

Ethan frowned. "How come?"

"Because," said Juniper Jones, "you're the quiet type. Not too noticeable. Not in a bad way, of course—it's just that I think back where you're from, you don't have a problem fitting in." She paused, suddenly troubled. "But not here. Here in Ellison, things are different, and you stick out like a sore thumb."

*

Juniper's watch read noon when Ethan realized that his aunt and uncle didn't know where he was.

"Relax," Juniper assured him, "Mr. and Mrs. Shay *love* me. They won't care. But if you really wanna, we can head back to shore."

Ethan nodded, distracted now because the thought of his aunt and uncle had reminded him of the broadcast the night before. The black schoolgirl had been gone from his mind for these few hours—now, she suddenly reappeared. He glanced sideways at Juniper as she drew two more biscuits from the basket.

"Think fast," she said, and tossed one at Ethan. Hardly paying attention, he made a weak grab for the flying object, but it flew through his fingers and splashed into the lake. Juniper glared at him as she leaned over the edge of the boat to retrieve it. "Way to go, klutz."

Ethan said nothing for long enough that Juniper became preoccupied with the biscuit in her hands. When he finally decided to speak, her mouth was full.

"June?" he asked as she swallowed. "You know things about, you know . . . things."

"Yes, Ethan," Juniper replied solemnly. "I know many things. About things."

"Oh, cut it out. Look, I don't know if you watch the news—maybe not—but anyway, on NBC last night, there was this one report." He explained the situation, and she listened quietly. "And I just—is that really the way things are here?"

Ethan paused when he saw the way Juniper was staring at him, her eyes wide and her mouth slightly agape. She'd finished the biscuit, but she swallowed again.

"Yeah, Ethan," she murmured. "In Ellison it's a little different 'cause the town's so small, but in the big cities like Montgomery and Birmingham? It's the law. A place for colored folks and a place for white folks. Even on the bus. Everything is separate."

Ethan blinked slowly. He looked down at his hands, several shades darker than Juniper's, and thought about that bus. "Why?"

Juniper looked at him strangely. "Say, Ethan, where did you say you're from, again?"

"Arcadia," he said. "City up in Washington state."

Juniper tilted her head, her eyes troubled. "And when your dad got mad and decided to send you here, he never talked about, you know—what it would be like?"

Ethan thought about Arcadia—its roads dense with shops and houses, its sidewalks scattered with pedestrians. When he rode the school bus every day, he sat wherever he pleased. Growing up he'd had friends who looked like him and friends who didn't, and until Samuel Hill came along, he'd hardly noticed the differences at all.

"No." He laughed slightly. "Then again, he doesn't talk to me much about anything. But he definitely didn't mention any of this."

"Well," Juniper said with a long sigh, "I guess I don't know what to say. This is how things are around here, Ethan. All the time. For people like you."

It all played back in his mind: the stares, the women in the general store, the fight with Noah. All because he was colored. Here, he was a deviation from the norm—and that was a threat.

"I can't tell you why they're like that," Juniper went on. "I've been trying to figure it out too. The way I see it, you know, people are like the different paint circles on a palette. You've got your reds and blues and greens and yellows, and you need all of them to make a painting. But around here, they don't see it that way." She shrugged. "They never have. And last year, when that black boy came to town and there was the whole — "

Ethan frowned as she froze. "What?" he asked quickly, leaning forward. Juniper shook her head, settling back onto the bench.

"Nothing," she assured him, picking up the oars and slipping them into position. "We should go."

"Juniper. What boy? What happened?"

"It's not important," she said. "None of it is." She forced a dim and tired smile. "Listen, I'm real sorry your dad decided to send you here. Not because I don't want you here, but because they don't. And they won't let you forget it." She cut the oars expertly through the water, sending the boat forward. "But while you're here, I'm gonna do my best to make this a good summer for you. I pinky swear."

Seven

The forest paths were the greatest gift that Juniper Jones could have ever given Ethan Charlie Harper. That Sunday afternoon, he needed the time to think. The sun was high above the trees, and the air was thick and damp when he strapped on his sneakers and took off down the lane that wound away from Aunt Cara's house and into the trees.

It was Father's Day. Ethan had known it was coming, but was planning to feign forgetfulness and hope his aunt and uncle wouldn't notice. And they hadn't — after breakfast, they put on their church clothes and headed off to Mass with only a simple good-bye thrown over their shoulders. Ethan had relaxed then, and was just settling down with a comic when the phone on the side table rang.

Ethan hesitated, glancing a few times between the comic and the phone. The ringing continued. Finally, Ethan leaned over the love seat and lifted the blue phone receiver from its cradle. Wrapping the cord around his wrist, he said in his most inoffensive voice, "Shay residence, Ethan speaking."

"Hi, Ethan," came a familiar voice.

Oh. In the corner of the seat, Ethan pulled his knees up to his chest. "Hi, Dad," he said. After a long pause, he added, "Happy Father's Day."

"Thanks." Another pause. "I just wanted to see how you were doing. We haven't spoken in a while."

Not since you left me here, Ethan had thought, but held his tongue, instead saying, "Yeah."

The sun beat down on the back of his neck as he wound through the trees. Sweat coated his arms and dripped down his cheeks, but Ethan forced himself to run harder. He thought that if his entire body was focused on this movement, he would be able to distract himself. But with every slap of his sneakers against the dusty trail, his conversation with his father did another lap through his mind.

It had taken a moment for Ethan's dad to speak again. The two had never been particularly communicative with each other, but this awkwardness was new. It had started just after the incident with Samuel Hill and, Ethan could see now, had only gotten worse.

"So . . . how are things going?" his dad had asked at last.

Ethan had opened his mouth, then closed it again. Should he tell the truth? For some reason, the thought of admitting the torment he'd endured made Ethan's face hot with shame. It felt like losing to admit to his father that this scheme had worked—that he regretted what he did, that he wished when stupid Samuel Hill had said what he said, Ethan had just turned and walked away.

"Good," Ethan said at last. "Things are good. I, um—I made a friend."

"Oh!" His dad sounded genuinely surprised, but caught

himself in time to add, "That's great, Son. I'm glad. What's his name?"

"Her name. Juniper Jones."

"Jones," his dad said slowly, his voice growing distant for a moment. "Yes, that's right. I knew her parents, back in the day. Cara was friends with her mom in grade school."

Ethan frowned, realizing he'd never heard Juniper talk about her parents, only her aunt. He didn't know anything about her family. But this thought lasted only a moment, because then his father was saying, "If she's as cute as her mom was, you're a pretty lucky guy, Ethan."

Ethan bristled. His dad would do this sometimes, comment on the girls he befriended, and it made him self-conscious and uneasy in a way he couldn't quite place. "It's not like that, Dad," he said tightly, even as Juniper's smiling face flashed through his mind.

"All right, all right, sorry." Ethan could practically hear him holding up his hands in defense. "Hold on, Anthony and Sadie want to talk to you."

"Okay, well, I—" Ethan started, but his dad had already passed the phone.

"Hi, Ethan," the twins said in unison, their voices loud through the receiver. Ethan held the phone slightly away from his ear, as if their spit could travel through the telephone line.

"Hey, guys," he said. "How's summer school?"

"Summer *camp*," Anthony corrected him.

"Yeah, summer school is for losers," Sadie added.

"Right, sorry, summer camp—"

"It's *great*." Sadie interrupted him. "We go swimming and make crafts and take the kayaks out on the lake. Have you ever been in a kayak, Ethan?"

"Well, actually, my friend Juniper and I—"

But his siblings had already begun to talk over him and each other as they told him about the bugs they'd collected during lunchtime. Ethan smiled to himself. He had never been close to the twins, and often found them annoying, but he still had a soft spot for them. When their mom had left, he'd been the one to pick up many of the duties—changing diapers, giving baths, remembering which foods they wouldn't spit out all over the table. He'd been only ten then, and Anthony and Sadie certainly didn't remember it, but those memories made him feel closer to them anyway.

Now, running through a stretch of forest he'd never seen before, Ethan thought of taking care of Anthony and Sadie, sometimes teaching his dad how to parent them—and he thought of how it had always seemed like his dad had been more interested in them than him. He'd always brushed it off, figuring it was just because they were younger. But now, picturing their rosy cheeks and wavy hair, he couldn't help but wonder.

His dad had taken the phone from the twins soon after, and Ethan heard their laughter fading into another part of the house. "So, everything's going good?" his dad said after a moment. Ethan imagined him leaning against the kitchen counter where their phone sat, his elbows on the white tiles.

"Yeah," Ethan said.

"Good, good. Well, in that case—"

"Did Mom want me to come to Ellison too?" Ethan hadn't realized he was going to ask the question until the words were already out. His heart pounded loudly as his dad sat in a seemingly stunned silence.

"Well." His voice changed in the way it did when he wanted to brush aside a topic without explaining it, the way he had when Ethan was ten and asked where babies came from. "Well," he repeated. "Actually, your mother doesn't know that you're there."

Ethan pulled the phone away from his face and gaped at it, as if it could explain. He felt suddenly distant from his body, as if he was hearing himself speak from somewhere above his own head. "Sorry, what?" Ethan's voice was tight and low. "You didn't tell her that you sent me to this shit—"

"Language."

"—to this *shit* town?"

Ethan could feel his dad bristle on the other side of the phone. "When was the last time your mother called you, Ethan?"

"Two months ago. My birthday."

"Okay, and before that?"

Ethan paused, counting. "Maybe Christmas?"

"Exactly." He sounded smug.

"Exactly what, Dad?"

"Your mother is not around," he snapped. "She lives a separate life now. She calls you on holidays. I'm the one who takes you to school, who makes you dinner, who pays for your running shoes—"

"Dad, stop." Ethan squeezed his eyes shut, trying hard to call to mind his mother's face. He saw, instead, his own eyes, nose, mouth—his own skin. He remembered holding his mother's hand as a child, how the brown of their wrists made one unbroken line. It was so easy back then, when neighbors would comment on how much he looked like her and he'd beam with pride, turning his face skyward to show off the dark cheeks she'd gifted to him.

In Ellison, his mother's gift was nothing to be proud of. His dad had known this, Ethan was sure—it was the knowing that had made him so uneasy as he'd moved through Aunt Cara's house, the knowing that twisted up his features as he drove away. But it hadn't stopped him, because he would never understand. He could list all the things he had done for Ethan, gather mountains of material proof of his love, and still he would never know what it was like to be in Ethan's skin. Even Ethan didn't know completely what stood against him. But his mother did, and he was certain that if she'd known what his dad was planning, he never would have ended up in Ellison.

"I'm doing this because I care, Ethan." His dad was shouting now. "I care about the man you are becoming!"

"But she's my *mother*!" Ethan screamed, surprising himself with the volume. It seemed to shock his father, too, because when he spoke again, his voice was softer.

"I know," he said, as Ethan breathed heavily into the line. "I know, I'm sorry. She is your mother, and she loves you. But I'm your father and your legal guardian, and I make the decisions." He paused. "And for the record, I know your mother. And whether or not she knows that you're in Ellison, she wouldn't be happy about what you did either."

"You don't get to tell me how she would feel about this," Ethan said. "Not when you didn't even bother to ask her."

"Ethan—"

"Bye, Dad. Happy Father's Day, I guess."

He slammed the handset back into its cradle. The living room was so silent that the air seemed to ring. Ethan felt as though he were coming back into his body—his head spun. He gritted his teeth and clenched his fists until his nails left crescent marks in his palms.

He clenched them again, here, on the forest path. The sharp pain against his skin cleared his head enough for him to realize that his breath was coming in pants now, his mouth dry and gritty with dust. His body wasn't used to such an intense workout anymore, especially in this Alabama heat, and he could feel his vision blurring with dizziness.

At the next bend, Ethan came to a skidding halt and allowed himself to fall to his knees in the dust. He saw that his sneakers were coated with brown, his shirt and shorts soaked through with sweat. At this point, he couldn't bring himself to care—his lungs were burning, and his stomach lurched. He dry heaved onto the path until the stars in his vision rearranged themselves into winding tree trunks and shivering leaves.

"Okay," he gasped. "Okay."

✳

Ethan walked home. Or perhaps the proper word was *wandered*, and aimlessly at that, because every curve and fork and bend looked exactly the same, and it wasn't long before he wasn't sure whether he'd gone left toward town or right toward the lake, or if maybe the lake was left and the town was right. His breathing was ragged and tired and sad, and his muscles ached and his lungs shrieked, but he trudged on. At some point it started raining—a brief sun shower, which he'd learned often happened here in the summer—and then he was drenched in both sweat and sticky rainwater.

Juniper found him at the base of a hill. He'd strayed off the path somewhere along the way and had stumbled through the trees until he found himself in a clearing. The sun was in his eyes and sweat pooled under his arms. He didn't notice the ground had begun to incline until he once again tumbled to the ground.

At some point he must have closed his eyes, because suddenly there was a hand on his shoulder, prompting them open. Light blurred his vision. He spat out a few blades of grass and rolled onto his back. Juniper was staring down at him, looking a little bit confused and very concerned.

"Ethan?" she asked carefully, poking his cheek with one finger.

He coughed and slowly eased himself into a sitting position. She squatted beside him. "Juniper. Hey."

"Are you all right? You're all wet."

If he'd had the energy, he would have pointed out that she was all wet too—the rain had plastered her hair to her cheeks, turning orange into muddy crimson.

"I—" He had to pause for breath. "I went for a run. I think—I think I got a little carried away."

"No kidding. Look, I was going to save this spot for our next adventure, but there's no use trying to hide it from you now. Welcome to Alligator Hill! Ethan? Are you paying attention? Open your eyes."

Ethan groaned and kept them closed.

"Fine. That's your loss. Anyway, remember how I told you that the lake was my second favorite place in the whole town? Well, this is my first. Alligator Hill. The best place in all of Ellison, Alabama. The best place in Alabama period, probably. If you climbed to the top right now and looked out, you could see the whole wide world. Some people don't like it up here, because they say it makes them feel small. But I love it. It makes me feel big. Taller than everyone."

She sighed. "Anyway, not like it matters. Not like you can even hear me right now. Are you asleep? Ethan?"

Ethan grunted and threw a hand across his eyes. "You look drunk." Juniper snorted. "Maybe you won't remember this place after all. I'll bring you here sometime, and you'll see how great it really is. Just you wait, Ethan. Just you wait."

✳

Somehow, through his own power or perhaps a show of superhuman strength by Juniper Jones, Ethan found himself back in the woods, trudging alongside the energetic redhead as she chattered up a storm.

"—don't know what's gotten into you," she was saying, shaking her head so that her curls slapped Ethan in the face. "You gave me a real shock, showing up at Alligator Hill like that. I don't know how you even found it. You must have gotten real off track. What happened?"

Ethan hung his head, tugged at the hem of his shorts, and shrugged. Now, he was conscious enough to think clearly about what his dad had said—he couldn't stop thinking about it. The thought of his dad keeping all this from his mom made him feel sick to his stomach, as if he was caught back up in the same power struggle that had erupted in their home during the divorce. It made him want to disappear.

"Come on," Juniper said, nudging Ethan with her shoulder. "You can tell me."

Keeping his eyes on the path, Ethan took a deep breath. "My dad called today. We talked for a while, and he, um. He told me that my mom doesn't know I'm here. He didn't tell her."

"Oh," Juniper said, but sounded as if she didn't understand.

"They're divorced. I don't see her much. But he didn't even give her a say in all of this. As if she doesn't even matter, which is how he acts pretty much all the time. And the thing is, my mom is — you know. Like me." He lifted an arm, pointed to his arm. "Colored. And I just can't help thinking maybe he didn't tell her because she would have tried to stop him. And maybe then I wouldn't be here."

"Oh," Juniper said again, softer this time. "Sorry, Ethan."

Ethan shook his head and pinched the bridge of his nose. "I just want to go home," he mumbled. "Or — not even home. But not here. I'd rather be anywhere but here."

Juniper was silent, and Ethan didn't realize why until he turned and saw the stricken look on her freckled face. "No, I didn't mean — it's not about you, I — sorry," he said.

"No, it's fine," she said flatly. "I get it."

"Sorry," he repeated.

They walked on in silence for a while, until the path split in two.

"The lake is that way," Juniper told him, pointing to their left. "Just follow the path to the right and you'll end up back at your aunt's house. Can you find your way from here? My aunt's probably waiting for her afternoon tea, and — "

"I've just been thinking a lot about what you said the other day," Ethan blurted. "About the people here, and the way they think, and I feel like — like I can't ever belong here. And I feel like my dad knew that. But he didn't care." He dragged his hands across his eyes and sighed. "So I just want to leave."

Juniper said nothing for a long moment, studying Ethan as he stood hunched in the middle of the path. Her eyes flickered strangely, and after a moment of hesitation, she said, "Hey."

Her voice was sharp, and it startled Ethan. "I know it sucks. I know you hate it. But either way, you can't go home. And I want you here. So you're going to have to suck it up and let that be enough."

"June," he began, still staring at the ground, but she held up a hand.

"I can apologize for the people in my town," she said in a low voice, "but I can't change them. The best I can do is try to make things okay while you're here."

Ethan looked up, expecting to see a glare on her face, but instead found himself faced with a red-faced, teary-eyed, tight-lipped Juniper Jones. He was startled to see her on the verge of tears when he himself felt so zapped of emotions. He felt like he needed to comfort her, but for what? This was his pain to bear, not hers.

As Ethan looked on, Juniper balled her hands into fists and studied the ground, then, in a sudden explosion, threw her arms around Ethan's neck and squeezed fiercely. Her chin dug into his shoulder. She pulled away before he could return the embrace and backed down the path toward the lake.

"I'll see you around, Ethan Charlie Harper." She gave him a watery smile. "Count on it." And with a flick of her sunset hair, she turned and hurried away.

Ethan knew that she had tried to make him feel better, but he still felt the roll of nausea in his stomach. He was damp and grimy and tired down to his bones, but he cracked his fingers one by one and walked toward home. He could hear his heartbeat in his ears, angry and swelling, a discordant beat that drowned out the lonely sound of birdsong. He squeezed his eyes shut as he walked, feeling the dust that rose in his wake.

When he found his way back to Aunt Cara's, he stumbled straight to the shower, letting hot water pour over his head and wash the forest from his pores. Then he stepped out and put on his pajamas, refusing to look in the mirror. The tile floor was cold beneath his bare feet.

"Okay," he said to himself, his eyes pressed gently shut. And for the rest of the afternoon he lay on his bed, eyes to the ceiling, and played a Billie Holiday record—it was the saddest one he owned. He thought about his father, with his unassuming green eyes, and his mother, whose face he still struggled to remember. He wished to know what she would say if she knew he was here and what had happened to him so far. He wondered if she would tell him, as he had begun to suspect himself, that her blood, and therefore his own, was poison.

EIGHT

The unease from the conversation with his father hadn't worn off by the time Ethan went into work the next morning. The morning lull of the malt shop certainly didn't help. He ran the empty blender a few times just to fill the silence, then paced around the store, wiping the clean tables vigorously with a wet cloth.

It was a relief, then, when at twelve on the dot, Juniper Jones swept through the door in typical hurricane fashion. Ethan, who had been selecting a song at the jukebox, jumped at the sound of the bell and dropped his nickel. It rolled across the tile floor and into a tiny crack at the bottom of the counter.

"Jesus, Juniper!" he cried. Juniper stood just inside the shop in a bright-orange dress that made her look thoroughly like a carrot. She grinned, and in her crooked teeth he could see no indication that she remembered the tension of their meeting the day before. *This is how Juniper is,* he thought. *Moving on as quickly as she can from the feelings that distress her.*

"Good noon, monsieur," she said now. Ethan couldn't decide what was funnier: her botched French accent or the bow she took, dipping all the way to ground.

Shaking his head, he replied, "Hello to you too."

Juniper walked past him and up to the counter. She took a seat and looked at him expectantly. Ethan blinked at her, still standing next to the jukebox.

"What?" he asked.

"Well," she said, "I'm visiting you at work because one of my goals for this invincible summer is to try every flavor of milk shake at the Malt. In one day. Today, on this fine June afternoon, I am going to drink milk shakes until I explode."

Ethan tried to keep a straight face, but seeing Juniper sitting at the counter, hands positioned determinedly on her hips, made the laughter bubble up in his stomach. He let out a loud snort.

"Gotcha! I am an expert at making people laugh, Ethan Charlie Harper, and don't you forget it."

He held up both hands in mock surrender. "All right, I won't," he said, making his way back behind the counter. "Anyway, which one do you want first? Chocolate, strawberry, vanilla and . . . that's it, actually." He squinted up on the menu posted behind the counter. "I'm surprised you haven't tried them all already."

Juniper suddenly looked very serious as she beckoned Ethan closer to her. "Thing is," she whispered once he had leaned in, "I've actually never had a milk shake."

"That's not true. I made you a milk shake last week—the special of the day, remember?"

Juniper snorted. "That was barely edible. And anyway, it had soda, so if anything, it'd be a float."

"Fine, it was a float," Ethan said. "But still—how have you never had a milk shake?"

"I'm a root beer float kinda girl," she retorted. "But today, I'll have a vanilla milk shake. Gosh, this is such an adventure."

Ethan raised an eyebrow and shook his head, but turned to the prep station and assembled the ingredients. Juniper leaned as far over the counter as she could to watch his every move, asking more questions than Ethan thought was possible about the making of a milk shake.

"Is that vanilla bean ice cream or French vanilla ice cream?

"How much milk are you putting in?

"*More* ice? Really?"

She'd move on to her next question before Ethan had time to respond to the previous one, so he just listened to her exclamations with a small smile on his face. When he topped the shake off with whipped cream and a bright-red cherry, Juniper gasped gleefully.

"Wow," she marveled. "That's *beautiful*. You're much better at milk shakes than you are at daily specials."

"I have my strengths." Ethan dropped in a straw and slid the tall glass across the counter to her.

"No, no," she said immediately. "I'm not drinking this by myself. This is *our* summer. We have to try all the flavors together."

"Thanks, but I'm really fine without—"

"Ethan Charlie Harper. Have you tried all the milk shake flavors at this malt shop?"

"Well, no, but—"

"Then grab a straw." She gestured at the container of straws behind the counter. "Come on, don't be shy."

"Fine, fine," Ethan said, sticking a straw of his own into the drink.

Juniper straightened in her chair. "Perfect," she said. "Now on the count of three, we sip. One, two, three—"

Forty minutes and three milk shakes later, Ethan and Juniper were slumped at the counter, their stomachs heavy with ice cream. Their final ranking had been chocolate as the best, then vanilla, then strawberry. Both had agreed that the flavored syrup in the strawberry milk shake, while delicious, was a little too sweet for their liking.

From the chair next to Juniper, where he had moved after milk shake number two, Ethan mopped his forehead with his apron. "I didn't know drinking milk shakes could be so tiring," he said.

With a hand on her stomach, Juniper nodded. "I know those were my first milk shakes and all, but I'm thinking that's gonna be it for me. Like, forever."

"I don't blame you," Ethan said, laughing. He spun slowly in his chair and had just made one full rotation when the shop bell rang. Assuming it was his uncle since it was almost one o'clock, he called, "Hey, Uncle Robert."

"Sitting on the job, huh?" came the response, but not in his uncle's voice. Cold horror creeping down his spine, Ethan spun back toward the front of the shop to see Noah O'Neil standing in the doorway with Alex slouching beside him.

"Scram, Noah," Juniper said, crossing her arms.

"Who, me?" Noah laughed. "Y'all can't make me leave. It's a free country." He dropped heavily into a chair at one of the tables and Alex sat beside him, grinning.

"Sorry, can't sit here unless you buy something." Ethan wasn't sure if that was true, but he was hoping Noah didn't know either.

"Oh, really?" Noah said. "Fine. Then make me a milk shake. Chocolate."

"Make me a milk shake too," Alex piped up a beat later.

Ethan gritted his teeth and remained in his seat. Noah snapped his fingers. "Well, what are you waiting for? Two chocolate milk shakes. Or should I tell your uncle you refused to serve me?"

Ethan looked at Juniper, who stared back, wide eyed. Finally, hands clenched at his sides, he stood up from the stool and marched behind the counter, barely aware of his own movements. The malt shop was silent except for the sounds of Ethan scooping ice cream, pouring milk, running the blender. Juniper sat frozen at the counter, staring at the wall. Noah and Alex lounged in their chairs, totally at ease.

It seemed to take ages for the shakes to be done. Once he had poured them into the glasses — sloppily, so some dripped down the sides — he gave each one an angry spurt of whipped cream and tossed a cherry unceremoniously on top. Then he walked as if floating through the swinging counter door and over to Noah and Alex's table, where he all but dropped the drinks in front of them.

"There," he said roughly.

Noah examined the milk shakes, leaning over so that his cheek nearly brushed the table, and everyone seemed to be holding their breath. Ethan watched, quietly fuming, wishing he could overturn the drinks onto Noah and Alex's laps.

Instead, after several quiet moments, it was Noah, with a quick swipe of his hand, who knocked both glasses onto their sides. There were two loud clanks as the glasses fell over, then the creamy liquid poured onto the table and then the floor. Juniper jumped out of her seat, Ethan stared with a mix of shock and fury, and Alex and Noah laughed so hard their entire bodies shook.

"Noah, how dare you!" Juniper cried, rushing toward

them. She stopped just short of stepping in the quickly growing puddle of milk shake.

"It was an accident," Noah said. He stared straight at Ethan, who returned the glare with his fists clenched tightly at his sides.

"Yeah, it was an accident," Alex echoed. "Cool off, psycho."

Ethan blinked, then followed Alex's gaze to Juniper, whose lips were suddenly trembling. "I'm sorry," he said slowly. "What did you call her?"

"He called her psycho," Noah said. "I don't know if you know, Ethan, but your pal Juniper Jones is a bit—you know." With his eyes crossed, he waved his finger in a circle around his ear.

"Get out."

Noah looked up, a challenge sparking in his eyes. "You sure you want to talk to me like that?"

"You heard what I said." Ethan looked at Noah, and the anger pulsing through his body made him feel like he could pick up the older boy by the finger and hurl him through the wall.

Alex eagerly watched as Noah held Ethan's gaze and, with infuriating slowness, leaned back in his chair and lifted each of his feet onto the soaked table, fingers linked behind his head. He didn't say a word, but the message was clear: *Make me*.

In Ethan's mind flashed an image of Samuel Hill, staring at him with the smugness of someone who knew they had the upper hand. The memory made Ethan see red. He hardly knew what he was doing as he grabbed the table with both hands and toppled it.

Three things happened at that moment. First, the table fell into the puddle with a loud thump, sending milk shake splattering over all of them. Second, Noah's legs were flung into the air, and despite a desperate attempt by Alex, Noah's chair tilted backward and onto the floor, where he lay momentarily stunned. And third, with a shrill tinkle of the bell, Uncle Robert walked through the door.

After the crash, the silence was complete. Nobody moved or spoke for a long moment—then Uncle Robert shouted, "*What* is going on here?" and suddenly everyone was talking at once.

"Your *nephew* attacked me—"

"—but Uncle Robert, I swear he started it—"

"Noah was minding his own business when—"

"—so Mr. Shay, you gotta believe that it wasn't Ethan's fault!"

Eventually, Uncle Robert, his face red, held up a hand. "Juniper," he said, turning to her. "What happened?"

Juniper took a big, shaky breath as everyone turned to her, and all the words came out in a rush, "Noah and Alex came in being all mean and told Ethan to make them milk shakes and then Ethan did but Noah knocked the milk shakes over and they spilled everywhere and then he wouldn't leave when Ethan told him to and so Ethan flipped the table over but Noah deserved it!"

From the ground, Noah yelled, "She's lying! I was being a perfectly civil customer, and your nephew just came after me. I don't know what's wrong with him, Mr. Shay, he's so violent." All the while, Alex nodded emphatically.

Uncle Robert turned to Noah with a look of disdain that surprised Ethan. It seemed to shock Noah too, because the boy stared up in wide-eyed silence.

"Noah, Alex, go home," Uncle Robert said.

"But—"

"Get up. Go home."

"Fine," Noah snapped. Alex reached out an arm to help him up, but Noah swatted it away and pushed himself to his feet. The back of his jeans was damp with spilled milk shake. He backed toward the door, but not before casting Ethan a baleful glare.

"You don't even know what I could do to you," he said. "I could make you regret this for the rest of your life."

Ethan opened his mouth to respond, but Uncle Robert beat him to it. "I can handle my own nephew, Noah. Go home."

With one last scowl, Noah shoved his way out the door, Alex on his heels. When they were gone, Ethan immediately began to speak.

"Uncle Robert, I know what it looks like, but I swear he came after me first. He knocked over the milk shakes and I just got so mad—"

"He was sticking up for me," Juniper interrupted, and both Ethan and Uncle Robert turned to her. "Noah and Alex were calling me names, and Ethan stuck up for me. That's why he knocked over the table. Don't blame him, Mr. Shay. Please."

Uncle Robert was quiet for a moment, his gaze trained on the fallen table and wide puddle. Finally, he sighed. "I believe you," he said. "Noah O'Neil is a nasty kid. Always picking on the underdogs." Ethan let out a breath he didn't know he'd been holding. "But you shouldn't have done that," Uncle Robert continued, giving his nephew a hard look. "You have to be careful how you act around here."

Ethan glowered, staring at the ground. "Yes, sir."

Uncle Robert sighed again, then walked slowly to the counter. "I'll handle the mess," he said. "You kids go home."

"Are you sure, Mr. Shay? I can—" But Uncle Robert cut

Juniper off with a shake of his head and waved them toward the door. Ethan stepped over the puddle as Juniper circled around it and they left the store.

Back in the glaring sunlight, they rushed out of the center of town. They didn't even have to look at each other: they both just immediately began speed walking down the street, their heads down. If people stared as they passed, they didn't notice.

Once they'd made it beneath the cover of the trees, Juniper stopped. She looked down at her skirt, which was splattered with brown streaks.

Ethan looked at his own stained pants and shook his head. "I'm real sorry, June," he said. "I overreacted."

She tilted her head to look at him. Instead of responding, she said, "Wanna go to the lake?"

Ethan paused for a moment, then nodded, and silently she led the way. They emerged from the trees several minutes later, this time on the opposite side of the lake from Gus's boathouse. Here, a few large rocks stuck out of the water, and Juniper dropped down cross-legged onto one of them. Ethan lowered himself down carefully beside her, his legs dangling over the edge.

For a while, neither spoke, just watched the lake glitter in the sunlight, its gentle waves lapping against the bottoms of the rocks. Ethan still felt on edge, his heart racing, as though Noah and Alex were going to burst through the trees at any moment. He felt angry, still, but mostly afraid. He hadn't expected to lose control that way—he'd barely realized it was happening. He thought about his uncle's warning, then of Samuel Hill's smirking face. He was scared to think of what might have happened if Uncle Robert hadn't walked in when he had.

Ethan was deep in worry when Juniper shouted his name. He figured it hadn't been the first time she tried to get his attention. When he looked up, she was watching him with concern.

"Hey," she said, face serious. "I don't know if you feel like talking, but I do. I wanted to say thanks. For standing up for me back there. Noah and Alex and other kids make fun of me a lot, and usually I just kind of take it because what else can I do, you know? But it was really nice to have someone on my side."

Looking back at the water, Ethan shook his head. "It wasn't good," he said. "It was stupid. I shouldn't have done that."

"It was brave," Juniper insisted.

"Then being 'brave' is exactly what got me stuck here in the first place. And what Noah said, about what he could do to me—I don't want to end up somewhere even worse."

He fell silent but felt Juniper's questioning gaze on his face. As cicadas chirped somewhere across the lake, she softly said, "You said you got sent here because you got in a fight with a kid. But there's more to the story, huh?"

Ethan squeezed his eyes shut. Behind his eyelids the memory played, as it did almost every time he closed his eyes. Samuel Hill, getting close up in his face, saying those words, and Ethan, drawing back his arm—

He took a deep breath.

"There's this kid at my school," he began. "Samuel Hill."

Samuel had never liked Ethan—it'd been tense between them ever since they were kids. Sam, with his light-brown hair and blue eyes, would throw sand at Ethan in the playground and dump pencil shavings onto his desk. But they were young, and some kids were bullies. Besides, Ethan had had plenty of friends. He had hardly minded Samuel Hill at all.

Then, when Ethan was ten, his mom had left. The word had spread quickly through their elementary school, and for some reason, Samuel couldn't let it go. He began to tease Ethan incessantly, escalating through middle school, so that by high school it was nearly unbearable. But Samuel's insults were always shallow, nonspecific. He'd call Ethan a loser, or a moron, and that was all.

"We'd get in each other's faces sometimes," Ethan recounted to Juniper, kicking at the water. "Nothing major, you know—I never even touched him. It was all talk."

Until May of his freshman year. It had been three weeks until summer, and kids were getting restless. They'd been in line for lunch at the cafeteria, Samuel with his friends just in front of Ethan with his. In math class that morning, Samuel had spent an hour sending spitballs into Ethan's curls, so Ethan kept his distance now.

Ethan's friend John, a klutzy kid who'd gone through his growth spurt earlier than the rest of them, had leaned over Ethan to grab an apple from the lunch lady. It had happened quickly—John lost his balance, knocking into Ethan, who stumbled, his empty tray shooting forward out of his hands. A few people quickly dodged, but Samuel, talking to his friends, hadn't seen it coming. The tray had struck him right in the behind.

"Shit," Ethan had said, trying to melt back into the crowd of his friends. But Samuel, who had whirled around, had already seen him. His eyes were bright with anger.

"You threw that tray at me, Harper?" Samuel had demanded, pointing at the plastic culprit on the ground. Students scattered, forming a loose ring around the two boys. "Fight!" someone had cried from the outskirts.

"I didn't throw anything," Ethan had said. "Calm down."

But Samuel had persisted, stepping forward to nudge Ethan in the stomach with his own tray. "Calm down? When you hit me with that shit?" He nudged Ethan again.

It was a reflex: as Samuel moved to push his tray into Ethan once again, Ethan had swept out an arm and sent the tray flying. It grazed Samuel's shoulder and clattered to the ground a few feet away.

The cafeteria was silent. Ethan had looked at Samuel, thinking it was over—instead, Samuel's sneer grew deeper. "You think you can disrespect me like that?" he had demanded, pushing his chest into Ethan's. "Huh, half breed? You think you can disrespect me?"

Ethan had been trying to dodge the boy's advances, but he remembered thinking that "half breed" was a new one. "Samuel," he had said, annoyance growing. "Can you cut it out? I said I didn't throw it."

Samuel had ignored him. "Well, guess what?" he said, raising his voice for the benefit of the growing crowd. "You *can't*, Harper. You can't disrespect me. Not when you're a half breed and your mom's a goddamn nigger."

Someone had gasped—maybe several people had. Remembering the moment now, Ethan couldn't be sure. He had been seeing red. Because that word, he knew. He'd seen it written in books, heard it whispered by adults, and when he had been young, his dad had told him never to say it. And here it was, being spat in his face.

The rest Ethan knew only from what his friends had told him later. Samuel Hill had stepped back, grinning smugly. Ethan, furious, wound up and swung. He punched Samuel three times, right in the face, until his nose gushed blood. Later, in the nurse's station, he had washed that blood from his bruised knuckles as he'd tried to explain to the principal what had happened. It hadn't mattered. Not to the principal, and not to his father.

"I got suspended for the rest of the school year," Ethan said. "My dad was pissed. I've never seen him so mad about anything my whole life. He didn't talk to me for a week. Then he came into my room and told me I was spending the summer in Alabama. To 'build character,' he said. Learn some 'real southern values.' That was it. Now I'm here."

Ethan didn't look at Juniper, just up at the top of the trees, where the sun was bright and high. Talking about it now made his stomach clench the way it had when his dad had come to pick him up from the principal's office that afternoon, his face bright red and furious. Ethan had opened his mouth, about to tell him what Samuel Hill had said, but his dad had cut him off. He said, "I don't care. That is not how you handle a problem."

There was a part of him that had been satisfied by the shock on Samuel Hill's face when he sat there on the cafeteria floor, clutching his bleeding nose. But there was also a part of him that was afraid of what he'd done. Ashamed. Because he knew, had always been told, that anger was the wrong thing to feel—and that when it made an appearance, it should never be acted on. His dad had always told him to be the bigger person, to walk away, to hold his tongue.

Juniper, who had been silent for a while, finally cleared her throat and scooted closer to Ethan on the rock. "You shouldn't feel bad about that," she said slowly. "About punching Samuel Hill or knocking the table over onto Noah. They deserved it."

Ethan shrugged.

"I think—" she went on, "I think it takes a real strong person to stick up for themselves. Maybe even more than it does to stick up for someone else." She put a hand on his arm. "You don't have to be nice all the time, Ethan. Not when people aren't nice to you."

"Thanks, Juniper." Ethan kicked at the water with his heel, just barely skimming the surface. "But I guess it's not that simple."

Juniper said nothing for a long time. They both stared out over the lake. Then, eventually, Juniper said, "I'm sorry."

Ethan nodded. "Thanks," he said. "Me too." He closed his eyes, thinking about Samuel Hill and Noah O'Neil, until their faces blurred together into one fair-skinned monster rising up in his mind. He clenched his fists, imagined himself bracing against their attack. He wished that was enough.

NINE

Juniper showed up at Ethan's window the next afternoon, just as she had that first morning they'd spent on the lake. Ethan was half asleep and listening to a record when the sound of Juniper's fist against his window sent him jolting out of bed. When he turned, she was standing at the glass with a wide grin on her face and a ratty wicker basket in her arms. She motioned for him to open the window, and he obliged.

"Hey," he said, as she pushed the basket through the window and scrambled in after it, "whatcha doing?"

Juniper looked at him in surprise and opened the basket to reveal stacks of paper in all sizes and colors, a roll of tape, and two perfectly sharpened pencils. "It's time to get planning," she said. "Summer's almost a third of the way over!"

She sat down cross-legged on the floor and looked at him expectantly. Ethan sat down beside her. Juniper began to guide him—*Tape this sheet to that one. No, not that one, that one, and turn it the other way*—and he followed her instructions with a laugh. She didn't mention the incident the previous day, not even once, and Ethan was relieved. He was worried that everything he had told her might have given her second thoughts about being his friend, but as she scrunched her nose at his taping skills and reprimanded his sloppy handwriting, she didn't seem to feel any differently about him at all.

"Ethan?" Aunt Cara called after Juniper had been there for about half an hour. "Are you talking to someone?" She opened the door before he could respond, and did a double take. She first seemed to notice the floor, almost completely covered in papers now—then she looked up and saw Juniper Jones, sitting in the middle of the mess with a big smile on her face.

"Hi, Mrs. Shay!" Juniper said brightly.

Aunt Cara looked at her for a moment, then fixed them both with a confused smile. "Hi, Juniper," she said, shaking her head. "How—when did you get here?"

"Oh, not too long ago. I climbed through the window!"

"I see. That's right, Robert mentioned the two of you were friends."

Ethan grimaced, expecting his aunt to be upset, but to his surprise, she seemed to be holding back a laugh.

"Ethan's my *best* friend." Juniper corrected his aunt. "As of a couple weeks ago. See, I have this plan to have this amazing, invincible summer, so anyway, I told Ethan about my plan and he agreed that it's an *amazing* plan, and now we're best friends and we're gonna go on adventures and have the best summer anyone has ever had, ever."

She finished with a gulping breath.

"Well," said Aunt Cara, smiling, "that is certainly some story."

"Sorry, Aunt Cara," Ethan said sheepishly. "I shoulda told you she was here."

But Aunt Cara shook her head. "No, that's all right, honey. I'm glad to see that y'all are friends. But next time, Juniper, maybe you could use the front door?"

Juniper grinned and gave Aunt Cara a mock salute. "Will do, ma'am," she said. "Just call me Juniper Starfish Uses-the-Front-Door Jones."

✳

It took a week to plan their invincible summer. A week of meeting after Ethan finished at work, of sitting by the lake or at Aunt Cara's kitchen table with biscuits and chicken sand-wiches, and of pieces of paper secured together with tape. Soon, it was a blend of his messy scribbles and her neat cur-sive loops, barely legible even to their eyes.

"Community garden," Juniper would shout, and Ethan would scrawl it onto the page. "Discover a new planet! Write a book! Compose a song on the mandolin!"

"See Frank Sinatra in concert," Ethan suggested one day.

Juniper scoffed. "*Bo*-ring. See Elvis Presley in concert."

"No way, I can't stand Elvis. I don't understand the whole hip routine." He stood up on the grass beside the lake and attempted to demonstrate a pelvic thrust.

Juniper winced. Leaning over the paper, she added, "Convert Ethan to an Elvis fan. Also, teach him to dance."

Other days, they would be starved for ideas, biting on the backs of their pencils and staring at the makeshift scroll with furrowed brows.

"How about," Ethan would suggest, then trail off into silence.

"Oh!" Juniper would exclaim, jumping to her feet. "What if we—wait, actually, maybe not . . ."

It wasn't until a week later, sitting on Aunt Cara's front porch with stomachs full of chicken sandwiches, that they put the finishing touches on their list.

"We, Juniper Jones and Ethan Charlie Harper," Juniper wrote in curling script, "hereby declare that we will follow this list to the best of our ability and that we will have what is, for all intents and purposes, an invincible summer."

She signed her name, two big *J*s with a lot of wavy lines between, then slid the paper over to Ethan. Rolled out flat, it stretched all the way across Aunt Cara's front porch. He wondered, absently, how many days of summer it would take to finish everything. He never once considered it impossible.

He scratched a signature next to Juniper's.

"I feel like I just signed the Declaration of Independence."

"No, Ethan," she chastised him, sticking a finger in his face. "You've signed something much, much more important. This is the most important document in the history of mankind."

She looked at Ethan seriously for a long moment before bursting into loud, shaking laughter. Ethan grinned, rolling his eyes.

"You're such a nerd," he teased. "Come on, let's roll it up."

It took their combined efforts—and a lot of tape—to roll their earthshaking decree into a tight scroll. "I hope you remember what was on here," Ethan remarked, "because we won't be unrolling this anytime soon."

"Of course," Juniper said dismissively, looking at Ethan through the scroll like it was a telescope. "And anyway, if we forget, we can improvise. This invincible summer has already set sail, Ethan. It can't be derailed."

Ethan looked at her in amusement. "Boats don't sail on train tracks, Starfish."

"Whatever, Chameleon. Maybe I'll invent one that can."

"I don't doubt that you will."

Juniper grinned smugly and handed Ethan the scroll. "Anyway, two things. First of all, it is absolutely urgent that you come with me right now to a super-top secret location. It's a matter of life and death." She ignored Ethan's skeptical frown. "Second, I have another super-top secret location where we can hide this scroll, but we can only do that after we visit the first secret location, because . . . well, that's just how it works. So go tell your aunt that we're leaving, and I'll meet you around back in five minutes." She held up her hand, palm flat, fingers splayed. "Five minutes, Chameleon. Don't you dare be late."

"Aye-aye, Starfish."

As Juniper scurried off to get her bike, Ethan cradled the scroll to his chest and stepped inside the house. It was early evening; the sun was just beginning to dive into the horizon, and Aunt Cara was listening to the second episode of a five-part series of *Yours Truly, Johnny Dollar*. She sat on a stool in the kitchen, her fingertips resting on her stomach and her neck craned toward the little green radio.

"*Expense account item number twenty-four,*" came Bob Bailey's smooth voice. "*Two dollars and thirty-three cents. A cab to downtown Los Angeles.*"

"Aunt Cara," Ethan whispered, as insurance investigator Johnny Dollar launched into the next description of his case. His aunt looked up, blinking away the glassy expression in her eyes. "Juniper and I are going out," he told her. "I'll be back for dinner."

She offered him a tiny, crinkle-eyed smile. "Have fun," she

mouthed. She was more relaxed, it seemed, when Juniper was around. Ethan hadn't seen Aunt Cara smile so wide as when she came into the kitchen to find him and Juniper seated at the table, and she'd asked him almost every morning that week whether Juniper would be coming over that day. She seemed relieved that they'd found each other.

After waving good-bye to Aunt Cara, Ethan hurried into his room, thrust open the window, and launched himself to the ground, Juniper style. He expected to land the three-foot drop without a problem, but found himself losing his balance and, seconds later, flopping flat onto his back.

"Ouch," he muttered, and squinted to see Juniper looking down at him, a mocking smile on her lips.

"Two minutes and forty-three seconds." She tapped the face of her watch. "Not bad. Not bad at all." She pulled Ethan to his feet, and he followed her to her bike a few feet away, where he dropped their scroll into the basket. As had become their custom, she climbed on, he took the pegs, and they both held on for dear life as she pedaled at top speed down the forest lane.

Ethan knew fairly quickly that they were heading toward the lake. He was still confused by most of the forest paths, but this one he knew; after all the days he and Juniper had spent planning by the grassy shores, this route had become almost second nature.

Still, he called "Where are we going?" into Juniper's ear.

She reached up with one hand, still pedaling, and smacked him upside the head. "No questions, Harper," she snapped, though he could hear the smirk in her voice. "You'll see."

When they arrived, Juniper eased her bike to a slow stop next to the boathouse. Ethan assumed they would be meeting Gus inside and going for another spin around the lake, but his redheaded companion marched right past the wooden building, and Gus was nowhere in sight. They walked along the perimeter of the lake, toward a new crowd of trees that Ethan hadn't yet explored.

"Juniper, just tell me where we're going," he implored, watching her leap clumsily from rock to rock in the shallow water.

"No can do," she replied. She paused for a moment, swaying precariously on one toe, before barely righting herself and hopping along to the next slippery stone.

"Well, at least stop that, then. You're going to break your neck."

"Negative. I was an acrobat in a past life, you know." She attempted a ballerina's leap and just barely cleared the water. "I was in the circus and I wore a costume covered in glitter and people came from miles around the country to watch me."

And with that, she slid from the rock with a shriek and dropped heavily into the water. Both she and Ethan were silent for a moment, staring at each other in surprise—then, before Ethan could even try to say "I told you so," she was scrambling to her feet, her slim frame racked with earth-splitting laughter.

"Are you okay?" Ethan asked. He watched, half horrified, as she clambered back onto the grass and wrung a good bucketful of water out of her skirt. Her entire backside was drenched and muddy.

"Better than ever," she hummed cheerfully, glancing over her shoulder to examine the damage. "Good thing today is laundry day." She gave her still sopping skirt a final shake and kicked off her oxfords. "These need a good drying too, so I'll just take the rest of this adventure barefoot. Let's hope I don't get bitten by a rattlesnake."

She sounded so chipper that it made Ethan pause. "Juniper," he said slowly.

She whirled to face him. "Calm down, city boy—there are no rattlesnakes in this part of Alabama. Probably. Anyway, if there are, I have a special dance that will scare them off. Trust me."

He shook his head. "Whatever you say."

Though still skeptical, Ethan had figured out by now that there was no way to stop Juniper Jones once she put her mind to something. So he shut his mouth and followed her into the thicket. It seemed like they had only taken a few steps before the trees thinned again, revealing a closet of a house perched right on the lake's edge, only a few wooden support beams away from sitting straight in the water. Gus stood just behind it in the grass, looking too big to fit through the door. At the sound of the kids' rustling, he whirled around, blocking something behind his hefty frame.

"Ethan, Juniper." He greeted them warmly, lacing his fingers at his stomach. "Fancy seeing you here."

"Hey, Gus." Juniper, as usual, was bright as a lightning bolt. She regarded Gus with a conspiratorial grin, then turned to Ethan. Her crooked teeth seemed eager to leap right out of her mouth.

"What?" Ethan questioned, suspicious anticipation tickling his gut. "What is it?"

"Ethan Charlie Harper," Juniper began, "also known as Ethan, Ethan Harper, Chameleon, and Ol' Harper-sichord—"

"What?"

"—I present to you, an extra special, very cool, extremely-secret-but-not-really gift that will change the rest of your summer forever. Gus?"

Smiling his half smile, Gus stepped aside for the big reveal.

"Ta-da!" Juniper cried, throwing her hands in the air.

Ethan found himself staring at a scuffed-up red bike, its handlebars slightly rusty and its paint peeling at the edges.

"It's old," Gus said gruffly, "but works just fine. Tires pumped, gears oiled. Ready to ride."

Ethan had still said nothing, and Juniper's smile faltered slightly. "Well? Do you like it?"

He paused for another moment, his mouth half-open in reply, then, finally, he grinned. "It's cool," he said. "Really, really cool. Thanks, Gus. Thanks, June."

Gus held up his weathered hands. "Don't thank me," he insisted. "Was all her, really. Found it in the junkyard outside of town, brought it to me. Did most of the fixin' up herself." He glanced proudly at Juniper. She blushed a pleased pink.

"Well, what are you waiting for, Ethan?" she asked. "We all know you can't beat me on foot, but maybe now that we've evened the playing field . . ."

"Oh, is that a challenge, Jones? Bring it on."

Juniper set her jaw in gleeful determination. "Prepare to get pounded, Ethan Charlie Harper!" she shouted. "Just let me grab my bike." And she whisked away, leaving a wind-blown Ethan and Gus in her wake.

Gus watched her go, that small smile still curving his lips. "Great girl," he noted. "Wonderful, really. Always means well. But doesn't always understand." Then he looked Ethan in the eye and delivered the first full sentence of their friendship: "You take good care of her, son. Do you understand?"

"Yes," Ethan said quickly. "Yes, sir."

∗

Ethan did not win the race. This was partly because it had been a while since he'd used a bike instead of his legs, and partly because he had absolutely no idea where they were going.

"Follow me!" she'd called as they'd taken off away from the lake.

"Then how am I supposed to win?" Ethan had yelled back, but his voice was lost in the breeze. He'd resigned himself to defeat pretty soon after that, and instead just tailed Juniper as close as he could without tangling his tires with hers. She veered down fork after fork, around bend after bend, and he squinted to keep from losing sight of her so deep in the thicket.

"Coming up ahead!" she announced at last, and by then, Ethan was hunched over his handlebars, panting. She made a sharp left turn straight into the woods so suddenly that Ethan almost missed it, and careened down a hill with an echoing yodel.

"By the way, watch out for the trees!"

Ethan, who had just swerved to avoid meeting a hulking pine head-on, shouted, "Yeah, no kidding!" As their tires bumped over the needle-strewn mulch, they came to a slow, rolling stop.

"I won," Juniper informed Ethan as he walked his bike to her side. "But we're here." She pointed in front of them to a tiny, nearly perfectly circular clearing, fenced in on all sides by towering trees. A softly murmuring brook ran straight down the middle.

"Whoa," Ethan mumbled, raising his eyebrows. "This forest is just full of surprises."

"Sure is," Juniper agreed. "Welcome to my hideaway, and also, my third favorite place in all of town."

Ethan counted off on his fingers. "Number one, Alligator Hill. Number two, the lake. Number three, this place."

"You've been paying attention." Juniper grabbed the scroll from her bicycle basket. "Follow me." She took a running start and leapt over the creek—not that it would have mattered if she had walked right through it; her skirt was still damp with lake water. Ethan followed, his arms flailing above his head. Juniper disappeared behind a tree, and when Ethan circled to the other side, he saw that the gargantuan fir had a hollow large enough for him to crawl inside.

"Cool, isn't it?" Juniper said proudly, squatting at its entrance. Ethan nodded. She reached into her pocket for the roll of tape and, leaning into the hollow, carefully secured the scroll to the inner wall of the tree. "Here it'll be safe. Every tree in this clearing is hollow, you know. I'm convinced that this clearing was built by fairies, and they used to have their houses in there, before the people came." She straightened and beckoned to him, and he trailed her in a circle around the secret grove. "This is where I keep some of my art supplies," she told him, pointing from one tree to another. These were smaller than the first, just large enough to stick a head in. "My easel here, brushes here, paints here . . ."

She was continuing her list when Ethan cut her off. "You paint?" he asked.

Surprised, she tilted her head. "Well, yeah. I don't talk about it much, I guess. My dad did too, so I guess it just runs in the family."

It was the first time Ethan had heard her mention either of her parents. He studied her carefully as she pushed her hair out of her face with a half smile. "I think that's really cool," he said finally.

Juniper blinked. "Really?"

"Yeah. I've always been useless at art, so I mean—I don't know, I just think it's cool. I never understood how it worked."

A slow smile spread over Juniper's face. "Well, then, Ethan Harper," she said, "today's your lucky day."

*

Ethan sat cross-legged on the damp grass to watch as Juniper set up shop. She dragged out a small wooden easel and unfolded it next to the brook, propped a canvas against it, and wriggled into a paint-splattered white smock.

"All of this really fits in the trees?" Ethan asked dubiously, craning his neck as Juniper appeared with a fresh palette of primary colors.

"Of course," Juniper replied with a sneaky smile. "I told you: it's magic."

Once everything was in place, she raked her hair up into a ponytail. Then, grinning at Ethan, she picked up a paint-brush in each hand, knelt in the grass, and said, "Watch and learn."

Leaning back against one of the trees, Ethan silently studied Juniper as she squinted, bit her lip, raised one hand, then the other, and finally dunked both brushes into the palette. It took a moment for it to register in his mind that she was painting with not one but two hands.

"Wait, wait, wait. How—what—how are you doing that?"

Juniper raised an eyebrow in bemusement. "I'm ambidextrous," she said, "I *could* paint with just one hand, but this is much faster. And anyway, having to choose one or the other? What fun would that be?"

Ethan shook his head.

"Shh," she hissed, waving her left hand and sending blue paint splattering toward the trees. "Art is happening."

It wasn't long before not only the trees, but also the grass, the dirt, and Juniper's face were splattered in flecks of every color of the rainbow. But she didn't seem the slightest bit aware of the mess she was making; every part of her was solely focused on the canvas in front of her. She didn't even seem to breathe. Ethan couldn't look away.

Ethan thought he was watching the entire time but found himself opening his eyes a while later to a darkening forest and Juniper, kneeling patiently in front of him. He blinked up at her, ethereal in the evening light, and wondered how he had ended up befriending someone like her.

"Wanna see it?" she asked, pointing at the canvas beside her.

"Yes," Ethan said, sitting up. "Of course."

She held out the canvas in front of her, and Ethan leaned close. He recognized the scene immediately. It was the clearing where they lay—the soft green grass, the brook, the hollow trees. Inside the largest hollow, he could just make out two tiny winged figures, floating in the darkness.

"That's us," Juniper said. "But as fairies."

Ethan nodded. He thought the painting was beautiful. It was chaotic, sure, and kind of messy—but the colors seemed to explode off the canvas, and everything was captured in just the right shade.

"It's incredible," he said.

"You really think so?"

"Really."

She beamed at him. There was still paint on her face, glowing in the dusky light.

"I think your freckles turned green," he said, squinting. Frowning, Juniper put a finger to her forehead, wiped off an especially large glob of paint, and smeared it on his nose.

"I think your nose has turned green too," she said seriously.

They stared at each other for a moment with straight faces, then burst into laughter.

"All right, nerd, it's almost eight." She held out a hand. "We should probably get going." She pushed herself to her feet and held out a hand to help Ethan onto his. "Hurry up, slowpoke!" She leapt over the quiet creek, humming the tune of some Elvis Presley song and dancing wildly in circles. On her way out, she paused to lay the painting gently inside a small hollow. Her feet were still bare and caked in grime.

Ethan sighed as he clambered slowly to his feet, wishing, suddenly, that they could just stay in this little forest sanctuary forever. The town was out there, somewhere, and in it, Noah and his friends, and the whispering townspeople—and somewhere else, far away, Arcadia, Washington, his family, and home. But here was Juniper Jones, in her muddy skirt, wearing paint on her cheeks like a badge of honor and spinning through the grass with her arms wide enough to embrace the moon. Ethan thought that if the world were to disappear at that very moment, and this was the last sight that he ever saw, he wouldn't mind at all.

July 1955

TEN

It was the Fourth of July, and the lake was as full as Ethan had ever seen it. Picnic tables hauled in just for the occasion dotted the grass to the edge of the forest, side by side with dozens of colorful blankets. People milled about in swimsuits and sun hats, drinks and American flags in hand. The greasy scent of hamburgers and hot dogs hung over the makeshift park—Ethan thought that for the first time, it smelled a little bit like home.

The barbecue was already in full swing by the time Ethan arrived with Aunt Cara and Uncle Robert, lugging two ice chests filled with the ingredients for root beer floats. This was a town tradition. All the town businesses contributed something: drinks from the Malt, food from the general store, tables from a logger who lived at the edge of town—and of course, fireworks, courtesy of Gus. That was the best part, according to Juniper: when Gus took his motorboat out to the middle of the lake and set the sky on fire.

"Over here, Ethan," Uncle Robert called, dipping his head

toward the boathouse, where Abrams was standing in front of a gigantic grill flipping dozens of burgers. Ethan grunted, hefting the chests in his grip and teetering after his uncle.

"Careful, sweetie," Aunt Cara implored, hurrying at his heels. He wiped the sweat from his forehead with the sleeve of his T-shirt.

Abrams looked up as Ethan approached and set the coolers in the grass. Uncle Robert was already a few yards away, dragging a table toward them, and did not notice the bearded man's gaze.

"You're got some real nerve, kid," he said. "Coming out here with the whole town to watch you. You've noticed, I'm sure, that you're the only colored person on the whole beach."

"I realize," Ethan said coolly. "Thanks, Abrams."

The man shrugged and turned back to his grill. The truth was Ethan had been dreading this day ever since his aunt and uncle had informed him of the occasion. Nothing sounded worse to him than putting himself in full view of the entire town—all of their stares on him at once. His only relief was that Juniper was coming, and he was already itching to find her.

"Ethan, give me a hand, would you?" Uncle Robert was still by the table, struggling to pull it closer to the bench.

Together, the pair of them managed to wiggle the bench closer to the rest of the food and unload the materials for the first round of drinks. Uncle Robert scooped and Ethan poured, and it wasn't long before they had a table full of ice cream sodas.

Uncle Robert looked up for Aunt Cara, only to find that she had wandered off. "Don't know where that woman's off to," he muttered, "but if we don't start passing these out soon, the ice cream will melt." He turned and started loading the glasses onto circular black trays. "Would you mind, Ethan? Just, you know, try to keep your distance from the O'Neil boy."

Ethan balked at the thought of running into Noah as he wound his way through the crowd, and Uncle Robert seemed almost embarrassed to be asking. Still, he forced himself to nod. A moment later, he had a tray in each hand and was stepping straight into the chaos.

A local teenage band was playing on a makeshift stage of wooden planks, all lazy guitar strings and voices that cracked on the high notes. People swayed as they walked without even realizing it. Ethan thought he would hand out a drink to anyone who looked his way, but everyone seemed too pre-occupied with the music or looked quickly away the moment they caught his eye. He noticed that wherever he walked, there was a gap between him and everyone else in all directions.

It was only through surprise that Ethan managed to rid himself of one tray, sneaking up on one person or another so that they took a float before they had time to think about it. Now he was down to four glasses, and the ice cream was melting fast. As the sweat began to pool at the collar of his shirt, he thought he might just down them all himself. Just as he was considering how sick four root beer floats would make him, a voice stopped him near the water's edge.

"Ethan Harper," Noah said. "Actually doing your job today, I see."

Ethan felt his blood chill. He hadn't seen Noah since that terrible day at the Malt, and after spending so much time planning with Juniper, he'd almost been able to forget the boy existed. He clutched the tray tighter and tried to con-vince himself that here, with all these people around, Noah wouldn't try anything.

"Noah," Ethan replied curtly, turning to face the other boy. Here, only a foot away, he could see Noah's face up close—the close-set brown eyes, the acne on his forehead, the blond wisps of hair beginning to grow on his upper lip. As he watched, Noah's lips twisted into a sneer.

"I want one of those," Noah said, nodding at the floats. "And so does my family. My mom and dad and little brother. Why don't you come and serve us?"

Ethan fought the urge to tip the tray of floats right into the lake, but managed to steady himself. He bit his tongue and followed in angry silence.

"You know, Ethan," Noah said as they made their way through the throng of people. "I think we could've been real good friends. If it wasn't for the whole"—he pointed to the skin of his cheek—"you know."

"There's nothing about you that would make me want to be your friend," Ethan muttered.

"What did you say?" Noah demanded, whirling. The look on his face was cruel, just as it had been before he'd knocked those milk shakes over.

Ethan gritted his teeth. "Nothing."

"Whatever," Noah said, turning back around. A few paces later, he stopped suddenly and nodded to a group of people seated around a picnic table. "Anyway, that's my family. You behave now. They like it when the help has manners."

Ethan fumed silently as he trailed Noah to a picnic table, where a fair-haired family sat eating hamburgers. A man, a woman, and an angelic little boy. When they turned around, Ethan realized that this was the same family he had encountered on that first day of work at the Malt—the same woman who had bemoaned his presence to Aunt Cara in the general store. And now, too, they were staring him in disgust.

"Noah, honey," the woman said, her voice nasal. "What is this boy doing here?"

"Root beer floats," Ethan said quickly, before Noah could interject. "I thought you could use a few."

The man's eyes turned stormy, and he narrowed them in Ethan's direction. "Where are your manners, boy?" he demanded. "Didn't anyone teach you not to speak unless spoken to?"

"Our Noah has fantastic manners," Mrs. O'Neil announced proudly, then glanced at her younger son, who was ripping pieces of bread from his hamburger bun and tossing them to the ground. "And Daniel, well . . . he's learning. Don't do that, sweetie, come on now."

"Root beer floats," Ethan repeated miserably.

Noah barked a cruel laugh. "Mom, Dad, come on," he addressed, lifting his hands as if to placate his parents. "The boy barely knows what he's doing. Let's just take these floats."

Ethan's stomach twisted as the O'Neils nodded and he realized that in this family, it was Noah who had control. They all reached up to grab a drink when he gestured, then turned back to their food when he told them they'd looked long enough.

"Well, Ethan Harper." Noah reached over and plucked his own float off the tray. "Great to see you, really. Happy to know you can actually do your job."

Ethan didn't miss the icy note behind Noah's feigned cheerfulness, the way his eyes were dark and hard. Still, he clutched the now-empty tray a little tighter and stood his ground.

"Sure, Noah," Ethan said. "And try not to spill your drink this time." The words out, he turned and hurried away before Noah could respond. Fear pulsed in his stomach at the thought of the older boy coming after him, but when he finally dared to turn around, all he saw was the crowd milling about.

He couldn't tell what was scarier—facing Noah up close or in a sea of people who looked just like him. Here, Noah had acted with restraint but seemed to be only barely hanging on to that forced civility, as if any wrong move from Ethan could send him flying into a rage. But for now, at least, Noah was gone, and by the time Ethan returned to Uncle Robert, his heart rate had lowered to a manageable pace.

"There you are," his uncle said briskly. "Pass these out too, and hurry. We don't have all day."

Ethan heaved a resigned sigh and nodded, turning back to face the crowd. "Aye-aye, Captain," he muttered to no one.

✳

It seemed as if hours had passed before Ethan finally found Juniper Jones. Or rather, before she found him. He had just handed his last float to an old woman reclining on a beach chair when something red, white, and blue rammed into him from behind and jumped onto his back. He looked up, and her curls fell into his face.

"Hey!" she cried, jumping back onto the grass. "Happy Independence Day!"

Ethan managed a smile for the first time that day, raising his eyebrows as he took in Juniper's patriotic attire. "Happy Independence Day." It felt strange to say; even as he relaxed in Juniper's presence, he felt a tenseness in his shoulders. Independence Day, sure—but with so many townspeople around him and Noah O'Neil not far away, he hardly felt free. He envied the ease with which Juniper sashayed across the grass, completely unconcerned about the space she filled.

"Ask me about my dress," she said, swishing her skirt.

"What about your dress?"

Juniper grinned. "I'm *so* glad you asked. I've been running around all day, trying to get everyone to ask, but they just keep giving me funny looks." She twirled in a circle, showing off the dress that was, essentially, an entire American flag. The bodice was navy blue and dotted with stars, and the skirt was thick candy-cane stripes. Her lips, ruby red, clashed wonderfully with her hair.

"No idea why," Ethan said. "You're stylish as can be."

"Oh, put a sock in it." Juniper rolled her eyes. "Can you please just admire my dress? I made it myself. There are forty-eight stars on the whole thing, you know. Here, count!" She spun in circles, too fast for Ethan to even register the stars, before he stopped her.

"Okay, enough!" he cried. "So, what, you're the American flag?"

Juniper shook her head. "*No*, of course not. I'm Betsy Ross after she accidentally sewed herself into her own flag."

Ethan burst into laughter. Juniper looked so proud of herself, her chin jutting out smugly, that he couldn't bring himself to tell her that in Betsy's time there were a good thirty-five fewer stars on that flag.

"All right, Ms. Ross," he conceded. "What do you say we go get some floats of our own before they're all gone?"

"That sounds just dandy," she replied, curtsying. "And also some hot dogs. I would quite enjoy a hot dog."

Ten minutes later, the pair sat on a picnic blanket by the water's edge, away from the celebratory commotion. Two root beer floats and a plateful of hot dogs sat on the blanket between them. Juniper had drowned hers in ketchup and mustard.

"The thing about hot dogs," she said, her mouth full, "is that they're the best food in the whole wide world. You can have them for breakfast, lunch, and dinner, you can add extra flavor to them, and you don't even need a fork and knife to eat them."

Ethan watched her in amusement as she stuffed the rest of the hot dog into her mouth and licked some stray ketchup off her lips. He was only halfway through his first one, and she was just about to get started on her third.

"Someone's hungry," he commented.

Juniper nodded vigorously as she slathered mustard on the bun. "When it comes to hot dogs, I am always hungry."

Uncle Robert came over just then, finally finished with ice cream-soda delivery. There was a hamburger in his hands. "How are you doing, Juniper?" he asked, offering up a rare smile.

"Mr. Shay!" She dropped her hot dog onto the blanket and leapt to her feet, darting over to squeeze Ethan's uncle in a tight embrace. "Happy Independence Day!"

"Same to you. You sure are looking patriotic today."

Juniper twirled proudly in a circle, her skirt billowing out around her. "She's Betsy Ross after she accidentally sewed herself into her own flag," Ethan explained, rolling his eyes. His uncle laughed.

"Junie, there's just no end to your ideas," he said affectionately. "All right, well, you kids have fun. I'll see you around here later today." He turned, then paused for a moment and looked over his shoulder, his eyes suddenly serious. "And be careful, please," he added. "A lot of people out today."

Juniper and Ethan shared a solemn glance as Uncle Robert walked away, but neither acknowledged the warning. Silently, Juniper returned to her place next to Ethan and ate two more entire hot dogs before she declared that she felt full.

"I don't know how you do it," Ethan said, swallowing the last bite of his third and final hot dog.

Juniper grinned. "I'm like an elephant!" she cried. "They eat a *ton*. Did you know that's because they don't have stomachs, only intestines? They eat and eat and the food just goes right through them." She stuck an arm out next to her nose and waved it around like a trunk.

"Juniper Starfish Elephant Jones," Ethan said.

"It has a nice ring to it, don't you think?" Before Ethan could respond, she turned and yelled, "Hey!" as she suddenly grabbed Ethan's arm. "They're starting a dance floor over where the stage is! Come on, Ethan, we absolutely have to go dance, this band is *so* good."

Ethan thought that for all their enthusiasm, the band was crap—still, he didn't protest as Juniper grabbed him by the arm and dragged him toward the edge of the dance floor.

"Do you know the Charleston?" Juniper asked over the din of guitar strums. Ethan shook his head. "Me neither! In fact, I'm not really sure what dances I do know. I just throw my arms around and hope for the best. Like this."

Ethan leaned back as she closed her eyes and flailed wildly to a rhythm just a few beats off from the music.

"Ethan, dance with me!" she shrilled, grabbing him by the wrist.

"No, I really don't—" he attempted, but she was already twirling him around.

"Don't fight the music," she scolded, then, "I love this song!" as the band launched into a cover of "Rock Around the Clock" that was slightly out of tune.

As uncomfortable as he felt, Ethan focused on Juniper,

her cheeks bright red as she shuffled back and forth in the muddy grass, and tried to copy her wild routine. When she lifted an arm, so did he. When she did what seemed to be some variant of the hokey pokey, he hopped in a circle on one foot and tried not to fall over. She couldn't dance any better than he could, and though the couples around them clearly had more experience, he began to feel more at ease. On the crowded dance floor, in the middle of all the noise and chaos, people didn't seem to notice him. For the first time in Ellison, at his most conspicuous, Ethan felt blissfully invisible.

A few songs later, Juniper dropped her hands to her knees, panting. "I'm exhausted," she announced, wiping sweat from her forehead. "Wanna go sit down?"

Ethan nodded, feeling his heart knocking heavily against his rib cage. He took a half step back, about to follow her off the dance floor, when his foot caught on something and he went sprawling onto the grass.

"*Oof.*" He blinked the air back into his lungs. Looking up, he saw Juniper's concerned face—and next to it, Noah's. Grinning.

"Sorry," he sneered. "Guess my foot slipped."

"You're a jerk." Juniper glared up at Noah as Ethan pushed himself to his feet. "Go away, Noah."

"I was just trying to dance," Noah said. "He got in my way."

"Well, then, you're a bad dancer," Juniper retorted.

Ethan said nothing, still a bit stunned by the fall. Before Noah appeared, Ethan had been feeling like he was finally living up to the nickname Juniper had given him—Chameleon. Blending in, as much as he could. But now, as Noah loomed over him, Ethan felt that security slip away—he could feel everyone's eyes on him.

"And you're a freak," Noah responded. "Maybe even a bigger freak than blackie over here."

Ethan bristled. In front of his family, Noah had been cold but not rude—he'd kept up his manners. Away from them, all bets were off. Ethan knew he had to get out of here before the situation escalated.

Thankfully, a soft voice called out, "Come on, Noah, lay off," and Ethan turned to see Courtney a few feet away, her arms crossed over her chest. "I just wanna dance. Let's go."

Noah glanced between Courtney and Ethan, seeming ready to hurl another insult before Courtney raised an eyebrow. He glowered, then spat onto the grass. "Fine," he muttered, stomping toward his girlfriend. "See ya, freaks."

The warmth and exhilaration of dancing had long left his body by the time Ethan watched Noah walk away—despite the summer sun bearing down on them, he felt a sudden chill.

"They're stupid," Juniper said. "Just ignore them."

Easier said than done, Ethan thought, but followed Juniper off the dance floor. They made their way back to the picnic blanket and Juniper flopped down on her back, her hair trailing into the lapping water. He knelt beside her and squinted out over the lake, watching people in rowboats racing swimmers through the gentle waves. As he swatted absently at the bugs that hid among the reeds, he tried to forget about Noah for a second time that day.

"Hey, Chameleon," Juniper said after a while, tugging the leg of Ethan's pants. One freckled arm was draped across her eyes.

"I don't want to talk about it."

She shook her head sleepily. "Okay. That's not what I was going to say, though."

He glanced down at her.

"I was just going to say, I really like the Fourth of July. It's the only time of year when"—she yawned—"the whole town comes together like this. It feels like I'm part of something."

Ethan wished he could agree. It was hard to feel patriotic in a place where he wasn't welcome. It seemed impossible that this could be his country, too, when he so obviously did not belong. As if sensing his unease, Juniper felt around for his hand and, when she found it, squeezed it tightly and didn't let go.

"Wake me up when the fireworks start," she mumbled, then rolled onto her side and fell asleep.

✳

Darkness crept in a few hours later, and Juniper was still fast asleep, snoring lightly. Ethan had brought along a novel and was sixty pages in when the sun sank too low for him to make out the words on the pages.

He tapped Juniper with his foot. "Wake up." She groaned loudly and rolled away from him. "June," he said, leaning over so that his lips were a few inches from her ear. Covering his mouth with one hand, he attempted to make a staticky sound, like a radio interference. "This is Chameleon delivering a secret message for Starfish. Come in, Starfish. Do you read me?"

After a pause, Juniper rolled over, smiling slightly, but didn't open her eyes.

"Starfish, HQ has informed me that the entire country is at risk and will probably explode if you do not accept this message."

Juniper lifted a hand to her mouth and opened her eyes.

"This is Starfish reporting for duty," she said. "What's the message, Chameleon?"

Thinking quickly, he blurted, "The boatman is in the torpedo. I repeat, the boatman is in the torpedo. Detonation scheduled for T-minus ten minutes."

"Well then, Chameleon"—Juniper grinned and sat up—"I guess it's time to move out." She turned and glanced over her shoulder at the lake, where Gus was standing on the deck of a sturdy wooden motorboat, steering it toward the center while holding a package of fireworks under his arm. Above him, the sky had gone dark.

"Come on," Juniper urged, jumping to her feet and pulling Ethan with her. "We have just enough time to get up there before the show starts."

Ethan raised an eyebrow as she tugged him through the crowd and toward the trees. "Get up where?"

She glanced back at him and smirked, a twinkle in her eyes. "The best seats in the house," she said. "You'll see."

Ethan gave a silent thanks that he was a runner as she took off through the dim forest, dust flying up in her wake. He kept on her heels, marveling at the ease with which she navigated through the trees, when to him every trunk and branch looked exactly like the last. Somewhere behind them, he heard the dim sounds of the barbecue, but Juniper's billowing flag skirt pulled him deeper into the woods.

When they emerged from the trees, panting, they were standing in a small meadow. He recognized it vaguely as the place where Juniper had found him after his phone call with his father—he could hardly remember how much time had passed since then. And there, perched majestically before them, was Alligator Hill, sloping gently skyward.

"Look at the moon," Juniper marveled, pointing to the

top of the hill. It loomed in the sky, low and huge and nearly full. Ethan thought that if he stood on the hill and reached up, he could pluck it from the sky and hold it in his hands.

Juniper seemed to have the same idea, because she cried, "I'll race you up there!" and took off sprinting up the grassy slope.

"Oh, no, you don't!" Ethan shouted, his arms pumping as he took long strides toward Juniper. He'd always been good at running uphill, and it wasn't long before he was side by side with her, then passing her, sticking out his tongue as he reached the top and dove to the ground, his heart racing faster than his legs ever could.

Juniper surfaced a few moments later and dropped down beside him, panting heavily. "All right, Ethan Harper, you win," she breathed. "This time."

"Every time," he retorted.

She slapped his arm. "Shut up and look over there." He followed her arm as she pointed ahead of them. They were high enough above most of the trees that they could just make out the moonlight reflected on the lake and a few people milling around. Even here, so far from the crowd, Ethan could just barely make out the sound of the band.

"Shh," Juniper whispered, though he hadn't spoken. "It's starting."

Right on cue, a familiar drumbeat rose up from the trees, getting louder every moment. Juniper clambered to her feet and placed her right hand over her heart, facing the lake. After some hesitation, Ethan did the same. He wasn't sure how, but when a girl's powerful voice began to sing the lyrics to "The Star-Spangled Banner," the words cleared the forest and floated right into his ears.

"That's Courtney, Noah's girlfriend," Juniper whispered in

his ear. "She's been singing it every year since she was twelve. She may be friends with terrible people, but she has some voice."

For all anyone could tell, the entire state of Alabama went silent as Courtney sang. Ethan wasn't feeling particularly full of love and pride for his country, but he could imagine every person from Montgomery to Birmingham stepping out of their houses and turning toward Courtney's voice. Beside him, Juniper had tears in her eyes.

It wasn't until the very last note that Ethan heard the faint whine of fireworks, and as Courtney's *"brave"* petered off into silence, the sky exploded in light. He couldn't help but gasp as the fireworks flew up above the lake, seeming only inches away as they burst into colorful, glittering streamers. As one faded, another would take its place, and even Alligator Hill shook with the shattering *booms*.

As the show went on, Ethan and Juniper sank back into the grass. The night sky shimmered under the watchful eye of the moon and Juniper tilted her head skyward, drinking in the moonlight through the trees. Suddenly, as if inspired by some omnipotent force, she let out a triumphant howl. The sound of it brought chills rising on Ethan's arms.

"Wow," he said. "Maybe we should add wolf to your list of animal nicknames."

She did not respond, but smiled, and the fireworks reflected in her eyes.

Juniper had told Ethan that Gus had an endless supply of firecrackers, and that seemed to be true. Whenever he thought it was over, that whining sound would pierce the air again, and sparks would fly above the trees. Time seemed to slow and then stop completely as they lay on top of Alligator Hill and watched the sky. Between explosions, Juniper would point out the stars.

"That's Orion's Belt, I think," she said, tracing her index finger along a row of three twinkling pinpoints. "Remind me to add that to our list, okay? To learn the constellations?"

Ethan nodded sleepily. "Deal."

Eventually, there was a suspenseful screeching louder than all the others. Juniper reached out and gripped Ethan's hand. "This is the grand finale," she whispered.

And was it ever. The entire sky seemed enveloped in this last display, an explosion of confetti rockets that reached out past the forest, the cities, and the oceans to touch every corner of the Earth in a dizzying swirl of color. Even after the fireworks had faded away, and the night air had found silence, Ethan's ears still rang.

"By gosh," he murmured, still looking up.

"Yeah," Juniper agreed. "By gosh."

Down below, they could hear the faintest sound of the band striking up a celebratory melody, but it was years away. The moon was right above their heads, seeming to offer them a smile. Juniper sighed. They closed their eyes and breathed as stardust fell from the black satin night sky and settled on their cheeks.

ELEVEN

That was the beginning of many good days. Something changed in the air—a shift in the wind or a settling of the dust—and it seemed that the entire town had taken a deep breath and let it out in a sunny stream. Ethan wasn't sure if his eyes were playing tricks on him or if Juniper's face really was especially radiant when she skipped into the Malt that next afternoon, with a wicker basket in one hand and a watering can in the other.

"Hurry, hurry, hurry," she urged, dancing from foot to foot as Ethan slung his apron on the peg. "Project Invincible Summer starts right now, and anything slower than top speed is way too slow."

"Okay, okay," Ethan said. "I'm coming." With a nod to Uncle Robert, who had just emerged from the kitchen, he followed Juniper out the door. They circled to the back of the store, where their bikes leaned against the wall, and he asked, "So, what's the plan for today?"

Juniper shook the basket before hanging it from her

handlebars. Ethan glanced inside and raised his eyebrows, surprised to find that it was filled to the brim with black seeds. "Sunflowers," she declared. "By the time we're done today, there will be sunflowers ready to grow all over town."

Ethan made a face. "I don't get why you chose sunflowers. They're basically weeds."

Juniper frowned at him as she mounted her bike. "They're misunderstood," she retorted. Then, as an afterthought, "But still beautiful." Then she pedaled off down the lane, and Ethan had no choice but to follow.

Their first stop was a patch of dirt near the edge of downtown. The few blades of grass that poked from the earth were a sad, brownish hue, and Ethan wondered how anything could ever grow from such a helpless plot of land. But Juniper was already on her knees, her yellow skirt no doubt becoming ridden with stains. She scooped a handful of seeds from the basket and dropped half into Ethan's outstretched palm.

"You know how to do this, right?" she asked.

Ethan shook his head. "My little sister tried to grow some tomatoes in our backyard once. They all died."

Juniper winced. "All right," she said. "Well, then, I'll show you. Come on, kneel down." Ethan did so carefully, making sure to avoid the dirtiest parts of the ground. June, utterly oblivious, shifted comfortably in the mud.

"First, you have to pull out the weeds," she began, tugging at a few serrated stems and tossing them into the road, "or they'll stop the plant from growing. Then"—she jumped up, reached into her bike basket, and pulled out a small bag and a shovel—"you have to add some fertilizer." She reached into the bag and drew out a fistful of white pellets then sprinkled them onto the soil. "Swirl that around, would you?" she said, and Ethan did. "I've been watering spots all over for the past few days to make sure the soil is ready, so now we can just plant."

Leaning over the small plot, she dragged the shovel in a straight line, creating a long, shallow ditch. When she finished, she tossed the shovel aside and dropped seeds in. She nudged Ethan, and he did the same.

"Next, you cover it with soil," she said, smoothing loose dirt over the seeds and patting it gently down. "Then water it—you can do that." Obligingly, Ethan took the watering can from her handlebar and tilted it over the row so that water flowed down in a gentle stream. Juniper grinned when he was done.

"That's it?" he said, squinting at the wet dirt.

"That's it," Juniper confirmed. "All that's left to do is wait. Now come on." She gathered her supplies and loaded them onto her bike. "That's one spot down, but we've got a whole lot more to go."

They pedaled slowly toward the lake, taking their time in the lazy afternoon sun. "Where'd you learn to garden?" Ethan asked as they rode.

"I didn't," Juniper replied, then explained, "My mom had an amazing garden when she was my age. Rhododendrons, camellias, orchids, daffodils—you name it, she planted it. What's it they call someone who's good with plants? Oh right, a green thumb. Well, she had one of those, all right. She even won some prizes. Imagine that! Here she was, a girl in Ellison, winning prizes. She was something, my mom was. Or so I'm told."

For a moment her smile faltered, and Ethan slowed his bike, unsure what to say. But before he could decide, Juniper shook her head and stood suddenly on her pedals, coasting for a moment before glancing back with a grin.

"Anyway," she continued, her voice bright, "no one ever taught me how to do this stuff, it was just kinda natural. I guess I was just born with flower petals in my blood."

Ethan nodded thoughtfully. "Yeah," he murmured. "I guess so."

By the time the sunset smeared pink and orange across the horizon, they had planted sunflowers in thirty-two spots around town and, despite his efforts to stay clean, Ethan was covered in dirt. Now he and Juniper sat on the dock, their bare feet dangling in the lake and tall glasses of lemonade—courtesy of Gus—in their hands. Juniper had a streak of soil on her forehead.

"The town will be so pretty when it all grows in." She sighed and took a long sip. "I'll betcha when you come back next summer, you won't even recognize the place." Ethan didn't reply, and she frowned. "I mean," she said quietly, "you are coming back next summer, right? At least to see the sunflowers?"

Ethan paused. Truth be told, for the past few weeks he hadn't thought of his life more than a few hours in advance. The summer seemed endless in Ellison. But in less than two months, he realized, he would be in the car headed back up to Arcadia, back to his dad and the twins, to the track team and his friends, and even Samuel Hill. It would be his sophomore year. But as he sat by the water and sipped his lemonade, that life seemed a thousand years away.

He glanced over at Juniper, who was staring at him with watery blue eyes, still waiting for an answer. He chewed on his bottom lip and felt the silence between them as a weight on his shoulders. His glass was sweating into his hand.

Finally, with a small sigh, he shook his head. "Well," he said softly. "I guess I don't know."

"What do you mean, you don't know?"

Ethan shrugged, keeping his gaze focused on a ripple in the center of the lake. Juniper pulled her feet out of the water and hugged her knees to her chest. The dirtied hem of her skirt landed in a damp spot on the wood.

"Maybe I asked the wrong question," she said softly. "Maybe what I shoulda said is, what don't you know? Whether you can come back, or whether you want to?"

Ethan felt shame warm his cheeks under Juniper's prying stare.

"Well?"

Setting down his glass, Ethan turned to her. "I meant what I said, okay?" he said, harsher than he intended. "You're great, June. All of our adventures so far—they've been great. But it's not easy to be here. For me."

"You think I don't know that?" She ran the heel of her hand against her freckled forehead. "I'm trying my best. And for the record, it's not easy for me to be here either."

"It's not the same."

"How is it not—" She paused. "Know what? Never mind. I'm being unfair."

"June," Ethan began, but she held up a hand.

"Really," she insisted. "This isn't about me. I should know better than to expect anyone to wanna stick around. Anyway, no use thinking about all that now, right?" She pushed herself to her feet and picked up her half-filled glass. Her lips curled back into a small smile. "Back in a flash. I'm gonna get some more lemonade."

*

"How high did you say it was?"

Ethan craned his neck to stare up at the towering hickory tree. Juniper sidled up beside him, shielding her eyes with one hand.

"A hundred and twenty feet," she said. "It's a doozy." She walked in a circle around the thick trunk, thoughtfully eyeing the lowest hanging branches.

"Wow." Ethan whistled. "And remind me again—why is it called Big Red? I'm pretty sure this thing's not a redwood."

"It definitely isn't," Juniper agreed. "There's this old town story, though—sort of a legend—about how it got its name. See, back like a hundred and something years ago when Ellison was founded, there weren't a lot of people living west of the Mississippi yet. So people didn't know the trees out west real well. Anyway, two guys from town were out exploring and they found this tree, and they saw how tall it was, and one of them said to the other, 'Say, this is one heck of a tree,' and the other one replied, 'Sure is, wonder what kind,' and the first one had a cousin or uncle or someone who'd been to California, where there are redwoods, and so he said, 'You know, I heard that there are these real huge trees called redwoods in California. I betcha it's one of those.' And so they called it Big Red, and that's the name it's kept to this day."

She let out a breath, and Ethan fought back a smile. She had provided a very animated re-enactment of the scene, complete with ridiculous voices and robotic arm movements.

"Anyway," she continued, rubbing her hands together in preparation, "that old legend doesn't matter. Today, we just have to climb."

"Right," Ethan agreed, nodding. "Just climb."

Juniper took a deep breath, licked her lips, and took a

few long paces back. With her eye on the nearest branch, she sprinted forward, launched herself into the air, and missed completely, collapsing to the ground with a surprised grunt. Ethan stared at her for a moment as she sat in silence and stared dazedly at the ground, then burst suddenly into laughter.

"June," he gasped, "you missed by a mile! Come on, you can do better than that. If I didn't know better, I'd think you'd never climbed a tree in your life."

Juniper pursed her lips, getting to her feet and dusting off the seat of her blue jeans. "Well, you see," she began, offering Ethan a sheepish smile. "That's kind of—sort of—a little bit the case. I have no idea how tree climbing works."

Ethan gaped at her, thoroughly appalled. "So, let me get this straight. You, a girl from a forest lake town, not only can't swim, but have also never climbed a tree?" He shook his head in disbelief. "I've gotta hand it to you, Juniper Jones. You're the only person I've ever met who makes less and less sense the longer I know you."

"Good." Juniper grinned widely, her teeth uneven between her rose petal lips. "Making sense is for nerds and grown-ups. I am way more interesting."

"And you also can't climb a tree," Ethan reminded her. He held out his arms. "All right, come on. I'll give you a boost."

He squatted down beneath the branch, lacing his fingers into a secure foothold. Juniper looked at him dubiously.

"I just—I just step on?"

"You just step on. What, are you chicken?"

"I am not chicken." Juniper stuck out her tongue, then put one hand on Ethan's shoulder and one foot in his out-stretched hands. Grunting with effort, Ethan stood, raising Juniper high enough to climb onto the branch easily. She shrieked the whole two seconds up and scrambled hurriedly onto the tree. With a quick running start and a lucky leap, Ethan pulled himself up beside her.

"There you go," he said, smiling at her. "That wasn't so bad, was it?"

"Not at all. Let's keep going." She got to her feet, her arms spread as she teetered precariously on the branch. Thankfully, the branches were fairly close together, good for climbing, so she found a handhold above her and stepped up to the next level. And the next one, and the next. Soon, Ethan was staring up at her from ten feet below.

"Would you look at that, you're a regular monkey," he remarked. Juniper looked down, first with a grin—then her gaze strayed past Ethan to the faraway ground, and he could've sworn that she turned nearly the same color as the leaves on the tree.

"Ethan," she said meekly, her eyes wide. "We have a problem. I think—I think I'm afraid of heights."

"Oh God." Ethan stood and climbed as quickly as he could to where Juniper sat, straddling a thick branch and hugging the trunk for dear life. "Come on," he said, attempting to peel her arm away from the bark. "Come on, let's climb down."

But Juniper shook her head fiercely. "No," she snapped. "I'm not coming down. I'm going to climb this tree if it kills me. Which"—she glanced down again and gulped—"it very well might."

"June," Ethan started, but she cut him off.

"Don't 'June' me. I'm climbing this tree, Ethan Charlie Harper, with or without you."

After a moment of hesitation, Ethan found a hold above his head and reached his free hand out to Juniper. "Well, then," he said with a sideways smile, glancing skyward. "What are we waiting for?"

They didn't make it all the way up the tree. At about the three-fourths point, Juniper made the mistake of looking down and promptly vomited onto the branches, only narrowly missing Ethan's head.

"I think we should stop here," she croaked, wiping her mouth with the back of her hand. Ethan nodded, and, climbing to a sturdy branch closer to her, stood up and surveyed the view.

"Whoa," he murmured. "June, you have to see this." He lifted a hand to shield his eyes from the sun and scanned the treetops. Beside him, he heard Juniper pushing herself to her feet.

She gasped. They hadn't climbed all the way up, but they were still above the rest of the forest. For miles they could see only a carpet of green—and just in the distance, faintly outlined against the afternoon sun, were the buildings of some faraway city.

"Incredible," Juniper whispered, her voice wobbling slightly.

"Yeah," Ethan agreed, turning just in time to see the sun hit her eyelashes and turn them gold. "Yeah, sure is."

✳

"Do you realize," Juniper said, as they pedaled away from the Malt, "that if we check another thing off the list today, we'll be a whole quarter of the way through? How crazy is that?"

Ethan raised an eyebrow, swerving to avoid a pothole. "You've been keeping track?"

"Of course. I go back to the clearing every day after our adventures and check another one off the list. And we're almost half of halfway there. At this rate, we'll definitely finish before you have to go home. And if we don't, well, I'll just get Noah to hold you hostage in town until we do."

She shrugged, grinning that crinkle-eyed grin.

"Then we'd better get going," Ethan said, shaking his head. "What do you say today I teach you how to swim?"

Juniper waved her hand dismissively and shook her head. "We can do that anytime. I actually have something else in mind." With a sudden skid of dust, she made a sharp right onto a side lane. "Follow me," she called over her shoulder. "We're going to Alligator Hill."

That was the first time Ethan had properly seen Alligator Hill in broad daylight. As they rolled their bikes to its base, he looked at the giant slope and thought there was no way anything could actually be so green.

"Come on," Juniper piped, laying her bike carefully in the grass and beginning the trek to the top. Ethan followed. Clovers bowed beneath his feet, leaving a vague impression of footsteps up the side of the hill.

When she reached the top, Juniper was panting heavily. She stood still for a moment, her arms wide and her face turned up to the sun. Unlike everywhere else in the town, there seemed to be a cool breeze up here. And no dust. With every breath he took, Ethan felt only fresh air.

"All right, then," Juniper said, softly for once, almost reverently. "Let's get started."

She dropped suddenly to the ground and sat cross-legged. She nodded at Ethan, and he did the same.

For a long moment she said nothing, and simply stared at some point over his shoulder. He glanced back and saw nothing but treetops. "June," he tried, "are we—"

Juniper shook her head and blinked as if awakening from a trance. "Sorry," she murmured. "I just get lost up here.

Anyway." In typical Juniper Jones fashion, she clapped her hands twice. "This is the one thing on our list that I've actually done before, but everyone who comes to this town needs to do it at least once. I think you'll love it."

Ethan narrowed his eyes. "And this is . . ."

"Easy." She flopped back into the grass, limbs askew. "We're going to roll down Alligator Hill. And I promise you, it is the best hill roll that you will ever have. Lie down."

With some trepidation, Ethan lowered himself carefully into the grass. As much as he was questioning the sensibility of rolling down this very steep hill, he had to admit that the grass was incredibly soft. He curled his fingers through it and squinted up at the sun.

"Are you ready?" Juniper asked, nudging him with her foot. "You're going first."

"I—what?"

"Oh, don't be a baby. You'll be fine, I promise."

Nodding slowly, Ethan inched closer to the edge, where the calmly-sloping top dipped suddenly into nothingness. "You sure about this, Juniper?" he asked, his voice thick with doubt.

"As sure as I am that root beer floats are the best drinks ever known to man."

"Fair enough." And before he could hesitate, he flipped over onto his side and took off rolling down the hill.

There was something about rolling down hills that all kids, and anyone who has been a kid, could attest to: no matter how hard you tried to keep your mouth shut so that grass didn't fly in, you couldn't help but laugh. It bubbled out of your lips in golden spurts, and maybe you got a few daisies caught between your teeth, but in the moment, it just didn't seem to matter.

That was how Ethan felt as he rolled down Alligator Hill, locked in a tunnel of green, his heart racing ecstatically in his chest in a way he hadn't felt in a while. When he reached the bottom, he was dizzy and panting and suddenly, inexplicably happy.

He lay there at the base, one hand on his chest and the other fiddling with the blades of grass beneath him. His eyes were closed, and he could have drifted off to sleep just then — but before he could, a shrieking orange tornado hurtled down the hill. Juniper's ponytail whipped furiously and her pink checkered dress was tangled in her legs. Ethan snorted, so amused by the strange sight that he forgot to scramble out of the way and Juniper rammed right into him.

"Ow!" he cried as her elbow caught him in the stomach.

Juniper leapt to her feet, then, with a dizzy stumble, fell immediately back to the ground.

"Ethan," she gasped, shaking her head, "you're supposed to move." He glared at her from where he lay.

Sighing, she offered him a hand and pulled him into a sitting position. He pressed a hand to his stomach as she eyed him eagerly.

"Well?" she demanded. "Wasn't that just a blast?"

"I'm not sure if my stomach hurts more from the spinning or from your incredibly bony elbow," Ethan muttered.

Juniper rolled her eyes. "Please, you had fun. Just like I knew you would." Shaking a few blades of grass out of her hair, she jumped up again, pulling Ethan with her. He felt the ground tilt beneath him just a little bit more.

"Come on," she beckoned eagerly, squeezing his hand. "Let's do it again."

She took off running up Alligator Hill and Ethan watched, stupefied, as she sprinted straight into the sun.

TWELVE

Juniper was sitting across the counter of the Malt in what Ethan had come to think of as typical Juniper fashion. Her hair curled loose and long down her back, falling over her shoulders every now and then as she leaned forward to take a sip from her vanilla milk shake (she had finally gotten over her milk shake overload and couldn't get enough of the vanilla). Her hands were damp with the icy sweat slipping down the side of the glass, and she hummed along with the song blasting from the jukebox while swinging her feet against her stool to a completely different rhythm. Ethan glanced at her out of the corner of his eye every now and then as he wiped the counter or flipped another page in his comic book.

It was still quiet in the mornings, minus the occasional primary school kid who would run into the shop flushed and clutching a quarter, breathlessly reciting their order to Ethan before they could even look at him. And Juniper, of course, was a regular customer, always insisting on paying no matter how often Ethan said that her drinks were on the house.

Today was a Tuesday, and the two of them sat in companionable silence, sweating in the seemingly airless shop as the minute hand on the clock inched toward one o'clock at a snail-like pace. Every few minutes Juniper would ask for the time and Ethan would mumble a response before wiping a new layer of sweat from his forehead. By the time Uncle Robert arrived, Ethan's shirt was clinging to his back.

Uncle Robert grunted a hello to Juniper and Ethan, shifting a full brown paper bag out from under his arm and onto the counter. "For you and your aunt," he said to Juniper. "Cara asked me to bring it for you. There're some pies in there, I think, maybe some chicken."

Juniper grinned, peering into the bag. "That's so kind, Mr. Shay! Tell her thank you very much."

"Don't think she just did this out of the goodness of her heart," Uncle Robert teased. "You've just been 'round our house so much gushing about her cooking that she wanted to show off her skills a little more."

"Whatever the reason, I'll take it," Juniper said. "In fact, I think I'm going to run these home right now. Ethan, can we postpone our snail race an hour or two?"

Next on the summer list was to pick snails from a particularly damp area by the lake and race them across a big rock. Juniper claimed she had already scoped out the options and selected her champion.

"Actually," Ethan said, as he hung up his apron, "what if I come with you? You've been to Aunt Cara and Uncle Robert's house a bunch of times, but I've never seen yours."

Ethan was surprised to see Juniper's smile falter. She glanced quickly at the bag of food, then back at Ethan, as if wondering how quickly she could grab the bag and run.

"I mean, unless you don't want to, I guess," Ethan added.

"Like, no pressure. It's just that we've been friends for almost two months and I still don't know where you live."

If Uncle Robert was listening to this conversation, he gave no indication. His focus was on the freezer he was cleaning out, as he always did, because Ethan had yet to master the proper technique. Juniper watched Uncle Robert wipe the icy walls for a long moment before she responded.

"Yeah, okay. Sure." She nodded too quickly. "Yeah, you can come over for a little while. But just a little while — I still have a snail race to win."

Ethan smiled. "Deal."

When they slipped out the back door of the malt shop, Ethan felt anticipation building in his stomach. It had been weeks, and though Juniper talked nonstop, she never seemed to talk about herself. For all that Ethan knew about her personality, he hardly knew anything about her history. He knew she lived with her aunt, and Uncle Robert had once alluded to her parents passing away, but the circumstances were unclear. He'd never seen her aunt or heard the woman mentioned in any detail. And though Ethan wasn't one to pry, he was curious about the past of this redheaded girl who seemed to live in her own world.

He was buzzing with excitement as he mounted his bike, but Juniper was uncharacteristically subdued. She set the food gently into her basket and silently adjusted her yellow skirt so it swished beneath her like cotton rays of sunshine.

"All right," she said. "This ride is a bit of a long one, just so you know. I live a little out of the way."

"Don't worry about it," Ethan assured. "Look at me. I'm practically Superman. I can handle it."

Finally cracking a smile, she rolled her eyes.

Ethan couldn't help but notice that she pedaled unnaturally slow the entire way there. Usually, Juniper was like a rocket on her bike; she went careening through the forest paths as if she was being chased by a wild animal, especially when she had a destination in mind. Today, she moved along at a leisurely pace, glancing back every now and then as if she thought Ethan would suddenly no longer be riding at her tail. As if she almost *hoped* that he wouldn't be.

She had been telling the truth though: it was a pretty long ride. They passed the houses nestled in the trees close to downtown—those people who actually had neighbors—before finding their way to a significantly less populated area. The trees seemed denser here, as if they sensed the lack of inhabitants and were slowly closing in. The way the branches sulked overhead, blotting out the sunlight, made the hairs on Ethan's arms stand on end.

"This way," Juniper called, after they had been riding for about fifteen minutes. She made a sharp left onto a skinny, almost invisible path. If she hadn't given the signal, Ethan would have pedaled right past it. The path they ended up on was bumpy and incredibly narrow; too thin to fit even a small car. It didn't seem possible that there could be a house all the way out here.

But the moment that thought skated through his mind, Juniper came to a jarring stop. Ethan let out a surprised cry, braking quickly and swerving to avoid crashing right into her.

"We're here," she said softly.

Ethan looked up through the small break in the trees to find that they'd reached the end of the path. In its place, swelling at the center of the forest in a mass of color and light, was the most magnificent and lonely house he had ever seen.

Juniper had already begun to walk her bike toward it, but Ethan was frozen in his tracks, his mouth agape as he took in the ethereal structure. It was like an enchanted garden out of a fairy tale—as far as the eye could see, there were only flowers. Sunflowers, daisies, roses, bluebells, buttercups, and other species that Ethan had never even seen before. But they were not planted in neat little rows, like the community gardens Ethan had seen back home—these flowers had run wild, growing over each other, their stems twisting together and reaching skyward to the gauzy sun. The entire house was enveloped in a bouquet.

"Ethan," Juniper said, jarring him from his wonder. "Are you coming, or what?"

"I—yeah," Ethan stuttered, wheeling his bike after her and nearly tripping on a pothole. "I'm coming."

Up close, he could see that a white picket fence had been built around the garden in a fruitless attempt to keep the flowers in. They spilled over, their petals bowing to meet the grass. Juniper leaned her bike against an almost clear patch of fence, and Ethan did the same. Then, without a word, she hefted the bag of food in her arms, unlatched the gate, and walked inside. Ethan scurried after her.

The forest seemed to disappear. The flowers were held back here by tall wooden trellises, but they still reached far above Ethan's head. He felt immersed in the beautiful jungle.

"Sorry, June—" He hurried to catch up with her on the winding cobblestone path, and she turned around. "All of this," he whispered in unintentional reverence. "Why? And—and how?"

"It's my job," she said, shrugging. "Every morning I cut fresh bouquets and bring them down to Mr. Abrams, and he pays me for them and sells them in the general store. We've had the deal for a while now."

Ethan shook his head. "But how is this possible?" he asked. "How can there be so . . . so much of it?"

Again, Juniper shrugged. "My mother. I told you she had a green thumb, remember? Fourteen years ago, these were all seedlings, but once they started growing, they just didn't stop."

And with that, she began to walk again.

It was like a maze trying to reach the house. The pathway went left and right and back again seemingly a dozen times before it finally deposited them at the front door, where a tired two-story house stared down at them. Its sagging clapboard walls and faded, peeling white paint were a stark contrast to the lively garden. It had clearly been beautiful many years ago—now, Ethan thought, it kind of just looked old. A wide, covered porch led up to the front door, and on it were two wicker chairs. Even from the ground level, Ethan could tell that one had a cushion worn with wear; the other looked brand new.

He followed Juniper up the steps, and as they reached the front door, he noticed a pot on the table between the two chairs. Juniper was pulling her keys out of her pocket, but he squinted and moved closer. Inside the pot was a tiny tree, a speck of a thing compared to the forest around them. He tilted his head curiously.

"That's a bonsai," Juniper said, nodding at it as she noticed him staring. "It's the only thing in this whole house that wasn't planted by me or my mother. It was a present from my dad; he was deployed to Japan during the war, and when it ended, he brought this back for her." She paused, then added, "It's a juniper tree. The regular, big kind were always my mom's favorites. That's how I got my name."

"Oh," was all Ethan could say. Juniper was oddly still,

staring at the plant as if she had no intention of ever going inside. She didn't move until Ethan said, "So, do I get to see the inside?"

At his forcibly light tone, Juniper cracked a half smile. "Right, of course," she said, then, bag balanced on her hip, stuck her key into the lock and turned it gently. The door swung open with a soft click, but she didn't step inside right away; first, she frowned and leaned forward, turning to listen for something. When there was no sound from within, she let out a breath and led the way inside.

"Welcome to my humble abode," she said quietly. "Keep your voice down a bit if you don't mind. My aunt's probably napping."

Ethan took in his surroundings, not at all surprised by the homey clutter. They had entered a foyer, and the worn, stained bench next to the coatrack was piled with scarfs. A few coats were hanging on the rack, but most were draped across the small table in front of the wall mirror. Juniper was unapologetic about the mess, and in fact, didn't even seem to notice it as she headed deeper into the house, jumping lithely over a pile of shoes in the hall.

She turned left into the living room, whose main feature was a giant patchwork couch, which looked to be bursting at its mended seams. A coffee table sat in front of it, squat and wide, framed on either side by two plush armchairs. On top of it, right in the center (and surrounded by cups and papers), was a radio. And on the wall, hanging haphazardly, were several paintings that Ethan recognized immediately as Juniper's—the thick brushstrokes and colors that seemed alive. There was the lake at sunset, the front of the general store, some flowers that might have been from her garden. Scenes of Ellison, so normal yet so beautiful through her eyes.

"Wow," he said.

Juniper followed his eyes up to the wall. "Thanks," she said, grinning. "Some of my best work."

"I'll say." He followed her through a doorway and into the kitchen, which was just as messy and outdated as the living room. The stove and refrigerator, with their curved, vanity-like legs, were a decade old at least, but probably more. Ethan figured that her family wasn't the type to get rid of things.

"Sit wherever you'd like," Juniper said, depositing the bag on the square table in the center of the room. Ethan dropped into one of the wooden seats surrounding it. Silence hung over the kitchen, but he couldn't think of anything to say. Thankfully, Juniper broke it by peering into the bag and saying, "Let's see what your aunt packed, shall we?"

She took out the items one by one and laid them on the table. A half dozen chocolate chip muffins, their tops crusted with sugar. A container of grilled chicken and another of mac and cheese. Two pies—one blueberry, one apple. Juniper squealed with delight, momentarily back to her usual self.

"All my favorites! How did she know?"

Ethan happened to know that all of these dishes were staples in Aunt Cara's house, but just shrugged and said, "She must be a mind reader."

Juniper nodded distractedly, already unwrapping the blueberry pie. "By gosh, this looks delicious. We've gotta have some." She hurried to the cabinet and pulled out two plates and two forks.

"Blueberry pie is my *favorite* pie," she said, dishing messy slices onto the plates. "Actually, maybe pumpkin. Or rhubarb. What's your favorite pie?"

Ethan thought for a moment as she pushed a plate in front of him. "I'm gonna go with key lime."

"How fancy! I didn't know I was in the presence of royalty."

"Okay, new question," Ethan said, laughing. He scooped up a large forkful of pie. "What is your favorite color?"

"Easy," she said, her mouth full. "Teal." Ethan quirked an eyebrow in question. "Because it's the color of the lake, *obviously*."

"Fine, fine," Ethan shook his head. "Favorite book?"

"Oh! Oh! *Twenty Thousand Leagues Under the Sea*, definitely. The sea monster is my favorite character ever."

"Really, the sea monster? But Captain Nemo is such a cool guy!"

Juniper gasped suddenly. "You've *read* it? That's amazing! You must be the first person I've ever met who's known what it is."

"Obviously," Ethan mimicked her previous tone, and she smacked him across the arm.

For the next half hour they sat at the table, plowing through the blueberry pie and firing questions back and forth. In between bites, Ethan learned that her favorite movie was *Holiday Inn*, simply because it was the last movie she had seen, over ten years before. He told her that he loved button-up T-shirts and Ella Fitzgerald, and had a pretty big crush on Debbie Reynolds.

"Okay," he said slowly, poking at the crumbs of his pie. "What do your parents do?"

"Oh, they're dead," she replied casually. "Died in a fire eight years ago at their flower shop in town."

She popped a blueberry into her mouth, seemingly unconcerned, but Ethan froze. "Oh wow, I didn't—I'm so sorry."

Juniper shrugged. "No sweat—it's not that big a deal,

really. People die all the time. And anyway, I'll see them again someday." Her tone was careless, light, even, but when Ethan stole a glance at her from the corner of his eye, he saw that she had stopped moving and was staring down at her plate as if wondering what it was doing there.

"I guess," he murmured, and then they were silent.

"No need to kill the mood," Juniper said after a moment, startling Ethan with her chipper voice. "Your turn—what do your parents do?"

"My dad works in advertising," he said. "And my mom . . . well, I'm not really sure anymore. She was a nurse when I was little. But ever since she moved back to Montgomery, I haven't—"

"Wait a second," Juniper interrupted. "Did you say your mom moved back to Montgomery?"

"Yeah, that's where she's from. It's where she and my dad met. Why?"

"Ethan"—she laughed—"that's only, like, two hours away from here! The way you've talked about her, I thought she was out on a desert island somewhere."

Ethan bristled. "Yeah, well, she might as well be. What, you think my aunt and uncle are just going to take me to see her? If I make them uncomfortable, she'll make them ill."

"I don't think you make them uncomfortable, Ethan."

"Yes, I do," he snapped. "Sure, things have gotten a little better. They're nice enough. But they always look at me like I'm a bomb about to explode. Like they're just waiting for something to happen or for me to do something. My dad's the only reason they tolerate me. Of course you don't notice it, but I do. All the damn time."

"What do you mean, of course I don't notice it, I—"

Juniper was flushed and halfway through her retort when

a floorboard creaked loudly above their heads. She jumped, her knees smacking against the underside of the table.

"Oh God, not now," she muttered, pushing her chair back from the table.

"What?" Ethan demanded. He was answered by two long, slow creaks of weight on the stairs and felt a sudden twist in his gut.

"Just wait here." She backed toward the living room. "I'll be back in a minute, okay? Just let me—" She was cut off in the middle of her sentence when a woman suddenly appeared in the doorway and they collided with a soft thump. Juniper shrieked, whirling quickly around with her hands held defensively in front of her.

"Aunt Annabelle," she began, her voice gentle.

Ethan was struck motionless by the sight of this woman, who was the last person he'd ever have expected Juniper to have as an aunt. He thought that any relative of Juniper's would be bright, eccentric, energetic—the way she made her parents out to be, and the way she herself was. Annabelle Jones had blue eyes and gray-streaked auburn hair just a bit darker than Juniper's, but that was where the similarities ended. Her shoulders were hunched, nightgown stained, face sagging—it was clear that life had hit her too hard too many times. She was probably in her seventies, but she looked even older. Even in the way her hands twitched, wringing together nervously, Ethan could sense the profound sadness. He felt a compelling urge to run from the room, to keep running and not stop until her crumbling image was razed from his memory.

"Aunt Annabelle," Juniper repeated. She swallowed hard. "I didn't realize you were awake. Why don't I help you back to bed?"

"You didn't make me my tea." Aunt Annabelle's voice was loud and halting. "I was waiting for my tea."

"I'll get you your tea, okay? Just let me take you back upstairs."

She gently took hold of her aunt's arm and was just tugging her back through the doorway when the woman's eyes, scanning the kitchen, locked with Ethan's. And she screamed.

Ethan pressed himself against the back of his chair, ears ringing. Aunt Annabelle was pointing at him, her finger quivering in time with her lips, her words mangled.

"B-B-Boy!" she stuttered wildly. "Nigger boy, in *my* kitchen!" In her anger, her southern drawl had thickened. "Junie, get him out! Get him out!"

Juniper turned quickly to her aunt and put her hands on the woman's shoulders. "No, Aunt Annabelle. It's okay. There's no one there." She began to steer her aunt back into the living room. "Come on," she said firmly. "We're going back to bed." They disappeared into the room, and a few moments later, Ethan heard the stairs creak.

He was shocked, feeling as if his entire body had been pinned in place. The light, streaming brightly through the kitchen windows, burned his eyes. He squeezed them shut, only to see Annabelle's words seared into his memory. He pushed his hands into his forehead and left them there until Juniper returned several minutes later.

When she came back, she didn't look at him. She rushed through the door in a flurry of skirt and filled a kettle with water, then set it on the stove to boil. She kept her eyes averted as she leaned against the kitchen table next to her half-eaten piece of pie. Her eyes were red and swollen.

"You should go," she said.

Ethan wanted to leave—he couldn't wait—but instead of

relief in his chest, he felt anger. "I should go?" he echoed testily.

"Yes. My aunt isn't well."

"Yeah, okay," Ethan scoffed. "*That's* the problem."

Juniper looked at him finally, her eyes fiery. "*What*, Ethan?" she demanded. "Are you still mad about me saying you should visit your mom? Fine, I'm sorry. I'll stop suggesting things that might make you feel better."

Ethan had forgotten about that, but now he felt mad about it all over again. Still, he shook his head. "No, June. I'm mad because of what your aunt said."

Juniper frowned, seeming genuinely confused.

"June, she called me a nigger," Ethan said, nearly choking on the word. "Didn't you hear her?"

"No, I guess I didn't, but I'm sure she didn't mean it and—"

"And you didn't say anything about it! You didn't defend me, you didn't tell her not to say that word, nothing."

"Okay, well, sorry!" Juniper cried, throwing up her hands. "I told you, she's not well! She barely knows what she's saying."

"When it comes to that word, people always know what they're saying," Ethan said. He stood up and turned away from the table. "That's what Samuel Hill said, and he knew."

Juniper was silent for a long moment, but if Ethan was expecting a heartfelt apology, it didn't come. Instead, when she spoke, her voice was tight. "I'm sorry that happened," she said. "But what are you gonna do, punch my aunt in the face? She's old, Ethan, and sick to boot. I can barely get her to understand what's for dinner, much less how she should treat colored folks."

Ethan turned back to her, crossing his arms. "That doesn't mean you shouldn't try."

"You know what?" Juniper's face was so red that her freckles nearly disappeared. Her hands were clenched in fists by her sides and the sun through the window made her hair look like fire. "It's not all about you, Ethan. I have other people to care about, and I can't change everything in my life to make you feel better all the time. I'm trying to be supportive. I'm trying to be your friend. But my aunt is the only family I've got."

Ethan thought then about his own family—how distant he'd felt from them at times even when they were under the same roof. He thought about Juniper's aunt, who, even in her age and illness, still bore a resemblance to her niece. Ethan was tall like his father but didn't share his thin nose, light complexion, or pale eyes. He didn't even really look like his mother, whose skin was a deep brown, her eyebrows thick and cheekbones high. And certainly—certainly—he didn't look like anyone in this town. Annabelle was all the family Juniper had, but why couldn't Juniper understand that she was all Ethan had here, period?

He said as much to her, in a low mumble, his eyes pointed at the floor. Juniper threw up her arms. "I'm sorry it's hard for you here!" she yelled. "I'm sorry, I'm sorry, I'm sorry! How many times do I have to apologize for this town?"

"Until I can walk down the street without feeling like every single person wants to point a gun at my head and pull the trigger."

"I can't do that, Ethan! It's not my job."

"Well, it's definitely not mine either!"

They stared at each other for a long moment, red faced and teary eyed, the pie on the table between them long forgotten. Finally, Ethan shook his head and turned to the doorway. "Whatever, Juniper. I'm leaving."

"Fine," she called at his back, her voice breaking. "Leave, then. See if I care."

Ethan paused for a moment in the kitchen doorway, a sudden pain welling up in his chest. She had said she would be there for him—she had promised. And he had convinced himself to trust her, because otherwise, he would have been all alone. He felt shocked, betrayed. The loneliness washed back over him, and though Juniper stood only a few feet away, he felt as though he was seeing her through a long tunnel.

"Maybe you're not who I thought you were," he whispered. Then, before he could stop himself, he hurried to the front door. When it shut behind him, all the air went out of his chest in one long stream and he nearly collapsed onto the scratchy doormat. The bonsai tree, on the table to his left, seemed to taunt him.

It was in a daze that he made his way through the floral maze. Several times he imagined Juniper, sitting there alone in that sad, sad house, and almost turned back around—but another emotion, anger or maybe fear, drove him away again, made him forge ahead until he burst through the gate of the white picket fence and left it all behind him.

Juniper's bicycle had fallen to the ground; he picked it up and leaned it against the fence, then picked up his own. He cast one last glance back at the house, feeling his heart pounding heavily in his chest. Anger made his vision pulse with red. There was a rolling nausea in his stomach; he didn't want to be here anymore. Forcing his gaze away from the house, he climbed onto his bike and pedaled away down the narrow path. The trees seemed to sigh in relief.

THIRTEEN

The dust swelled in Ethan's wake as he pounded down the path. Arms pumping, head tipped forward, legs carrying him in long strides. By now he knew these paths by heart. At the next turn, he'd see the old magnolia whose branches bent nearly to the ground. There was a fork coming up: to the right was Alligator Hill and to the left, the lake. He knew the spots where the birds chirped the loudest, where the grass was filled with hidden burrs, where the path became almost smooth and the dust nearly disappeared. Juniper had taught him well.

But it was Juniper he was trying to forget today as he ran. There was a state he could reach sometimes during his longest distance races when his mind went blank and all he knew was the way his heart beat in time with his footsteps. He couldn't quite get there now, but he was close, his skin burning with the effort. Just another mile, maybe, and he could forget that he hadn't spoken to Juniper in nearly four days.

He made it half that distance—maybe less—when a rumbling sound cut through the forest, seeming to come from the trees themselves. It had been cloudy all day while Ethan was at work, but now, with a flash of lightning, hot rain poured down between the branches. The trees offered little protection; in a few paces, Ethan was soaked. He swiped a hand across his eyes and turned right at the next fork, toward home. Now, as he ran, dust was replaced by spurts of mud and his sweat mingled with rainwater. By the time he reached Aunt Cara's front porch, his curls were plastered to his forehead and his sneakers felt like they were filled with water.

Aunt Cara met him at the door with two towels, motioning for him to stay on the porch until he was dry. "First real storm of the summer," she said, peering out at the downpour. Ethan didn't respond as he scrubbed the towel across his face, wrung out his hair, and kicked off his shoes. Even with two towels wrapped around him, he still dripped all the way to the bathroom.

"Lunch is ready when you're done!" Aunt Cara called as he stepped inside.

"Okay," he said to the closed door. "Thanks."

One hot shower later, he emerged into the kitchen in sweats. Though it wasn't cold outside, Aunt Cara scooped him up a bowl of thick bean soup and set it at the table. She hovered for a moment as he silently began to eat, then blurted, "So, Juniper hasn't been around lately."

Ethan paused, spoon halfway to his mouth. "No," he said carefully. "She hasn't." He didn't look at his aunt. He was worried that she would catch on after half a week without Juniper stopping by the house at least once, but he'd hoped that his disappearances during his now-daily runs would be mistaken for meetings with Juniper.

"Is everything all right?"

Ethan considered—if he told her, she'd keep asking questions. Then again, if he didn't tell her, she'd probably still keep asking questions. He set down his spoon and said, "Actually, we're kind of in a fight."

"Oh, honey." One hand on her swelling stomach, Aunt Cara-lowered herself into the seat across from Ethan's. "What happened?"

"I was at her house the other day and her aunt called me something." He turned away, cheeks burning, unable to repeat it. But Aunt Cara seemed to understand.

"Oh," she said. "Oh dear." Ethan felt one of her hands close around his. "I'm sorry, Ethan."

He shook his head. "I mean, it's not the first time I've heard it. It's just coming from her aunt—I mean, I know I'd never met her, and it shouldn't mean anything. But it hurt."

"Of course it hurt. How could it not?"

"Not the word," Ethan said. "The fact that Juniper let her say it."

Aunt Cara was silent for a while, her head turned to the window. Rain streaked down the glass and thunder rumbled in the distance.

"I didn't see a colored person till I was seventeen," she said. "It was your mother. We'd grown up sheltered here in Ellison, but your dad went off to college in the city and met your mom while she was waitressing to put herself through nursing school. He didn't think anything of bringing her back home. Our parents had a cow. *I* had a cow. I'd only seen black people in movies, and now here one was, standing on my front porch."

Ethan said nothing.

"I thought he was crazy when he marched on in here at

just twenty-three and said he was going to marry her. Our parents thought he was irredeemable. They said since his marriage wasn't legal in the state of Alabama, it might as well not be legal anywhere. They refused to speak to him again after that, not even when they were on their deathbeds. And your poor mother, Lydia—I can't imagine that visit was easy for her."

At the mention of his grandparents, Ethan felt cold. His father had rarely mentioned them, had only shown him a few dusty photographs of them in the thirties, young and blond and sitting at the edge of what Ethan now knew was Ellison's lake. Never had he heard that they had disowned their son for his choice of partner. He imagined, with growing anxiety, his parents sending them his baby pictures, only to have the images thrown away without a glance. To them, his existence would have been shameful. But they had both died before he turned three, so thankfully, he would never know.

"And as much as I hate to admit it," Aunt Cara went on, "I didn't talk to your dad for a long time either. Almost a year. But he wrote me letters from Washington when they moved up there to get married. He told me about Lydia, how kind and patient and tough she was. And about the life they were building together. And about how, when it came down to it, she was just a person, and all colored folks are just people. And slowly, he changed my mind."

"What?" Ethan muttered. "My dad's a hero because he married a Negro woman? And the twins and I are miracle kids?"

Aunt Cara shook her head, frowning as she gathered her thoughts. "No, he's no hero. He's a good man, but it's separate from that. My point is, he was accepting, and open minded, and he really did love your mother. But there's a lot he doesn't understand, still, I know. There's a lot more that I don't understand. But we're trying, Ethan. And Juniper's trying too. Even if you can't always tell."

Ethan laid his hands on the table, palms up in a gesture of helplessness. "Trying doesn't make them stop staring," he said. "Trying doesn't make me feel safe here. And I guess I just think there's only so much trying you all can do. There are some things about me and my life that you'll never understand." He paused, looked into his quickly cooling bowl of soup. "And probably there are things about my mom and her life that I'll never understand. Or that girl who got arrested on the bus. Because of who my dad is, and the parts of him that are in me, even if they're small."

Ethan was surprised to find himself being so open with Aunt Cara. These were probably the most words he had said to her since he'd been staying here. To her credit, she didn't try to argue with him, just nodded thoughtfully and looked out the window again. The rain was less intense now, just soft patters on the roof.

"I'm sure you're right," she said eventually. "About all of that. And I wish I knew what to say. In the general store that day, I wish I had . . . I don't know. I don't know what to say, Ethan, or how to help you. I wish that I did."

"It's okay," he said, and realized he meant it. "I don't need you to have all the answers. Thanks for trying. And for lunch. It was good, I'm just not really hungry anymore." He pushed back from the table and carried his half-full bowl to the sink. Aunt Cara was still staring out the window as he ducked out of the kitchen.

Just as he was making his way to the hallway, she called, "You could call her sometime, if you want."

Ethan paused, turned around. "What?"

"Your mother." Aunt Cara was looking at him now, a small, sad smile on her lips. "You know she's back in Montgomery now. Uncle Robert and I have her contact information. I could give you her telephone number, if you'd like to call her. Maybe it'll help you figure some things out."

Ethan's heart skipped in his chest—never since his mother had left had he been able to call her. She'd moved around a lot those first few years before settling back in Montgomery, and between changing phone numbers and an increasingly unstable relationship with his father, it had never worked out. She always called him, as his dad had pointed out, on birthdays and holidays. But now he could call her on his own terms.

His first thought was, *I have to do it*. His second thought was, *I have to tell Juniper*. Then he remembered her face when he'd left her house four days earlier, and his stomach sank. He thought about calling his mom and wondered what he'd say, where he'd start. Suddenly, without a friend by his side, the thought seemed daunting.

"Thanks, Aunt Cara, really," he said, forcing a smile. "I'll think about it."

Once he was in his room, he tumbled into bed, threw an arm over his eyes, and willed himself to fall asleep. He dreamt in confusing flashes of color—of his father's stern face, of his mother's soft hands on his shoulders, of bright orange hair flying, cape-like, in the wind.

✳

When he woke up, it was dark out. Squinting at the clock on his bedside table, he saw that it was nearly midnight; he'd slept right through dinner. The rain had stopped, and through the window, Ethan could see that it had left behind a clear sky. He lay there for a while, listening to any sounds throughout the house, but it seemed that Uncle Robert and Aunt Cara had gone to bed. He tried for a while to sleep again, but after his nap, he was wide awake.

Rubbing his eyes, he stood up and strode to the window, where he could see the half-moon hovering above the trees. His shoes sat by the wall, and he silently slipped them on. Like someone in a trance, he raised the window slowly and, just as he had with Juniper a few weeks before, climbed through and leapt out onto the grass.

By now, he could make the hike to the lake with his eyes closed — which was nearly what he did that night as, by the light of the moon, he put one foot blindly in front of the other and hoped that he would find his way. The ground was hard and damp from the storm, and the trees were dewy. Occasionally, a gust of wind would disturb the leaves and send droplets of water onto Ethan's shoulders.

Somewhere among the trees, as pebbles crunched beneath his feet and a light breeze nipped at his skin, Ethan felt himself fully waking up. He rubbed at the sweat already gathering on his bare arms and blinked himself back to life — by the time he was making the final turn toward the lake, his head was clear.

At this late hour, the lake barely looked real. Its surface glimmered as if it were made of crystals, and the water that lapped against the grass made the faintest whispering sound. He stopped at its edge and stared out at the midnight blue. He'd heard about lakes like this, nights like these, where the sky and water were so near in color that it was impossible to tell where one ended and the other began. For all Ethan could tell, he was staring out at a curving expanse of sky.

Shivering despite the nighttime heat, he removed his shoes, and, leaving them in the center of the path, made a barefoot trek to the dock that stretched out like a lonely arm next to the boathouse. Its dark wooden surface was slick with misty spray; he tiptoed carefully across the planks, wincing as they scratched at his feet. Once he reached the end, he contemplated for a moment the idea of diving in, clothes and all, and holding his breath—letting the water fill his lungs and drag him to the bottom of the lake, where his body would drift among the tiny minnows and waving plants until it surfaced several days later, bloated and pale.

Instead, he felt gravity tug him down until he was sitting on the end of the dock, his legs dangling over the side. Dampness from the wood spread across the seat of his pants. He cuffed his sweats and dipped his toes into the waves. A tree across the lake bent its branches as it was struck by a sudden gust of wind, and it looked to Ethan as if it were raising an arm in greeting. He hesitantly lifted his hand in return.

He suddenly wished that Juniper was beside him.

"Look!" she would have cried, pointing at the waving tree. "It's saying hello! Hi, tree! My name is Juniper Jones—I'm a tree, too, actually. A much smaller tree, but still a tree. We're family."

And Ethan would laugh, rolling his eyes as she forced him to introduce himself to the drooping willow, to shout across the empty lake and shatter its jeweled surface with his voice. But he would do it, of course. With her, that was the person he could be.

He looked sharply to his left, certain, for a moment, that he had seen a flash of carrot-red hair. But it was only a cattail, dancing among the shadows on the shore.

Juniper was shipwrecked in her worn house, surrounded by an ocean of flowers. And Ethan was here, sitting on this dock alone, because she had hurt him—and even though he knew deep down that she hadn't meant it, the pain was still there.

As if reprimanding him, a wave slapped his ankle.

"Couldn't sleep?"

The voice came from just behind him, piercing the still night air with a familiar gruffness. Ethan jumped, nearly falling into the water in that moment before he realized it was Gus. He looked up to see the older man standing a few feet away.

"Something like that," Ethan replied.

Gus nodded, then, with a grunt, lowered himself down beside Ethan, his legs in their faded jeans falling toward the lake. Some water sloshed over his thick boots, but he didn't seem to notice.

Ethan studied Gus out of the corner of his eye—the elderly boater was staring out at the lake with a quiet fondness, the slightest smile playing on his lips. Juniper might love this lake as a friend, but Gus loved it as a child. Anyone could see it in his eyes.

Somehow both unnerved and comforted by the silence, Ethan kicked at the reflection of the stars. His bare feet were numb and shriveled.

"Something's wrong between you and Junie," Gus said, a question that fell flat at the end. He didn't look at Ethan, but his face had changed. He knew.

"Yeah." Ethan sighed, rubbing his arms so that his hands would not be idle. He thought that if he did not do something, he would use them to hurl himself into the lake.

Gus nodded sagely. "She was here today. Didn't say much.

Didn't tell me what. But I could tell." Now, finally, he turned his head to Ethan, narrowing his eyes so that his bushy eyebrows formed a gray caterpillar across his forehead. "Want to tell me what happened?"

"No, not really," Ethan said, shaking his head. "It's not a big deal, really. I was just at her house, and her aunt was there, and she—and Juniper—"

Tears began to slip from his eyes before he realized it, and as he blubbered out a fragmented mess of the story, Ethan wasn't sure if he was crying over Juniper, or her aunt, or stupid Samuel Hill—he just knew that his entire body was shaking with the insurmountable sadness of *something*, and down to his bones, he was shattering.

Gus listened but made no move to comfort him. His hands remained stuffed into his pockets, his head bowed, moving only for the occasional nod.

"I see," he would mutter under his breath. "I see."

When he finished, Ethan felt as if he had been struck by lightning. Every limb felt in the wrong place and his face was raw from the tears. Embarrassed, he swiped angrily at his eyes, rubbing until they were sore and stinging and red, but dry.

"Sorry," he said, wishing he'd thought to bring his handkerchief. "You probably think I'm the biggest sissy right about now. Crying and all that—I know I shouldn't be doing that, I'm not a girl, for God's sake—I don't know where it came from, really—"

"Son." Gus cut him off with a hard syllable, sounding almost angry. "There's nothing wrong with a man cryin'. You go on saying that only the girls do it, and I shut you up myself. Understand?"

Eyes wide, Ethan nodded. Looking satisfied, Gus turned

back to the lake, cracking the knuckles on both hands before finally giving a response.

"That girl's proud," he muttered, shaking his head. "Don't seem like it, but she is. She's protective too. Lives to please the people she loves. You and Annabelle are two of the people she loves the most. When all that happened, I'll bet she just didn't know what to do. And that pride, it's stopping her from saying anything about it. She doesn't want to admit she hurt you."

That was the most Ethan had ever heard Gus say, and as the words left the man's lips, he wondered if they were true. He couldn't imagine Juniper—bird wings, sunshine Juniper—being weighed down by something so silly and material as pride. He couldn't imagine her being weighed down by anything; in his mind, she was a balloon, spiraling endlessly into the sky.

Gus must have seen the doubt on Ethan's face, because he added, "Listen, son, I'm not saying it's right. And I'm not saying you should forgive her just like that. I'm just saying, she's got pride enough for everyone in this town." He paused for a long moment, staring at something in the dark between the trees. "And also twice the heart," he said, quieter now, and looked at Ethan. "Hell, she's got enough heart for the whole goddamn world." Clapping Ethan on the shoulder, he clambered laboriously to his feet. "Don't worry 'bout her, son. She'll come around."

And with that, he clomped back down the dock, leaving Ethan alone and wondering whether it was the lake that Gus saw as his child—or if it was Juniper Jones.

∗

Sometime in the night, sitting on the dock, Ethan drifted off to sleep. He awoke just as dawn was yawning on the horizon. His body was stiff and freezing, sprawled out on the wooden planks, and his feet were still bare. In the night, it seemed, the air had chilled. It was only with deep, shivering effort that he managed to drag himself back to the path where his shoes waited patiently, facing northwest, the white canvas slightly damp with morning dew.

"Goddamn," he lamented, groaning as he bent to tie his laces and his body cried out in protest. At a slow, exhausted pace, he dragged himself back up the path, feeling the ice in his bones rattling with every step. His eyes were half shut, maybe frozen with the cold. It was a wonder, he realized once Aunt Cara's house was in sight, that he'd found his way back at all.

When he climbed through the window and fell against the hardwood floor, he looked up at the clock and saw that it read six o'clock, only a little while before Aunt Cara or Uncle Robert would wake up—he'd made it back before they could notice that he was missing.

Slowly, carefully, he picked himself up off the floor and gathered some wrinkled clothes from his closet, then made his way into the empty hall and to the bathroom. He turned the water in the shower on as hot as it could go and stood under it, his head turned up to the burning stream until the frigid night had been washed completely from his aching body. Then he remained there, washing away the tears and the old, invisible wounds that were peeling open again under the new, until it was all down the drain along with a thick layer of dirt and grime.

He didn't feel mended when the hot water finally ran out and he stepped out of the shower, but he certainly no longer felt like his bones were made of glass. He toweled off, put on his fresh clothes, and wandered back into his room.

It was hard to tell, after sleeping in the cold all night, whether that talk with Gus had really helped him at all. He trusted the man and his carefully chosen words, but when he thought about Juniper, there was a beam of bright orange sunset, followed by lonely blankness. With a moan that grew from his stomach and made his entire body vibrate, Ethan crawled into bed, under the covers, and pulled a pillow over his head.

It was here that his uncle found him, nearly two hours later, as the sun finally reared its head over the town of Ellison, Alabama, and everyone but Ethan rose for work and play. He heard Uncle Robert's voice through a hot, hazy fog, saw him through blurred vision.

"I think he's got a fever," Uncle Robert said, his voice crashing and grating against Ethan's ears. "He's boiling up."

Aunt Cara's cold hand pressed against his forehead and she confirmed, "That's a fever, all right. Poor child must have worried himself sick."

His head pounded, and he squeezed his eyes shut.

A few minutes passed—or maybe hours—and then he felt a cool cloth settle against his burning forehead. "Shh, there you go," Aunt Cara said, patting his shoulder. "You get to stay home from work today—Uncle Robert's got it covered. Just rest." She walked away, adding, "There's another bowl of bean soup on your bedside table, if you'd like it."

Ethan could smell it—the appetizing scent wafted toward him. But his entire frame rattled when the door was eased shut, and he felt too weak to reach for it. He lay where he was instead, drifting in and out of sleep, his body aching and shivering and punishing him for his rashness the night before.

In his more lucid moments, he would think about his conversation with Gus and find some semblance of comfort in the thought of Juniper coming back and showing up at his door the next morning when he was well again, smiling that crooked-toothed smile. At some point, in between restless sleep and check-ins from Aunt Cara, he thought he saw her walk through his door, kneel beside his bed, and smooth back his hair with one soft, freckled hand. He closed his eyes and smiled at the coolness of her touch. When he opened his eyes again, she was gone. He figured it must have been a dream.

FOURTEEN

Ethan's fever disappeared as quickly as it had come, and by the next morning he was feeling like himself again—although his shoulders were still sore from sleeping on the dock. Even so, when he showed up in the kitchen ready to eat breakfast before his shift, Uncle Robert waved him away.

"Take another day to rest," he said, mouth full of grits. "I can handle today."

Nothing sounded worse to Ethan than taking another day to rest. He knew if he did that, he'd spend hours cooped up in his room, thinking about his fight with Juniper and Aunt Cara's standing offer to call his mom. It would drive him crazy.

"No, I can do it," Ethan insisted. "I just wanna get out of the house today."

Uncle Robert thought for a moment, then sighed. "Tell you what. Come in around six, at closing. You can do cleanup and prep for tomorrow."

Ethan groaned. He'd been switched to the cleanup shift at

Steak n' Shake a few months in and it had been a nightmare. Uncle Robert raised an eyebrow.

"Really, son, you don't have to come in."

"No, no." Ethan shook his head. "I'll do it."

"Whatever you want," Uncle Robert said, wiping his mouth. "I'll see you at six."

*

The afternoon malt shop crowd was just thinning out when Ethan arrived at seven minutes to six. A couple of stragglers were finishing their milk shakes, and Uncle Robert was watching them with obvious impatience. They didn't look up as Ethan came inside.

"Afternoon." Uncle Robert nodded as Ethan slipped behind the counter. "Day go all right?"

Ethan shrugged. He'd spent the morning lying on the front porch reading comics and the afternoon playing records. "Could've been worse."

"Glad you could make it. Let me show you what you need to do." Much like he had on Ethan's first day, Uncle Robert walked through all the steps of closing. He pointed out the key ring on the hook just inside the kitchen, opened the cabinet with the cleaning supplies, and explained the prepping process. Ethan nodded along.

"Got it," he said, when the instructions were done. "No sweat."

"Great. I'll see you at home." He ducked out of his apron and hung it on the peg. "Did Cara say what's for dinner?"

"Pot roast and baked beans."

Uncle Robert grunted in what Ethan had come to recognize as a show of approval. He stepped out from behind the counter and glanced at the kids who were still drinking their milk shakes. "Hey, closing time," he said. "Get on home." The pair stood immediately, mumbling their apologies as they left. Uncle Robert tipped his head in Ethan's direction as he followed them out the door, flipping the sign to closed on his way out.

When the door shut, Ethan heaved a sigh of relief. There was something calming about work, even if it was work as annoying as washing dishes and scrubbing the floor. Arming himself with a wet rag in one hand and a broom in the other, he circled the store, attacking smears of chocolate on the tabletops and sweeping crumbs from the floor. He collected used glasses on the counter.

As he was fighting a particularly stubborn stain on one of the tables, the bell above the door jingled. A couple of soft footsteps crossed the threshold. Without looking up, Ethan muttered, "Sorry, we're closed."

Whoever it was didn't move. Ethan rolled his eyes. "Hey, I said we're—"

"I know," said a familiar voice. "But is it too late for a vanilla milk shake?"

Ethan looked up sharply. Juniper Jones was standing just inside the doorway, her eyes downcast. She clutched a single, giant sunflower to her chest.

"Juniper," Ethan said, colder than he intended. He set the rag down on the table. "What are you doing here?"

"I passed Mr. Shay on the way to your house. He said you were closing today."

Ethan sighed. "What do you want?"

"Apology flower." She held the flower out to him with both hands. When he didn't move, she shuffled toward him, arms still outstretched. "I'm sorry," she said. "Really, really,

really sorry. I'm not good at saying that 'cause I don't like being wrong. But I was this time. And I wasn't fair to you."

Ethan didn't take the flower, just looked at her with a frown. Part of him was still hurt, and angry that she thought a flower could fix that. But a larger part of him remembered what Gus had said, about how much she cared for him even if she didn't always show it the right way. And that part of him really, really missed his friend.

Juniper looked at him worriedly, her small smile wavering. "Ethan. Please?"

After another moment of hesitation, Ethan reached out and took the flower. "Thank you," he said. "I appreciate it."

"Ever since the other day, I've been thinking a whole lot. Just sitting in my garden with all the flowers and thinking about what you said. And you were right. I love my aunt, and she's my family. But"—Juniper took a deep breath—"part of being family is about making each other better people. And I can't make any promises that she'll change. But I'm sure gonna try my best."

She peered up at Ethan, who was staring down at the flower, a feeling of warmth sweeping over his chest. For all the anguish he'd felt the past few days, and as guarded as he felt still, he was relieved to see Juniper. He felt better when she was around. Absently, he twirled the flower in his hand.

"Thank you," he repeated. "Yeah. I don't know. Thank you. I mean it." He frowned. "And I'm sorry, too, for freaking out on you. I know you didn't mean to make me mad. I know you're trying, which is more than most people here are doing."

Juniper nodded. "And I know it's not always easy being my friend," she said, "so I know you're trying too." In a sing-song voice, she added, "We're all just trying the best we can," as she twirled in a slow circle.

Ethan felt a smile begin to creep up on his lips—noticing it immediately, Juniper grinned, pointing at his face. "I knew it!" she cried. "I knew I could get you to smile today. So, what do you say? Are we cool?"

She held out a hand, just as she had when she introduced herself to him weeks before, and Ethan shook it. "Yeah, Starfish. We're cool."

Juniper stuck around for the next hour, helping Ethan clean as he told her, at her request, about his past few days. There wasn't much to tell, of course, so while they mopped the floor Ethan found himself acting out the parts of a radio show he had listened to. They sang his latest favorite song as they washed dishes. When his voice cracked on a high note, Juniper burst into laughter.

"Hey, I'm trying my best!" He swatted suds in her direction and she blew the bubbles out of the air.

"Well, your best is *bad*," she said, wiping her hands on a towel next to the sink. "Hold on. I'll get us some proper cleaning music."

She disappeared into the restaurant and Ethan heard coins jangling into the jukebox. A moment later, a popular Elvis song—Ethan could never tell them apart—began playing through the speakers. Ethan groaned and covered his ears.

"Oh God, please no, anything but this," he begged as she danced back into the kitchen. "I hate Elvis."

"I know!" Juniper said, swiveling her hips in a wide circle. "And I take that as a challenge."

Scrunching his nose, Ethan turned up the sink so the water spattered loudly above the sound of the song.

"Don't fight it," she cried, shimmying her shoulders. "This is the best music in the world."

"That is definitely not true."

"Well, *I* think it's true. And you know what? I'm putting myself on official jukebox duty. Trust me, dishwashing goes much faster with a little music."

"Juniper, I swear, I'll kick you out of the store!"

But she was already dancing away to the jukebox. "Please, Ethan Charlie Harper! I'd like to see you try."

With Juniper's help—and, though Ethan would never admit it, the music—they finished in half the time it would have taken Ethan alone. When everything was done, they sat across from each other at a table and surveyed their work.

"Well," Ethan said, "I'd say we did a pretty good job."

"I'd say you're right." She slouched back into the seat, her eyes half closed. "Hey," she said with a yawn, "you never finished telling me about your week. You ended with your awful singing."

Ethan rolled his eyes but thought back over the days since he'd last seen her. He opened his mouth, about to insist he had nothing more to say, when he remembered Aunt Cara's offer from the day before. To let him call his mother. He didn't know how he'd managed to forget it for so long.

"Actually," he said, "Aunt Cara told me something kinda crazy." Juniper perked up immediately and her jaw dropped as he explained.

"Ethan!" she cried, jumping in her seat. "That's amazing news! You have to do it, you know you do. Now that you know your aunt and uncle are okay with it—I'll tell you, I knew they would be, but that's not the point, you *have* to."

"I don't know. I mean, my mom and I almost never speak. What if she doesn't want to talk to me? Or what if she does, but then I have to explain the whole Ellison thing to her, and then it turns into another big fight with my dad?" He shrugged. "Or, I don't know, what if she doesn't even pick up the phone?"

To his surprise, Juniper laughed. "Oh, Ethan, you big silly — I don't think you should call her. I think you should go see her."

"What?" Ethan blinked, unsure if he had heard her correctly.

"Yeah! I mean, why not? Montgomery's not far, and I'll bet Mr. Shay would drive you if you asked real nicely. Think about it, Ethan — wouldn't it make you feel better to spend some time with someone who understands?"

"No. Definitely not. I can't do that."

"Why not?"

"Because —" Ethan hunched into his chair. "Because I'm scared of what I might find out if I do. About my dad, and my parents' relationship, and our family. I don't know. It's stupid."

Juniper's face softened. "It's not stupid, Ethan. I get it. But when are you going to get this chance again?"

Ethan stared at the floor, considering. He hadn't seen his mom in person for over a year, when they'd had a quick two-day visit in Seattle. Those were the only days she could manage to get off work. He loved her and knew she loved him — but they barely knew each other. For as long as Ethan could remember, parents meant just his father.

But like Juniper had said, when would he get this chance again? And when, in this summer of loneliness and hurt, would he be able to tell someone what had happened here and have them say *Yes, I know. I understand.* And mean it. She was right; he had to do it. But not by himself.

"Will you come with me?" Ethan blurted. Juniper looked at him in surprise.

"Really? You want me to come?"

"Of course, June. I mean, Uncle Robert would have to agree to driving us first. But you're my best friend, right? This is definitely a best friend job."

Grinning, Juniper said, "Well, then. Count me in."

"Good," Ethan said, relieved. "Look, why don't you come over for dinner? Aunt Cara's making pot roast. I can ask Uncle Robert." He paused. "I think it'll help if you're there. They kind of have a soft spot for you."

"You had me at pot roast," Juniper said.

✳

When Ethan unlocked Aunt Cara's front door and Juniper followed him inside, both his aunt and uncle all but jumped up from their seats.

"I invited June for dinner," Ethan said awkwardly. "Hope that's okay." He stared at Aunt Cara, willing her with his eyes not to pry.

Instead, she rushed over to Juniper and enveloped her in a tight hug. "Oh, I'm so glad," she said. "When Ethan told me y'all were fighting, I was so worried. Rob was too."

"I was," Uncle Robert added, sauntering over to hug Juniper as well.

Ethan cringed, but Juniper just smiled. "Well, Mr. and Mrs. Shay, no need to worry. Everything's all square between Ethan and me."

"That's wonderful to hear." Aunt Cara smiled. "Come in then, please, take a seat. Dinner's almost ready."

It had been a while since Juniper had spent time at the house, and Ethan had forgotten how much warmer the place was when her voice was there to fill it. She spun stories for the table about a raccoon she'd met while gardening and a particularly intense game of solitaire she'd played with herself, and Ethan wasn't sure if they were true but laughed nonetheless. When Juniper was around, Aunt-Cara and Uncle Robert were warmer too—whatever kindness they'd learned to show him grew under Juniper's unintentional guidance. Even Uncle Robert managed to crack a few smiles.

By the time the pot roast was down to scraps and Aunt Cara placed a tray of chocolate chip cookies in the middle of the table, everyone was in a good mood. Juniper looked at Ethan, and before he could react, cleared her throat.

"Mr. Shay," she said solemnly. "Mrs. Shay, Ethan has something he wants to ask you."

"What is it, honey?" Aunt Cara asked, frowning.

"I, um—well—"

"Come on, Ethan," Juniper urged. "Just ask 'em."

Ethan looked nervously around the table, at Juniper's imploring eyes and his aunt and uncle's concerned gazes. If he backed out now, it would be uncomfortable for everyone. He took a deep breath.

"I was wondering if I could go visit my mom," he said quickly, then winced. "In Montgomery. June said it's not too far, just a couple of hours. I'd just need a ride there and back, and I could be quick, I swear."

"And I'd come too," Juniper added. "For protection." She clenched her fists, attempting to produce muscles in her thin arms.

"I know it's a lot to ask," Ethan went on. "And I know you already said I could call her. But I just—I just think it would help."

Aunt Cara and Uncle Robert looked at each other and Ethan held his breath. "I do have a shipment to pick up from the warehouse next weekend," Uncle Robert said, still facing his wife. "It's just outside Montgomery."

"And there are two extra seats in the truck," Aunt Cara said.

"Can't imagine Andy would be too pleased."

Aunt Cara shrugged. "Andy has no right to keep the boy from his mother."

Juniper was practically vibrating in her seat, cheeks red with excitement. Ethan clutched the hem of the tablecloth. Finally, Uncle Robert turned to him.

"I'd expect you to be on your best behavior," he said. "Both of you. I'd give you a time for pickup and drop-off, and you'd have to stick to it."

"Done and done," Juniper said with a mock salute.

"Ethan?"

"Yeah. Yeah, I can do that."

Uncle Robert nodded as Aunt Cara added, "And one more thing." She stood slowly and moved to the kitchen drawer at the edge of the cabinet. After rummaging through it for a second, she pulled out a spiral notebook and dropped it on the table in front of Ethan. The cover said Phone Book in purple script.

"Call your mother," she said gently. "Ask her if it's all right."

＊

It took a couple of days of doubting and second-guessing and berating from Juniper before Ethan was finally able to pick up the phone. Finally, on Saturday afternoon—a week from the planned trip—Ethan found himself sitting in front of the phone in Aunt Cara's living room, Juniper perched on the couch beside him and his mother's number in his hand.

With a long, shaky breath, he dialed. When the operator answered, he barely heard himself speak to her. Next thing he knew, the line was ringing, soft and slow. Juniper rocked beside him.

There was a click, then, "Hello?"

He almost hung up the phone right then. But Juniper, faintly hearing the response through the phone, punched him in the arm. He blurted, "Hi, is Lydia there?"

The other line was silent. "One second."

Ethan heard the sound of muffled conversation, then footsteps, and the gentle click of the phone being transferred from one hand to another. Then a warm, low, familiar voice said, "This is Lydia. Who's calling?"

Ethan suddenly found himself on his knees next to the couch, the phone cord stretched as far as it could go. Relief and sadness washed over him in waves as Juniper squeezed his shoulder and he struggled to speak.

"Ethan," he said. "It's Ethan. Hi, Mom."

"Ethan," she sounded surprised. "Are you at home? Is something wrong? Is it the twins, or your dad?"

"No, no, nothing's wrong," he assured her. He could barely think. "And I'm not at home, actually. I'm in Ellison, Alabama. It's a long story. I'm staying with Aunt Cara and Uncle Robert. And well, I know you're in Montgomery. I know it's not too far from here." He paused, heard his mother breathing on the other line. "And I was just wondering if you had plans next weekend. Because — because if it's okay, I'd really like to visit you."

FIFTEEN

Uncle Robert's '52 Chevy pickup could fit two comfortably—three with some effort. Ethan found himself squeezed in the middle of the tan vinyl bench, his uncle's elbow against his side and Juniper's hair slapping him in the face every time she whirled to look at something outside the window.

"Wow, look at all the trees!" she cried. Slap. "There are so many! And they're moving so fast." Slap. "Ethan, look!" Slap.

"Yeah, June. Real cool." Ethan sank low in his seat and crossed his arms over his chest. They hadn't even made it out of town.

Uncle Robert chuckled. "Just wait till she sees the buildings."

The road to Montgomery was uneven for the first twenty-minute stretch as they made their way off of the rural roads and onto the highway. Ethan braced a foot against the dash-board to keep himself in place, but Juniper allowed the jolts of the truck over potholes to launch her out of her seat again and again. Her hair was everywhere, including across Ethan's shoulders and in his mouth, but she didn't seem to notice.

And to be honest, Ethan was glad that she was entertaining herself and that Uncle Robert was characteristically silent as he drove. He needed the time—as bumpy and distracting as this time was—to think. He'd been replaying the phone call with his mother over and over in his mind since it had happened; how she had sat on the other line in stunned silence for a long moment after his question before saying, softly, "Of course, Ethan. Okay."

The plan had fallen quickly into place after that. Uncle Robert would bring Ethan and Juniper to Montgomery that Saturday afternoon when he met his suppliers at the warehouse. Ethan's mother worked during the day, so he and Juniper would spend the day in town and go to his mother's apartment for dinner. Ethan had the address—the location was circled in dark pencil on a map of Montgomery tucked into his pocket. Uncle Robert would pick them up after dinner and they'd drive back to Ellison. It was simple; it was his mother, the woman who had raised him for the first ten years of his life, and it was a city, where he felt at home. There was no reason for Ethan to be worried.

But he was. As Uncle Robert turned onto the highway and the road smoothed out for the rest of their journey, Ethan fought down the nerves writhing in his stomach. It had been a long time since he'd last seen his mother, and he was different now. Especially after this summer. He was scared to tell her, as he had promised, why he was sent to Ellison. Scared to see her disappointment, her agreement with his father's decision. And scared, most of all, that so many years apart would make it impossible for her to still see herself in him just as he, when he pictured her face, lately struggled to see himself in her.

Still hunched over in his seat, Ethan looked up at Juniper,

who had cranked open her window and was now hanging her head outside. Her hair whipped back in the wind like a streak of paint across a canvas and she squinted into the morning light. Feeling Ethan's gaze, she looked over her shoulder with a grin.

"Are you seeing this, Ethan? Mr. Shay? Is this not the best?"

Uncle Robert laughed. "Glad you're having fun, Junie."

"Oh, I'm having *so* much fun. It's going to be such a fun day! Ethan's gonna see his mom, I'm gonna see Montgomery—nothing could be better. Right, Ethan?"

Ethan forced a smile. "Right, Juniper."

As Juniper began a running commentary on the sights blurring past, Ethan willed himself to mimic her enthusiasm. It was his choice, after all, to visit his mother. She was the only one who would understand.

True to Uncle Robert's prediction, when they spied Montgomery from the highway an hour later, Juniper let out a shriek. She leaned forward so far, Ethan thought she might fly out the window.

"Look at that!" she shouted, pointing at a tall, white church. "And that!" Her finger swiveled to a street of four-story brick buildings. "Wow. Wow, wow, wow."

"Welcome to Montgomery," Uncle Robert said.

Ethan stared out the window over Juniper's shoulder, struck by a strange sense of familiarity. He knew little about Montgomery—his parents had rarely talked about it, and he'd never felt compelled to ask—but a part of him felt as though he'd been here before. It had surely changed from how it had been when his parents fell in love, and even probably from when his mother had returned after they fell out. But he knew this place, somewhere in his gut; and he was certain of it when Uncle Robert turned a corner and Ethan found himself mirrored on the sidewalk.

Two black men and three black women walked together, wide-brimmed hats on their heads blocking the sun. The truck passed them quickly. Ethan only caught the slightest glimpse, but it was long enough to see them lean together in easy camaraderie, laughing.

Juniper, her head inside the window now, saw it too. She reached over and squeezed Ethan's hand. Ethan held in a breath, releasing it only when Uncle Robert stopped behind a bus that had paused to let passengers off. He watched them exit, joining other pedestrians on the sidewalk, side stepping cars to cross the street. Some black folks, some white — not speaking, maybe, but existing together in the same space. He felt relief swell almost painfully into his throat.

"All right," Uncle Robert said, turning right onto a smaller side street and pulling over to the curb. "This is for you." With a gruff nod, he handed them each three wrinkled dollar bills. "Just in case. Spend it wisely."

Juniper took the money carefully and tucked it into the polka-dot purse in her lap. "Thank you, Mr. Shay," she said. "We absolutely will."

Ethan muttered a distracted thank you, his attention on the brick buildings outside the window. Down one of these streets was the apartment building where his mother lived. He had memorized its placement on the map, a small circle amid a spiderweb of streets. It wasn't far from downtown, not even a mile.

"You kids be careful." Uncle Robert tightened and loosened his grip on the steering wheel, over and over. "This isn't Ellison, but it's no Arcadia either. Keep your heads down and all that. And if you need anything, you've got my number at the warehouse, right?"

Ethan nodded—the number was scrawled on the corner of the map in his pocket. Uncle Robert sighed. "All right, then. This is where I leave you."

"Bye, Mr. Shay!" Juniper called, shoving open the passenger door and leaping out onto the pavement. To Ethan, all of this felt barely real. He murmured a good-bye to his uncle, sliding across the worn seat toward the door. As he did, Uncle Robert suddenly placed a hand on his arm.

"I mean it, Ethan," he said, as Ethan turned to look at him in surprise. "If you need anything at all."

If relief and apprehension had been battling in Ethan's gut, it was apprehension that won out now. Something in Uncle Robert's gaze sent a nervous shiver through his shoulders. But again, he simply nodded, offering his uncle what he hoped was a reassuring smile.

"Sure thing, Uncle Robert," he said, sliding out of the car. His uncle waited until they had reached the corner before shifting into gear and driving away.

It was a particularly muggy day, and they hadn't even walked a block when Ethan felt the sweat gathering on the back of his neck. A few minutes of wandering had brought them back to a busy street, where storefronts were arranged one after the other and pedestrians stopped to chat and window shop. Juniper's attention changed focus with each novelty that appeared. She cooed to Ethan over a couple walking their baby in a stroller, a window display filled with TV sets, the way the sun reflected from the mirrors of so many passing cars. And slowly, he started to relax. There was nothing he could do until he went to his mother's for dinner, after all, and that was three hours away.

"What do you want to do?" he asked Juniper, who had paused at the window of a bakery.

"A great question." She straightened, hands on her hips. "You know, I always said if I made it to Montgomery I'd do it all — trouble is, now I can't remember what I meant by that."

Ethan stepped back to make room for an elderly black couple, who nodded at him as they passed. "Well, let's think," he said. "What's something you've always wanted to do that you can't do in Ellison?" Juniper opened her mouth immediately, and he held up a hand. "A *reasonable* thing."

Juniper sighed loudly. "Ethan Charlie Harper, you're no fun." She resumed walking, slowly, and he followed a few steps behind. "Let me think," she said. "Climb up the fire escape of a building, try every flavor of ice cream in an ice-cream parlor, paint a mural—" She'd been ticking off the options as she walked but stopped suddenly as a drop of rain landed right in the middle of her forehead.

Ethan had learned after two months in Alabama that somehow the sky here could do this: open up and empty without warning. Juniper knew this even better than he did, but still she shrieked and covered her head with her arms as she took off down the sidewalk.

"Hey, wait up!" Ethan called, weaving through the other people also hurrying for shelter. Juniper laughed, dropping her arms and tossing her head back as she ran. Rain streaked down her cheeks and soaked her dress, but she did not weave through the awnings of nearby buildings. Ethan could have easily sped past her, but he ignored the wet curls flopping into his eyes and kept an easy jog. Juniper was, in this sudden sun shower on a city sidewalk, as in everywhere else, radiant, and he didn't want to leave her behind.

They only ran two blocks; the rain only lasted five minutes.

And yet, by the end of it, they stumbled to a breathless stop as if they'd run for miles. "You look," Juniper wheezed, "like you just got out of the shower."

"You look like you just took a swim in the lake," Ethan retorted. He wrung out the hem of his T-shirt, dripping water onto the sidewalk. Around them, the city was coming back into motion: umbrellas closed, heads peeked out from shop doors, first tentative steps were taken back onto the pavement. No one seemed to notice or care about the boy and the girl giggling on the sidewalk in front of the movie theater.

Ethan noticed the theater sign first, its overhanging sign affixed with the words MONTGOMERY CINEMA in boxy letters, with the current shows listed beneath it. It looked much like the theater he and his friends frequented back home, the one that was two blocks from school, and which was smaller than the others and had a projector that sometimes didn't work, but was ten cents cheaper and served the best popcorn in the state.

"Say, June," he said, skimming the titles, "didn't you say you'd never gone to the movies?"

"Sure did." She followed his gaze up to the sign and audibly gasped. "Did you plan this, Ethan?" she asked, playfully accusatory.

Ethan held up his hands in defense. "Hey, you're the one who was leading the way. But as long as we're here, we might as well catch a show, right? We've got just enough time."

"You don't need to convince me," Juniper said, gazing up at the titles in awe. "Oh, man—which one do we even choose?"

Ethan chuckled—there were only two options. "Your choice. Look, why don't you get the tickets? I'm going to look for a bathroom and try to dry off."

"It would be my *honor*," Juniper said. She darted off to the ticket booth, where a bored-looking cashier was tapping his hand against the counter.

Ethan glanced around for a restroom sign and eventually spotted one a few stores down, nestled between a pawn shop and an ice-cream parlor. The sign hung above the entrance to a narrow alley, and when Ethan entered it, he saw that it branched off into two hallways a little ways down, with two signs perched above two mismatched drinking fountains. As he got closer, he was able to make out the words. Above the drinking fountain to the right, which was large and clean, was a sign reading WHITE. To the left, above a dinky, dirty fountain that seemed moments away from falling off the wall was a sign with the word COLORED.

Ethan froze, his heart suddenly plummeting. He gripped the basin of the right-side fountain to steady himself. As he stood there in the center of the walkway, a man emerged from the "white" side, wiping his hands on his jeans. At the sight of Ethan, he raised an eyebrow.

"Excuse me," he snapped, nodding to the drinking fountain.

"Oh, right," Ethan mumbled, taking a few shaky steps back from the fountain. "Sorry."

The man did not respond, but eyed Ethan shamelessly as he bent to take a drink. He was a small man, dressed in a poorly tailored suit and gripping a briefcase under his arm. He seemed to find nothing amiss with the signs above the drinking fountains.

"Don't stare at me," the man said as he walked off, and Ethan jerked away. Just then, a black woman in a sun hat emerged from the "colored" hallway and studied him with concern.

"You all right there, sweetie?" she asked, her southern drawl thick and soothing.

Ethan opened and closed his mouth, floundering for words. "I—I'm not from here," he managed.

The woman seemed to understand, because she pointed to the aisle she had just exited. "That's where you want to go," she told him.

Muttering a garbled thanks, he edged past her and down the hall. At the end of it, he stumbled into the men's restroom, noting the sudden paleness in his cheeks as he glanced in the mirror. *Of course*, he thought. It was here that the girl his age was arrested from the bus for taking up space designated for whites. With his heart in his throat and the rainstorm forgotten, Ethan splashed water on his face. He had to be careful here, perhaps even more so than in Ellison. Here, the way Ethan had been treated for weeks was law.

"Just keep your head down," he said to his reflection. When he returned to the theater a few minutes later, Juniper was standing on the sidewalk, two tickets clutched in her hand. She saw Ethan approaching and grinned. She didn't notice the stiff way he walked or the fact that his hair was still wet.

Instead: "Got them!" she cried, waving the tickets in the air. Ethan forced a smile and reached out to take his ticket from her outstretched fingers. A new animated movie, Juniper told him, about talking dogs who fall in love.

"Sounds great, doesn't it?"

"Yeah, great," Ethan echoed, following her to the door. He was distracted as the ticket taker checked their tickets—first Juniper's, glancing at it and waving her through, and then Ethan's, taking it from his hand and staring hard at it for a moment before allowing him to pass. He said something as he returned the ticket to Ethan, but Ethan didn't catch it and simply nodded.

Juniper was already at the concession stand, making the cashier smile as she watched the popcorn machine in awe. She met Ethan at the doors of their theater a moment later, bag full of popcorn in arm.

"Hey, are you all right, Harper?" she asked, her mouth full of kernels. "You're being awfully quiet."

Ethan could think only of the bathroom signs, but he nodded and said, "Yeah, totally fine," as he followed her into the theater. It was nearly empty, with only a few other people scattered throughout the seats, and Juniper made a beeline for the center.

"I heard this is the best place to sit," she said in a loud whisper. But just as Ethan was about to follow her into the row, a loud voice behind them called out, "Excuse me! Boy!" and Ethan turned to find himself in the beam of a flashlight. It was the ticket taker, looking stiff and furious in his red uniform vest.

"What's wrong?" Juniper asked, making her way back to Ethan.

"Didn't you hear what I said?" the man demanded, his beam on Ethan's chest. "Coloreds up top." He pointed over his shoulder, where Ethan could make out a sad row of chairs, not even theater seats, lined up across a small balcony. Above it, a white sign labeled the area as COLORED SEATING.

"Sorry, I didn't realize—"

"Don't make excuses to me. Just get up there."

"Wait a minute." Juniper held up the hand that wasn't holding the popcorn, frowning. "He's with me. Why can't he sit down here?"

The man, who Ethan saw was barely older than twenty,

eyed her warily. "That's the rules, ma'am. You ought to know better than being out with a colored boy, anyway."

People were staring now, and Ethan felt his face grow hot. "It's fine, Juniper."

"No, it's not," she said. "He's my best friend, and I'm going to sit with him. I don't care what the rules are."

"Best friend, huh?" the man sneered. "That's what you call it?"

There was a familiar tilt to the way he held his body, leaning toward Ethan at just the right angle to pounce. He'd seen Samuel Hill do it a million times. He knew what could happen if it escalated.

Panic rising in his chest, Ethan stepped away from the vested man and from Juniper, who still stood tall with the popcorn under her arm. "Look, I'll just go," he said. "Sorry about the misunderstanding." He scurried away before either of them could say anything. Every step toward the door seemed to take a century, and he was nearly shaking by the time he stepped into the light of the lobby. He looked back only when he reached the stairs to the balcony. The ticket taker was standing by the theater doors, glowering. Juniper hadn't followed.

The balcony was small and dirty; popcorn kernels and dust littered the floor, and the chairs were scratched and wobbly. Still, Ethan took a seat, clenching his hands into fists in his lap and staring straight ahead as the lights dimmed and the movie began. He imagined Juniper in her seat in the middle row, glancing back up at the balcony occasionally, struggling to make him out in the low light. He didn't try to look for her.

Usually, Ethan loved the movies. He would sit, riveted, taking in every last detail that passed across the big screen.

But today, though his eyes never left the screen, he couldn't seem to follow a single scene. He heard sparse laughter from the audience as if through a wall, and the animated images passed right through his mind. All he could think about was the scene he'd caused, the way the man had dismissed him like a misbehaved child.

It was this, and not the film, that was playing itself in his head when the door to the balcony creaked open and quiet footsteps approached his chair. "Hey," Juniper whispered, pulling over the seat beside him. "This seat taken?"

Ethan shook his head and she sat. She held out the bag of popcorn and he silently took a handful. Maybe it was just the silence of the theater, but she didn't press him to speak, didn't say anything else at all. She just sat beside him, holding the popcorn bag within his reach, and stared ahead at the movie screen until it went dark.

SIXTEEN

Juniper didn't say anything until they'd left the theater and walked a block down the street. It was nearly six now, the sun lower in the sky but hot as ever. The streets had emptied since the afternoon, and only a few cars passed as Ethan and Juniper walked.

Finally, at a corner, Juniper stopped. "That was horrible," she announced, turning to face Ethan. "Absolutely horrible."

Ethan shrugged. "It's really not a big deal, Juniper."

"It *is* a big deal," she said. "You're a person, and you couldn't do a normal person thing like see a movie with your friend because what? You don't look like them?"

Her voice was rising now and she paced in a circle on the street corner. Sweat beaded on her nose. Ethan took a step back, worried again that her volume would attract attention. "June, please. I don't want to talk about it."

She whirled to face him suddenly, eyes flashing. "Well, why not?" she demanded. "Bad things happen and you say you don't want to talk about them, so you just sit there and be miserable about it?"

"What else do you expect me to do?"

"Scream!" she shouted. "Throw things! I don't know, Ethan—be *angry*. There's plenty of reason for it."

Ethan closed his eyes, taking a long breath. He *was* angry. He had been for as long as he'd been in Alabama, maybe even longer. But he kept the anger locked away in the space between his ribs; held it there tight. He was afraid to see what it would look like if he let it out.

When he opened his eyes again, Juniper was silent, standing there on the sidewalk and watching him with tired eyes. "Thing is, I know I don't get it," she said. "I'll never really get it. But we're about to go see your mom, and she'll get it. Maybe it doesn't make sense to tell me you're angry, but I know you are, deep down somewhere. And I'm just hoping that maybe you'll think about telling her."

She was looking at him more earnestly than Ethan had ever seen her, her eyes at once gentle and fierce. He could tell, in that single gaze, how much she cared. And he knew that she was right—that however long it had been since they'd seen each other, however infrequently they spoke, his mom would understand.

He sighed. "Okay. I'll think about it."

Juniper stepped forward and hugged Ethan so quickly that he was barely sure it had happened. Then she nodded. "No time to waste then," she said. "Your mom's expecting us for dinner. Do you have the map?"

They made it to the apartment twenty minutes later, after several wrong turns and a few instances of Juniper being distracted by a baby or a dog. It was an unassuming building, three stories of brick—underwhelming, Ethan thought. It looked like any old person might live here.

"This is it," Ethan said, staring up at it from the sidewalk. Beside him, Juniper nodded.

"How do you feel?"

"Nervous. Excited. Scared."

"Sounds about right." She held out a hand. "Well, I'm here no matter what. Let's go."

He took her hand and together they went up the steps to the small porch. There was a doorbell with his mother's unit printed beneath it: #2. Taking a deep breath, he pushed the button.

It was silent for a few seconds, then quick footsteps approached the door. When it swung open, Ethan found himself facing a girl a bit younger than him. Her dark curls were a halo around her head, and a pair of large, wire-frame glasses balanced on her nose. She took one squinty look at Ethan and ran back inside, yelling, "Auntie, he's here!"

Ethan and Juniper looked at each other, then back at the open door. Through it, they could see a set of narrow stairs.

"Well," Juniper said after a moment. "Should we go inside?"

Just then, a woman appeared at the stairs and hurried down them. She had tight curls pulled into a bun at the base of her neck, heavily lashed eyes, and a crooked smile. Now, with her standing right in front of him, Ethan wondered how he had ever managed to forget her face.

"Hey, Mom," he said. He hesitated in the doorway and so did she. It was only after a moment that she opened her arms, and after another that he stepped into them. He was taller than her now and he bent to press his face against her shoulder.

"Hi, sweetheart." She stepped back to look at him, her

eyes crinkling. "You've really grown." Her accent was thick and smooth, stretching out every syllable. "And you must be Juniper."

Juniper stuck out a hand and Ethan's mother shook it. "Yes, ma'am," she said. "Juniper Jones. Nice to meet you, uh—"

"Ms. Phillips is fine, honey."

"Then nice to meet you, Ms. Phillips."

Ethan and Juniper followed Ethan's mom up one flight of stairs and through an open door to their right. The apartment began with a short hallway that opened up to a living room and kitchen. To the right was another hall where two closed doors faced each other. It was a small space, and crowded with furniture, but tidy. The little girl who had greeted them now sat on the couch, staring owlishly at the grainy television by the window.

"Ethan, this is your cousin, Ramona. Ramona, this is Ethan and his friend Juniper."

"Cousin?" Ethan echoed.

"Hi," said Ramona, not looking up.

"My sister's daughter," his mom explained. "She's—how old are you, Mona?"

"Twelve and a half."

"Twelve and a half," she repeated. "Right. Well, go ahead, take a seat—dinner's almost ready." She gestured to a small dining table in the corner of the kitchen. "How does beef brisket with mashed potatoes and green beans sound to y'all?"

"That sounds *wonderful*," Juniper said earnestly, slipping into one of the seats. Ethan sat beside her. Ramona finally turned from the TV set for a moment, scrutinizing Ethan and Juniper before jumping off the couch and pattering off toward one of the bedrooms.

"Mona, dinner in five!"

"I know!" the girl called, already gone.

Ethan's mom shook her head, returning to a pot on the stove and stirring it a few times. Ethan watched her quietly. He felt a nervous energy from her, much like his own, and thought that maybe she was stirring to avoid an awkward silence.

"I didn't know I had a cousin," he said eventually.

Still at the stove, his mother chuckled. "Neither did I, till last year. My older sister had been gone in New York City for over a decade, moved back out of the blue with a husband and child in tow. They live here, too, but both of them work nights, so I watch Mona."

"I didn't know you had a sister," Ethan said. There was a lot he didn't know about his mother, he realized. He tried to take stock: he knew that she grew up in Montgomery, trained to be a nurse, then moved to Arcadia when she met his dad. Her dad died when she was in high school, and her mom passed when Ethan was only five—he just barely remembered his mom leaving home for a few days to attend the funeral. But with just about everything else, he was left to fill in the blanks. He was young when she left, and their phone calls had been so brief, so infrequent, that he'd never had time to ask. He didn't even know where to begin.

"Two," she corrected. "A younger one, too, living out in Mississippi." He tried to imagine two more women with his mother's pointed chin and crooked smile.

For a moment, watching his mother open the oven and pull out a pan of green beans, he caught a glimpse of what life might have been like if she'd never gone away. He would sit at the kitchen table in the morning before school, chatting with her as she made breakfast and the twins chased each other through the house. She would ask him about his friends, his current favorite record, and she would share her own in turn. There would be nothing they didn't know about each other. She would send him off to the bus with a packed lunch and a kiss on the nose.

The image faded. Here he was again, in this cramped kitchen, waiting for a dinner cooked by someone he hadn't spent real time with in years. Juniper sat behind him, eagerly inhaling the smells. When Ethan's mother placed the dishes in the center of the table, Juniper grinned.

"Thanks so much, Ms. Phillips," she said. "This looks delicious."

"Thanks, Mom."

"Oh, my pleasure." Leaning toward the living room, she called, "Mona, dinner!" and there was the sound of a door creaking, followed by footsteps. Mona rocketed around the corner and all but leapt into a seat. Ethan's mom took the fourth chair and began dishing the food onto each of their plates.

Ethan moved slowly—while Juniper rushed to shovel brisket into her mouth, he had hardly reached for his knife. His mother busied herself with Ramona's plate, but he could feel her watching him out of the corner of her eye.

"So, Juniper, how did you and Ethan meet?" she asked, cutting into her own food.

Juniper swallowed a hefty bite of mashed potatoes. "Ethan's been working at the malt shop, and I love root beer floats. I went in one day for a float and saw Ethan working there and decided right then and there that we were going to be best friends. See, I had this plan for a whole invincible summer, but of course I couldn't do it all by myself. And who better, I thought, than my new best friend?"

"I see." Ethan's mom smiled slightly. "Now, I haven't been to Ellison in—oh, two decades, almost. But I can't imagine many other folks in town feel the way you do."

"No, I wouldn't say so." For a moment, Juniper's face grew somber, but she quickly brightened. "It's all right, though, Ms. Phillips, because I'm looking out for him. I protect him against all the bullies in town."

Ethan rolled his eyes, taking a bite of his food. His mother, though, straightened. "People are bothering you, Ethan?"

"It's fine, Mom. Really."

Juniper scoffed, her mouth full. "Fine? Ethan, you don't have to pretend." She gave him the same imploring look as she had on the street corner.

"Okay," he said, looking down at his plate. "It's not fine. At all."

"I see," his mother said again, and that was all. After a beat of silence, she changed the subject, asking about what had been on their list for an invincible summer, telling them about a painting Ramona had made that week—filling the space with inconsequential chatter. Ethan was grateful for the interlude. He let Juniper do most of the talking and focused on eating his food, one bite at a time. For a little while, he let himself tuck the movie theater and the bathrooms away in his mind. He thought only about the meal in front of him and his mother across from him.

By the time their plates were empty, Juniper had, in predictably hilarious fashion, laid out their entire summer plan in great detail and described each of her favorite places in Ellison at least twice over. She even got Ramona to laugh a few times.

"Ramona," Ethan's mom said, after the plates were cleared and the table wiped down. "Weren't you saying you were a little stuck on the new puzzle you've been doing?"

Ramona nodded. "It's a picture of a big train."

"Juniper, you said you're an artist—I'll bet you have a great eye for puzzles. Why don't you go see if you can help her?"

Noting the gravity in Ethan's mother's voice, Juniper paused for a moment. She glanced quickly at Ethan, who immediately felt panic well in his chest—he realized now that as angry as he was, and as much as he wanted to express that, he was also scared. It felt as though if he told his mother everything, it would all be real, once and for all.

"Of course," Juniper said belatedly, standing up from the table. "I'll bet that puzzle is no match for a Ramona and Juniper duo." She gave Ethan an encouraging nod as she passed him, following Ramona through the living room and down the hall. A moment later, he heard a door close gently.

"Ethan," his mother said. He couldn't remember the last time he'd heard his name said so tenderly. He looked down at his hands, pressed flat against the table.

"I don't think I'm ready to talk about it," he said hoarsely, though part of him wanted nothing more than to let the words spill out.

"Okay," she said gently. "You don't have to talk right now. I will." She reached across the table and placed her hands over his. "I spoke to your father. Right after you called, in fact—I was so furious that I called him without thinking."

She laughed a little, and Ethan struggled to imagine his talking parents on the phone—he couldn't remember the last time he'd heard them have a conversation.

"What did he say?" he asked.

"Everything there was to say, I guess. He told me about the fight, the suspension, the plan to send you to Ellison—all of it." She sighed. "And I just kept wondering, what were you thinking?"

"Mom, it wasn't my fault. Samuel Hill said—"

"No, honey, not you." She smiled. "Your father. I asked him what he was thinking, sending you there. He said he thought it would teach you a lesson. For all that that man cares—and he cares deeply—he never learned what it means to raise a black child."

Ethan blinked. "You're not mad at me? For punching Sam?"

His mother laughed. "I remember Sam from your kindergarten class. He was always nasty, even then. I wouldn't be surprised if he said something that deserved a fist in the nose. And while I don't love the idea of you getting into fights," she went on, raising an eyebrow, "sometimes you need to be angry. A lot of the time, these days, you need to be angry."

It was strange, Ethan thought, to hear his mother speak this way. Except when he was young and she'd fought with his father, he'd never seen her angry a day in his life. She was the one who held her temper and kept her voice soft. But as he looked at her now, he saw that her eyes were bright with fury. She kept her anger quiet, held it differently, but it was still there, burning.

"Yeah," he said eventually. "Juniper's been saying that too."

"Then she's a smart girl. And a good friend." She tilted her head. "Now why don't you tell me what's been going on in Ellison."

Over the next hour, over tall glasses of sweet iced tea, Ethan talked about Ellison. He told his mom about Noah O'Neil, the moment in the general store, the way people stared. He seethed about his father. He talked about being angry, constantly, but also sad and, most of all, afraid. He felt the layers of hurt peeling away, if only for a moment.

"It's just that I didn't know what it would be like," he said at the end, picking at a splinter on the tabletop. "I thought Dad made me go to Ellison because it's hot and boring, not because it's—you know."

"You know, I'd guess that your father thought he was sending you to Ellison because it's hot and boring too." She sighed deeply. "Your dad has never talked to you about race." It wasn't a question. Ethan shook his head. "That's what all our fights always came back to. I wanted to talk about race with you and the twins, the way my parents did with me when they told me about my enslaved grandparents who were sold for auction at that big fountain in the center of Montgomery. It's important for us to know where we come from and what's been done to us, otherwise, how're we supposed to fight what's happening to us now? It's all connected."

It's all connected. This was the first Ethan had heard about his great-grandparents, but he remembered passing that fountain as he and Juniper ran through the rain. They'd learned about it in school, a little bit: the slave trade, the Civil War. And yet never had he connected the grainy drawings of black bodies in chains to his own history.

"But Dad didn't think so," Ethan guessed.

She shook her head. "A decade in Arcadia was enough to make him forget what the world was like outside. And Arcadia wasn't even perfect. But of course, he didn't see that." Frowning, his mother gazed over his shoulder, where the TV still played softly. After a moment, she went on, "He wanted you to stay innocent as long as you could. Problem is, colored kids don't get to be innocent. It's like you come out of the womb full grown, the way the world treats you. And your father means well, but he just can't understand. He'll be innocent till the day he dies."

Ethan thought of Juniper, with her brazen curiosity, the way she moved through the world with childlike ease. All this time he'd figured that was just Juniper Jones. And it was, sure. But maybe, also, it was because she was allowed to be this way.

"Is that why you left? Because Dad didn't agree with you?" He realized after the words were out that they were, to his surprise, coated with resentment. His mother was unfazed.

"It's more complicated than that," she said softly. "We knew we couldn't stay together. But when it came down to the divorce, your dad won custody. I couldn't afford to live in Arcadia on my own. I didn't want to leave. But I had to."

Ethan's resentment shifted now to his father. "This is all Dad's fault," he said.

"The blame here's not so simple, sweetheart. Your dad was doing the best with what he knows. This is what he thought was right."

"But it's *not* right. You know it's not right."

"I know," she said softly. "I know."

They were both silent for a while, thinking, maybe, about their fragmented family. For his part, Ethan was wondering how he might ever begin to forgive his father. How he could ever really believe that his dad had been as naive as he himself had been? He sighed, turning back to his mother.

"In town today," he said, "Juniper and I went to see a movie, and I had to sit separate from everyone else. And when I went to the bathroom, same thing." He looked down, somehow ashamed. As if to be distinguished in this way was a weakness.

His mother nodded slowly. "It's like that in all the big cities 'round here. Separate rooms, seating areas, sometimes even businesses for white folks and colored folks. Or take this apartment, for example. You couldn't pay a white person enough to make them live within a half mile radius of here. Some towns, I hear, you're not even allowed out on the street after dark if you are black."

"But *why?*" Ethan felt like he'd been asking this question all summer. To Juniper, to himself—and he couldn't find an answer.

His mother was silent for a moment, lips pursed as she gathered her words. Ethan watched the way her eyebrows arched when she was thinking, just as they had when he was little. The same way he knew his eyebrows arched too.

"For a long time, the law let white people treat us no better than cattle," she said finally. "And some of them realized that it was no way to treat a person—or at least, they realized that they couldn't get away with being so obvious anymore. So they got more clever, and they made laws that kept us down—even if we weren't in captivity. That's why my parents, your grandparents, worked on a farm for next to nothing for years and years, even though they were free. Because the law said they couldn't have a deed to their names."

"But why?" Ethan asked again.

"Because people are afraid of what will happen if we are really free." Her eyes hardened. "When you trap people for hundreds of years, make their lives a living hell, they're bound to get antsy. And furious. And so white folks think the harder they make it for us to live, the longer they'll be able to put off a revolution."

She said it so simply: a revolution. Gently, but with conviction, as if she knew it was coming. If it was, she'd be part of it. Ethan was sure of this. For years to come, Ethan would remember the revolution his mother spoke of—he'd see it in the people around him, and eventually in himself. But for now, the word sent an excited flutter through his stomach. And a certain relief, too, of someone finally giving him an answer.

"Mom, can I just stay here?" he blurted. It was clear from their mirrored surprise that neither expected those words. "I mean—I just—" Ethan struggled to explain. Of course, so much would be harder in Montgomery. There was more, he was sure, than what he'd seen. But sitting here with his mother, he realized how long he'd gone without having someone who understood him. He didn't say this out loud, just looked at her, but she seemed to understand.

For the first time Ethan could remember, tears gathered in his mother's eyes. Clumsily, she stood and rounded the table to collect him into her arms. "Honey," she whispered, "there's nothing I want more to have you and Anthony and Sadie with me. But it's not that simple." She stepped back, smoothing his curls back from his forehead. "Your dad is your legal guardian, and to challenge that would mean putting our whole family through hell. If I couldn't even get partial custody the first time around, there's no way any judge would give it to me now. Especially with me being back in Montgomery, and all—according to this state, my marriage to your father never existed."

Whatever relief Ethan had felt rushed quickly out of him. Tears slithered down his cheeks and his heart ached with every beat. "That's not fair," he said, turning to bury his face in his mother's shoulder. She held him close.

"I know, honey," she said. "It's not fair at all."

Ethan closed his eyes, wishing to hold still forever in the safety of that moment. He had spent two months, and really longer, looking out for himself—he'd forgotten how wonderful it felt to let himself be held. His mother didn't move, running her hand gently across his hair as he let his breathing slow to a calm.

Some time later, Ethan heard the doorbell ring. "I think that's your uncle," his mother said softly, and took a slow step back. Ethan straightened as she disappeared into the hall.

"Is that Mr. Shay?" came Juniper's voice, and a moment later, she bounded back into the kitchen, Ramona at her heels. The younger girl was grinning.

"We finished the whole puzzle," she said proudly.

"We sure did," Juniper said, giving Ramona a high five. "But really, it was all Mona."

Ramona's smile grew wider. From the hallway came Ethan's mother's voice: "Ethan, Juniper—Robert is here." A moment later, Uncle Robert appeared in the kitchen. It was strange to see him here in his mother's kitchen, these worlds colliding. But Uncle Robert offered him a smile and asked if he was ready to go, and Ethan smiled back and nodded.

"Thank you for dinner, Ms. Phillips," Juniper said, hugging Ethan's mom as Ethan stood up from the table.

"Anytime, sweetheart. If you ever find yourself back in Montgomery, you know you're always welcome here."

"Bye, Mona." Juniper hugged the younger girl, who squeezed her fiercely before running to Ethan and quickly wrapping her arms around him.

"Bye," she said, blinking up at them.

"Bye, Mona," Ethan said. Juniper and Uncle Robert were in the doorway now, and Ethan was left with his mother, who looked at him with teary, loving eyes.

"Thank you for coming, Ethan," she said, embracing him tightly. "I'll see you soon."

"I hope so," Ethan said against her shoulder.

"Know that if I could let you stay here, I would do it in a heartbeat. But even if I'm far away, I'm here for you, always. I'm your mom, after all." She stepped away, smiling sadly.

"I know."

"And I love you."

"I love you too," Ethan said, his voice cracking.

"Oh, and one more thing," she said, dropping her voice. "Juniper seems like a wonderful friend. Sometimes that's what you need to make it through. Keep her close."

Ethan nodded. "I will." He took a deep breath and gave her one last, quick hug before joining Juniper and Uncle Robert at the stairs.

"Thanks, Lydia," Uncle Robert called through the doorway.

"Anytime, Rob."

Ethan felt exhaustion sweep through him as they made their way out to the pickup. It was near dusk now, and the sky was streaked with the purples and pinks of sunset.

"Wow," Juniper breathed, tilting her head back. "Isn't that beautiful?"

Ethan nodded; it was. Seeing the wonder on her face, Uncle Robert smiled. "You know, I've got a few blankets back there. Why don't you kids ride in the bed?"

"You mean it?" Juniper asked. "Oh, wow, I can't wait. Come on, Ethan." She grabbed his hand, dragging him toward the truck's parking spot down the street. Heavy as he felt, Ethan couldn't help but laugh.

There were a few boxes strapped into the bed of the truck but just enough space to wrap themselves in blankets and lie back to see the sky. Ethan and Juniper settled in, shoulders pressed together as Uncle Robert started the engine.

"Y'all good back there?" Ethan flashed him a thumbs-up. The truck revved to life and Uncle Robert took off down the lane.

Both of them were silent as Uncle Robert wound through the streets of Montgomery and back onto the highway. Once they were out on the open road, though, trees rushing by them, Ethan turned to Juniper.

"I told her everything," he said.

Her head against his shoulder, Juniper nodded. "How did it feel?"

"Good. Really good." He paused. "And also sad. Because there's nothing we can do about it."

Juniper yawned. "Well, I don't know about that," she said sleepily.

"What do you mean?"

"I think it would be hard. But I think there's always something you could do. Just little things, like that girl our age who didn't get up for a white lady on the bus. Or you telling Noah O'Neil to leave you alone. The things that let the bad guys know you're not just gonna sit and take it." She looked up at Ethan, her freckles like stars in the dusky light. "And there's a lot I can do, too, I think. Because people look at me different than they look at you. I'm safe in my skin, I mean." She yawned again. "I don't know what yet, exactly. But whatever I can do, I'm sure gonna do it."

Love and gratitude swelled up in Ethan's chest, and he pressed his cheek against Juniper's hair. "I bet you will," he said quietly.

The sun fled quickly, and it wasn't long before they were bathed in darkness. Ethan whispered Juniper's name, but she was asleep. Carefully, he eased her head off his shoulder and lowered her onto the floor of the truck bed. She snored loudly, curled into a tight ball. Ethan smiled down at her, then crawled over to the rear window of the truck and rapped a fist against it. Glancing over his shoulder, Uncle Robert reached back to slide it open.

"Everything all right, son?" he asked.

"Yeah," Ethan replied. "Just wanted to say thanks for taking us to Montgomery."

Eyes on the road, Uncle Robert shrugged. "I mean, had to go for my shipment," he mumbled. "But how was it, anyway?"

Ethan leaned his chin against the cold metal of the windowsill and shrugged. "It was a lot of things," he said. "Great sometimes. Hard lots of other times."

"Well"—Uncle Robert scratched his head—"want to talk about it?"

"No, I think I'm all right."

"Okay." He was silent for a long time, then cleared his throat. "You know, I've been meaning to say for a while," he said after a moment. "I know your dad didn't tell you much. About race and all that."

"No, he didn't."

"I'm not saying things should be the way they are here. But I think white folks down here just don't know it any other way. And I know it's hard for you to be here. I just—I wanted to say, I get it. Even if I don't. I know it's not like that where you're from."

Ethan frowned, thinking about Samuel Hill and years of subtle comments from other kids that made his stomach churn in ways he couldn't explain. "I don't know," he said. "Maybe it's like that everywhere. Some people just hide it better." It was the first time he'd said it out loud, even thought it fully, but he knew immediately that this wasn't a maybe. Like his mother said, things were different for him, looking the way he did.

Out of the corner of his eye, Ethan saw Uncle Robert nod, then they both fell silent. Ethan stared over the empty seats and out the front window, at the road that chased the sliver of the moon ahead of them. Every now and then a car would pass from the other direction in a blur of headlights, but otherwise, it was just them and the trees. The fuzzy green landscape and soft radio music were hypnotic, and after a while, Ethan felt his eyes drifting shut, his cheek against the edge of the window.

"Hey, son, I'm sorry," Uncle Robert said suddenly. Ethan jolted awake. "I haven't always been fair to you since you've been here. Guess I just didn't really know how. Ellison hasn't got such a great track record with colored folks, and I just assumed—anyway, it wasn't right of me."

"Thanks, Uncle Robert. I appreciate it."

"It was because of Juniper, you know," he went on, the words spilling out now. "I saw the way she looked at you, how she knew so fast that she wanted to be your friend, and I thought, 'Well, Juniper Jones doesn't take such a liking to just everyone.' She's got the biggest heart of anyone I know, and I thought if she liked you, you must have a good heart too. And you do. I'm sorry I didn't realize that earlier."

"It shouldn't have taken Juniper," Ethan said, before he could stop himself. Uncle Robert frowned.

"Sorry?"

Ethan swallowed. "It shouldn't have taken Juniper being my friend," he said. "For you to see me as a person." He stared pointedly ahead, bracing himself for his uncle's defensive, angry response. Instead, after a long moment, the man nodded.

"You're right," he said simply. "It shouldn't have."

Ethan looked at his uncle then, really looked at him, for what felt like the first time. He saw past the scruffy face, trimmed hair, and wrinkled T-shirt to a man, good at heart, who was trying to unlearn what he'd been told for decades. Behind Ethan, Juniper snored suddenly in her sleep and rolled over. Ethan glanced back at her with a small smile.

"But I'm still glad it did," Ethan said. "However you got there. I'm lucky to have Juniper."

Uncle Robert glanced quickly back at them both, then back to the road. "You are," he agreed. "But you know, it goes both ways. She's lucky to have you too."

August 1955

SEVENTEEN

August descended on Ellison in a series of sweltering days, where the air sat heavy and people slowed to glacial paces. But for Ethan and Juniper, there was no change in speed. Every day after Ethan's shift ended, Juniper would ride up to the Malt on her bike and Ethan would practically throw off his apron as he ran out the door, ready for their next adventure.

One day, they made kites out of fallen sticks and old newspapers. They only stayed airborne for about five minutes, but the paper airplanes they made from the leftover scraps had some serious flight power. Another day, they borrowed yarn from Aunt Cara and tried to learn how to knit, ending up with a tangled mess of knots and loops. Juniper taught Ethan how to row a boat, and Ethan taught Juniper how to sprint a hundred meters. They both taught each other the words to their favorite songs.

It was quickly occurring to both of them, though they didn't voice it, that Ethan was leaving very soon. In a month he would be loading his record collection back into his dad's Mercury for the 2,500 miles back to Arcadia. For Ethan, this was at once relieving and incredibly sad. He'd been looking forward to going home all summer—now, home felt as foreign to him as Ellison had when he'd first arrived. He wasn't sure how to go back to his friends, to school, to track practice, or to his job at the burger joint, pretending as if nothing had changed.

He said this to Juniper one day, biking alongside the lake, and she looked at him strangely. "But a lot has changed," she said, slowing her pedaling. "Why do you have to pretend like it hasn't?"

"Because," Ethan began, then trailed off. It didn't matter why, because he couldn't go back to the way things were. Whatever his normal had been—if it had ever been—it had been irreparably altered. "It'll just be hard, is all," he said eventually.

Juniper braked, dropping her foot in the middle of the path. Ethan stopped a few feet ahead. "I know it will be," she said, when he looked back at her. "But easier than all of this, right?" She swept her hand in an arc above her head. Ethan nodded. "And anyway," she added, "I'll still be there for you. Well, not actually, but we could talk on the phone! I don't have a phone, but I'll bet Mr. and Mrs. Shay would let me borrow theirs. Oh, and we could write each other letters! Wouldn't that just be the coolest thing? Pen pals!"

Ethan laughed as Juniper leapt gleefully back onto her pedals and coasted a few feet down the path. He remembered what his mom had said, about keeping Juniper close. He intended to—he'd never met anyone quite like her and didn't think he ever would again.

As four more weeks in Ellison turned to three, Ethan

noticed his feelings begin to shift, ever so slightly. He'd noticed it before, in passing—brief moments where the sunlight would catch Juniper's hair so that it looked like fire, and he'd feel his stomach flip. Thinking back, it had probably been building for a while, maybe even since the first day she walked through the malt shop doors. And Ethan was filled, suddenly, with so much fondness for Juniper Jones that he felt compelled to show it to her, somehow. All summer, she had orchestrated their adventures. Now, he decided, it was his turn.

Which was how Ethan found himself biking through the forest just after sunrise that next Sunday morning, a back-pack slung over his shoulder, trying to remember the way to Juniper's house. Every push of his pedals sent him deeper into the morning heat—he felt the air like a blanket across his skin, and the dust from the road mingled with the sweat on his cheeks. His handlebars were slick in his grip. But he'd come to love the feeling of pushing through soupy air and feeling his breath hot in his lungs. It felt like the forest was holding him in a sticky embrace.

The forest paths were more familiar now, but every turn was still a guess. It was by luck alone that he eventually found the slim pathway up to Juniper's house. He slowed his bike, remembering the uneven ground. The trees rustled over-head, and a bird let out a wake-up call as he made his way down the path at a leisurely pace.

Somewhere between the main road and the house, he saw the sunflowers. He wondered, briefly, if Juniper had planted them in that small clearing between the trees because she knew that one day Ethan would look over and find them. He thought of the day she had shown up at the Malt with an apology sunflower. This, maybe, was the right occasion to reciprocate.

He dropped his bike and padded over soft grass to where the sunflowers stood, their leaves grazing the top of his head. With careful, determined fists, Ethan plucked out three flowers, leaving half their stems bowing toward the earth. Riding his bike was even more difficult now with the flowers in his hand. He squeezed them underneath his arm, wincing every time the wheels hit a dip in the road. Thankfully, Juniper's house came into view within a few moments, just as magical and forlorn as he remembered it. Standing outside, taking in the garden and the picket fence and the worn white walls, it looked like a castle in a fairy tale.

Ethan left his bike leaning against the picket fence, just like last time, and laid his backpack down beside it. He stepped into the garden, bouquet in hand. The smells of roses, daisies, and daffodils filled his nose—he was torn between sneezing and breathing in more. On the porch, Juniper's bonsai tree greeted him from its tiny pot. He knocked on the door and waited. Several seconds, and nothing. He knocked again. And again. Finally, there was a loud pounding on the stairs and the call of, "Hold your horses, I'm coming!" A moment later the door flew open, and there was Juniper Jones, standing in the doorway with messy hair, plaid pajamas, and a squinty look of surprise.

"Um, Ethan?" She yawned. "No offense, but what are you doing here at the crack of dawn?"

Ethan smirked. "You don't care what time it is whenever you come bursting through my window at some ungodly hour," he said. "We're going on an adventure. You coming, or not?"

Juniper lit up immediately. "Silly that you even have to ask," she teased. "Give me seven minutes."

"I'll be counting," Ethan called after her as she disappeared back into the house. "Oh, and bring a swimsuit!"

Ethan sat out on one of the wicker porch chairs to wait, tapping his foot against the old wood of the deck. The sunflowers lay across his lap. A few minutes later, footsteps pounded back down the stairs, and then there was Juniper, standing on the porch in a sundress, her hands on her hips. That was when she noticed the flowers and gasped.

"Ethan Charlie Harper," she said, "do you have a green thumb you've been keeping from me all this time?"

Ethan laughed. "Definitely not. I found these on the way. But here — for you. Apology flowers," he explained.

With some suspicion, Juniper took the flowers from his hands. "Apology flowers for what?"

Ethan grinned mischievously. "You'll see," he told her, pushing himself up from the chair. "Let's just say, this adventure might not be your *favorite* thing."

He jumped off the porch and started down the path, Juniper at his heels. "What do you mean by that? Ethan? You can't just walk away from me!"

"Fine, then — I'll run!" And he took off, sprinting the rest of the way across Juniper's garden and to his bike. She caught up, rolling her bike in front of her, just as he was shouldering his backpack and climbing onto his seat.

"What is that for?" she demanded, leaning against her handlebars. The stems of the sunflowers were wedged precariously between the wires of her basket.

Ethan shrugged. "You'll see," he said, and took off biking down the path.

"Hey!" But she pedaled after him, expertly avoiding the rocks and roots that caught his tires. He led the way out of the heaviest woods and onto the main path, making his way toward the lake. As the water came into view, he stopped, Juniper slowly beside him.

"Oh *God*," she said, staring at the jeweled surface. "Don't tell me this is why you told me to wear a swimsuit."

"Why else?" Ethan grinned. He reached into his backpack and pulled out two towels, one of which he tossed over to Juniper. She caught it but glared at him.

"This is *not* a fun morning surprise," she declared.

"But it's on your list! Don't tell me you're chickening out."

"Obviously not." She stepped off her bike, letting it fall to the side. "Come on, then. Let's get it over with."

When they approached the shore a few minutes later, Gus was sitting out on the dock, fishing. He waved at them. "Finally teaching Junie to swim, I see!" he called.

"Sure gonna try!" Ethan replied. Then he turned to Juniper. "You ready?"

Juniper took a deep breath, crossing her arms over the front of her polka-dot swimsuit. "As I'll ever be."

"All right, we'll start slow," Ethan said. "Just getting a feel for the water." He waded in, mud and plants squishing between his toes. The water was pleasantly cool. The lake stretched out before them in a blue-green expanse, willows bending to meet its surface in the distance. Ducks floated contentedly in the center, bobbing with the gentle waves.

Ethan took a deep breath, inhaling the clean morning air. Juniper still hadn't followed. She stood a few feet from the edge, her eyebrows knit in uncharacteristic apprehension. Smiling gently, he held out a hand. "Come on, it's okay," he said. "You can trust me."

Juniper looked at Ethan, then out at the lake, then back at Ethan. Finally, she nodded and took his hand. Fingers interlocked, they waded into the water. Juniper squealed at the first squish of mud and laughed when a fish brushed against her leg.

"Okay," she said. "It's not so bad." The water was just up to their knees.

"Didn't I tell—" Ethan was cut off when the ground suddenly dropped off beneath him, plunging him waist deep. Beside him, Juniper shrieked, splashing at the water as she sank beside him. "It's okay," Ethan said, as she clung to his arm. "Look, you're still standing!"

"Yeah, uh-huh," she replied shakily. "Anyway, I think that's enough for today. Good lesson, thanks, Chameleon!" She made to rush back out of the water, but Ethan grabbed her hand, keeping her in place.

"Come on, you can do it. What kind of starfish is afraid of water?"

"I'm not scared," she retorted. "Just careful."

"Why not be careful a little farther in?"

Juniper stuck out her tongue at him. "Fine, but we're going at my pace."

Inch by inch they scooted forward until they were in up to their shoulders. The shore seemed far away, and Ethan could see a few fish swimming lazily near them. Gus gave them a thumbs-up from the dock. Above them, the sun beat down and kept the water pleasantly warm.

"All right," Ethan said. "First lesson."

"There's *more*?"

"Of course! Come on, we're gonna tread water." He demonstrated, pulling up his legs and kicking furiously underwater. Juniper watched, wide eyed.

"Oh, no, no," she said. "I definitely cannot do that."

"Sure you can. Here, put a hand on my shoulder. That's it. Now lift your legs and kick."

Juniper kicked, her face scrunched in concentration. And she stayed above water—but she also gripped Ethan's shoulder with all her might. When she let go and stood back up, grinning proudly, he shook out his arm.

"Okay, that was a start," he said, rubbing his shoulder. "But maybe next time don't hold on so tight."

She sighed. "Right. Trying again."

It took nearly an hour of attempts, of standing in that one spot in the lake and of Ethan's skin being repeatedly subjected to Juniper's nails, but finally, she managed to tread water on her own. And although it was only for three seconds, she was so excited by the victory that she threw her hands in the air, spraying water everywhere, including into Ethan's mouth.

He spat, wiping at his face. "Some thank you," he said. "That was pretty good, but we've still got a ways to go. Why don't you try that again?"

Juniper crossed her arms. "But I'm tired! And we've been doing this for *hours*. Can't we take a break? I'm basically an Olympian now, anyway."

Rolling his eyes, Ethan relented. "Fine. But just a quick break! I haven't even taught you how to doggy paddle yet."

"Yeah, yeah!" Juniper called over her shoulder, already wading back to shore.

They lay on the grass, letting the sun dry them slowly. If he turned his head one way, Ethan could see Gus still on the dock, sitting stoically beside his fishing pole. The other way, and he saw Juniper's freckled cheeks as she examined the sky. When she smiled, eyes barely open, his heartbeat stuttered.

"Remember that first day we went out on the lake and looked up at the clouds?" she asked.

"Sure do," Ethan said.

Juniper yawned, loud and long. "That was fun."

"Sure was."

She looked at him suddenly, so they were almost nose to nose. Ethan's breath caught in his throat. Very seriously, she said, "I'm gonna miss you, Ethan Charlie Harper. A whole lot."

Ethan felt his stomach twist. Soon, he realized yet again, he'd be in a car driving back up to Arcadia. How could he leave her behind?

"Yeah," he mumbled. "I'm really gonna miss you too."

She looked away again, back up at the sky, and so did Ethan. For a while it was quiet, just them and their breaths and the occasional dragonfly buzzing past. When neither of them had spoken for several minutes, Ethan pushed himself up to sitting. "Ready for round two?" he asked. But when he glanced over at Juniper, he saw that she had fallen asleep, her hands on her stomach and her eyes peacefully shut.

EIGHTEEN

Ethan would miss Aunt Cara's chicken sandwiches. This occurred to him as he sat with Juniper by the lake, fishing one sandwich after another out of the picnic basket between them. His shift had just ended, and the sun was high and bright. Juniper lay next to him in the grass, shoveling ripped off sandwich pieces into her mouth.

"This is the perfect angle for digestion," she told him.

This was one afternoon of many they'd spent in this way over the summer, eating lazily by the water. But it was these moments that Ethan tucked away in his memory, that he would come back to years later and remember fondly. This was Juniper at her most relaxed and unguarded, her most honest.

"You know, I've been working on a new painting," she said now. "It's of Gus. And your mom. And the movie theater in Montgomery."

Ethan raised an eyebrow.

"It's complicated. I've always just painted, you know, land-scapes. The lake, Alligator Hill, the forest. But I realized that what means most to me in the world is the people I love. So I wanna learn how to paint people too. I'm not very good yet, but I'll bet by the end of the month, you'll be looking at the best portrait artist in all of Alabama."

"I'll bet," Ethan said, his mouth full.

"And also," Juniper went on, "we should talk about the next thing on our invincible summer list. I'm thinking either bake a cake as tall as we are or learn the jitterbug. I've been really itching to bake, but of course, I've also been really itching to dance, so I think you've gotta be the deciding vote. Of course, on the other hand, we could also do . . ."

She went on, gesturing wildly above her face from where she lay, as Ethan tried his best to follow. She was still talking when Noah arrived.

Juniper didn't notice him at first, and neither did Ethan. She was too caught up in her story, and he was too caught up in her freckled nose and the way her hands made little waves through the summery air. It wasn't until Noah squatted down on the grass beside them that Ethan jumped and Juniper stopped midsentence.

"Hi, Juniper," Noah said. "Hi, Ethan."

"What are you doing here?" Juniper demanded, sitting upright.

Noah leaned his elbows against his knees and grinned. "Some greeting," he said. "I just wanted to say hello to my two friends."

Ethan tensed, ready to spring up and run. "Well, you've said it. You can go."

"Oh, don't be like that. I'm just here to chat. Catch up a bit. It's been a while."

"Not long enough," Juniper muttered. She, like Ethan, was sitting with muscles clenched.

"So, heard you two went on a little trip to Montgomery the other day," Noah went on. "That's *fun*. What was it, some kind of date?"

Ethan and Juniper made eye contact across the picnic basket, both sensing the threat in his question. Noah seemed to take this as confirmation.

"Knew it!" He leaned forward, chin on his hands. "Wow, Juniper. That's bold, considering."

Ethan narrowed his eyes. "What's that supposed to mean?"

"You mean Juniper hasn't told you?" Noah said. "What, Starfish? Did you think he'd never find out?"

"Never find out what?"

"What folks 'round here do to people like you," Noah said. "To protect ourselves."

"Noah, don't do this." Juniper's face was ashen.

Noah just shrugged.

"What's going on? June?"

Juniper shook her head quickly. "It's not important."

"No, Ethan," Noah interjected. "It's very important."

"Noah," Juniper said. She gripped the cloth of her skirt in both fists.

"No, June, it's okay," Ethan said slowly, looking at Noah. "I think I should know."

The grin that sprang to the other boy's face turned Ethan's blood cold. If he wasn't so curious—curious and angry—he would have leaned away.

"It was last year," Noah said, evidently relishing the moment. "There was a girl in town, only fifteen years old at the time. Her daddy was a well-to-do man in town. They were good people. Honest people. Weren't asking for trouble. But then they hired a live-in family to help out around their property.

"They were called the Parkers. A mother and father, Judy and Leroy Parker, and two sons, Abel and Cole. Judy cooked and cleaned, Leroy worked out on the yard. Abel was a kid, only eight or so. Cole, though, was seventeen. Oh, and did I mention? They were Negroes. The whole lot of them."

"They were good people," Juniper interrupted, her cheeks flushed. "They were kind. They didn't deserve it."

Noah held up a finger, frowning. "I'm getting to that part." He cleared his throat. "Everyone in town knew the Parkers didn't belong here. But they were earning their keep, so we let them stay. Abel and Cole had to go to a different school next county over, but the rest of the time they'd be around town. Come to think of it, Cole even worked at your uncle's malt shop for a little while last summer."

Despite the sun beating down on them, Ethan felt suddenly cold. He just barely remembered his uncle telling him that the boy who'd worked for him the previous summer wasn't around anymore.

"That boy Cole was something real special. Real smart for a Negro, clever-smart. He could trick you just like that." He snapped his fingers in Ethan's face. "Never knew what hit you. And that's what he did with the girl.

"Long story short, he got friendly. Too friendly. Used to be that they'd say hello when they saw each other around. That's all anyone thought it was. But then her daddy found them together out in their garage. I think you can guess what they were doing."

Juniper clutched tighter at her skirt. "She *cared* about him."

"She thought she cared," Noah fired back. "He brainwashed her. It's what people like him do." Juniper was shaking now she was so angry, but he turned pointedly away from her, back to Ethan. "The dad chased him off the property, of course. But he didn't stop there—how could he? Running into the woods stark naked in the middle of the night isn't punishment enough."

Despite himself, despite Juniper's quivering lips, Ethan leaned forward. His heart was racing.

"Luckily," Noah went on, "he knew people. Ever heard of the Klan, Ethan? May not be big in Washington, but everyone knows them around here. They keep the Negroes in line. Anyway, this dad, he knew someone in the Klan. My uncle. Lives just a couple towns over. And he called my uncle, and he said, 'Rick, we've got a problem here,' and my uncle Rick came over right away."

Noah smiled, his eyes as heartless as Ethan had ever seen them. "The next day, they found Cole strung up in a tree down by the lake." He drew a finger across his neck. "Dealt with."

Ethan was silent. His heartbeat was loud in his ears.

"I just wanted you to know," Noah said after a while, "what happens when you try to mix things together. Try to say that this"—he pointed between Ethan and Juniper—"is okay. Because it's not, Ethan. I know you're not from around here, that's why I'm telling you. Just being a good neighbor."

"Noah O'Neil," Juniper hissed, low and hard. "You worthless piece of crap."

Noah simply smiled. "Oh, shut up, Juniper. You know as well as I do that Ethan's not welcome here. God knows why his father thought he could show back up to town with his half-breed child." He turned to Ethan, tilting his head to one side. "Things have been changing since the court's ruling last year, about that school in Kansas. The colored folks have been changing. They're saying that a revolution's coming, did

you know that? They're saying that things are gonna change."
He laughed. "But I'm not worried. Because my uncle, and all
the people like him, they'll keep everything under control."

When Ethan's mother, at her kitchen table in Montgomery,
had said the word *revolution*, it had made Ethan's heart lurch.
From Noah's lips, it sounded like a slur. Ethan didn't realize
it, but he was standing. He was dropping his chicken sandwich onto the grass. He was turning, arm outstretched, to
slap Noah O'Neil across the face.

There was a shattering clap as Ethan's palm connected
with Noah's cheek, then a moment where everything froze.
The lake, the wind, the hovering bugs — everything was suspended midair, midmovement. Everything was silent. Then
Noah toppled backward into the dirt and the sound came
rushing back.

"What the hell?" Noah cried, clutching at his cheek. He
lay stunned, looking up at Ethan with wide eyes.

Juniper, too, had leapt to her feet, and now looked fran-
tically between Noah and Ethan. Ethan stood panting, fists
clenched, ears ringing. As Noah regained his composure and
struggled to his feet, Ethan stumbled backward.

"How dare you," Noah growled, lurching at him. But
Ethan was faster, and he knew it. He whirled and took off
running toward the trees, heartbeat ricocheting through his
whole body. Noah didn't give chase, but Ethan heard him
shriek the same thing over and over: "You'll regret this. You'll
regret this!"

✳

Juniper found Ethan in the forest clearing some time later.
He was lying next to the brook, fists clenched at his side.

He stared up at the sky through a gap in the trees until she leaned over him and filled his vision with her freckled face. She carried the picnic basket, still half full of sandwiches.

"I thought you'd be here," she said. She sat down beside him, crossing her legs, and picked at the grass. Ethan said nothing.

"Okay, I'm guessing you're upset. That makes sense."

"Why didn't you tell me?" Ethan asked. He still stared upward, where the blue was so bright it hurt his eyes. Only minutes before he'd been looking at Juniper as they ate chicken sandwiches and thinking about how sometimes she made his stomach turn somersaults. And as if reading his mind, Noah had appeared and informed him that this could never be.

Juniper frowned down at her hands. "I guess I didn't want to scare you."

"I'm already scared, Juniper. I've been scared this whole time." It was the first time he'd said it out loud, but it was true. For weeks now, fear had been his default. Now, it just felt more real.

"I'm sorry," Juniper said.

"I know." Ethan lifted a hand and trailed it in the brook. Juniper, sitting a few feet away, seemed to fill the entire clearing with her anxious energy. He wondered if she was imagining, like he was, finding this boy he'd never met in a tree out in the woods, looking into his eyes and realizing how easily that could have been him. How easily that could still be him.

Juniper scooted closer. "I should have told you," she said. "No one else was going to, at least not in a nice way. But of course they've all been thinking about it. And I know you being my friend doesn't make it any better."

Ethan felt the urge to inch farther away, but there was nowhere to go. He was struck with the sick realization that his proximity to Juniper was a threat to both of them and it always had been. How foolish he'd been to let himself feel anything for her, thinking their friendship could be anything more.

"I don't want to hurt you," he blurted, looking up at her.

Juniper glanced at him sharply. "Why would you say that? I know you wouldn't hurt me."

"No, I—" He shook his head. "I'd never mean to hurt you. But I don't want it to happen by accident either. Like collateral damage."

"Ethan, you don't have to worry about me," Juniper said quietly. "Nothing's going to happen. Noah just talks big."

"I don't know," Ethan said. He could still feel a sting on his palm where it had connected with Noah's face. And he still heard the older boy's words repeating over and over. *You'll regret this*.

"I can't believe I hit him," he murmured.

Juniper snorted. "I can't believe it took you so long. Really, he deserved it."

"Yeah," Ethan said, sitting up slowly. "But it's not so simple, right? Deserving and not deserving. Hitting a white kid in Arcadia got me sent here. Hitting a white kid in Ellison could mean—" He couldn't finish the sentence.

Juniper shook her head. "Don't," she breathed.

"How can I not?"

Juniper was silent. Her cheeks were red, her eyes misty. Ethan looked over at her, his fierce advocate and loyal friend, and wanted nothing more than to keep her safe. But how, he wondered, when he wasn't even sure he could protect himself?

"I don't know what to do," he said, his voice breaking. A few tears came loose, trickling down his cheeks.

"Ethan," Juniper whispered. She leaned forward, gathering him into his arms, and he leaned against her.

"I don't know what to do," he said again.

Juniper squeezed him closer. "We look out for each other. As best we can." She pressed her face against his shoulder. "That's all we can do."

Ethan said nothing, just let himself be held as the sun filtered down through the trees and the brook trickled past them. Juniper's embrace was soft and warm, and her hair smelled like flowers. She was right, he knew. They would look out for each other, just as they had all summer. In some ways, they were each all the other had.

The wind shifted, sending a scattering of loose grass blowing toward them. Neither Ethan nor Juniper moved. He stayed there in her arms until she had almost convinced him that everything would be okay. Until he was almost sure.

NINETEEN

From the top of Alligator Hill Ethan felt like he could touch the stars. The crest of the hill wasn't very high, but the sky was so clear tonight that it seemed inches from his reach. Juniper was trying—she stood on her toes and stretched for the tiny pinpricks of light.

"I'll get one, one day," she said. "Just you wait."

They had come to learn the stars. It had been Juniper's whispered request to Ethan over a month before and he hadn't forgotten. Uncle Robert had an old constellation map and a handheld telescope, and with two weeks left in Ethan's stay, they were determined to memorize as many constellations as they could.

"Which way do you figure we're supposed to look at it?" Ethan asked, tilting his head. He'd rolled out the map on the flattest part of the hilltop, until it extended a few feet long. Looking at it now, it seemed impossible to read—hundreds of tiny dots connected by thin lines and labeled in cramped text.

Juniper knelt next to him, squinting at the map, then up at the sky. "This way," she said, then, rotating it, "actually, no— this way." She repeated this dance a few more times before settling it down at a diagonal. From this angle, they could see the dark banks of the lake in the distance.

"You sure this is it?"

"Oh, absolutely not," Juniper chirped, dropping into a squat. "But that's never stopped me before."

Ethan shrugged and knelt beside her. "Maybe we should start with Orion's Belt," he said, pointing out three stars on the bottom left of the map. "That's usually the easiest one to spot. Wanna do the honors?" He handed her the telescope, and she lifted it to her eye, squinting skyward. Ethan watched her, with her face awash in moonlight and stardust, and felt so completely at home.

"That's it!" she cried, dropping the telescope. "That's it, right?"

"Which one?" Ethan followed her finger to a few bright stars that seemed to be mostly in a row.

"Wait—maybe it wasn't that one." Juniper frowned, lifting the telescope again. She swung it left and right with increasing speed. "Gosh darn—I think I lost it! I swear I found it though, Ethan, trust me. I'll find it again." She stuck out her tongue in concentration and Ethan laughed.

She did find it again, eventually, and from there, they traced the stars to all of Orion. "Oh, I *totally* see it," Juniper said. "Look, you can practically see him mounting his horse."

Ethan took the telescope from her and peered through it. "I don't think he has a horse, June."

"In *my* story he has a horse."

They managed to spot Taurus after that, and what Juniper insisted was Ursa Major—and then they got stuck. All the stars seemed indistinguishable, and they went back and forth about whether one star was the top of Aries or the bottom of Pisces before Juniper finally said, "Y'know what? Let's make up our own."

She flopped backward on the grass, dropping the telescope to the side. Ethan lay next to her, staring up at the glittering night. "Okay," he said. "See that star right there?"

"That one?"

"No"—he adjusted her hand—"that one."

"*Oh*. Yeah, I see that one."

"And see how around it there are those four other ones, kind of in a zigzag?"

She squinted. "Uh—uh-huh."

"What constellation is that?"

"That is"—Juniper pursed her lips, thinking hard—"that's the lady washing her clothes in the river."

"Sorry, what?" Ethan snorted.

"No, look, it totally is! That's her knees, and her head, and that's her hand putting the clothes in the water."

Ethan tilted his head in every direction but couldn't make the image appear in his mind. He shook his head. "Yeah, I don't see it."

"Your loss. Okay, my turn." Juniper slapped one hand over her eyes and swung the other in a pendulum motion, counting under her breath before finally coming to a stop with her finger pointing out to her right, over Ethan's face. "Those ones," she said. "The four going down, kind of, and the three going across."

"Hm." Ethan followed her hand. "I don't know, a cross?"

"Wrong!"

"What do you mean, wrong? We're making them up!"

"Yeah, but that's just about the least creative idea I've ever heard. Haven't I taught you better than that?"

Ethan sighed heavily. "Fine, fine. It's a . . . tree?"

"You can do better."

"Can I?" He stared up at it again, until the pinpricks blurred in his vision and became a watercolor of white on satin black. And finally, in this haze, he saw it.

"A bird," he said. "A big bird with huge wings flying straight up into the sky."

Juniper frowned up at the stars for a moment, considering. Finally, smiling, she nodded. "Not bad," she said. "Not bad at all."

"Not bad? That was great!"

"Don't get ahead of yourself. You've still got a lot to learn."

Ethan nudged her with his shoulder, then reached over to grab the telescope. "Whatever. I'm gonna find one for you now, and it'll be *hard*." He swung the telescope around across stars that all looked the same to him, trying to find the perfect arrangement. It was as he followed this arc, sweeping the telescope low over the trees, that he caught sight of something moving in the distance.

"June." He sat up quickly, trying to get a better view. "I think there's a fire."

Juniper leapt to her feet, ignoring the telescope in Ethan's outstretched arm to stare out at the edge of the lake. Sure enough, when Ethan stood up beside her, he saw orange lights flickering in and out of view between the trees.

"Oh God," Juniper whispered. "Do you think it's a forest fire?"

Ethan didn't respond, but imagined the trees consumed by flames—how fast it would spread, with the brush so thick. It would overtake the town in moments. The image of destruction was so clear in his mind that it took a moment for him to realize that Juniper was saying his name, over and over.

"Ethan—Ethan, look." She grabbed his arm and pointed out over the trees. It wasn't the forest that was on fire, he realized quickly. It was torches. About a dozen torches, coming out of the forest and into full view at the edge of the lake. Bearing them, and walking in a slow procession, were hooded figures in white.

Ethan felt his heart drop. He would recognize these figures anywhere, though he'd never imagined he'd be so close to them. He thought immediately of what Noah had said, days ago, and wondered which among them was his uncle.

"Ethan," Juniper said very seriously. "We need to go."

But Ethan was frozen in place, unable to look away. The Klansmen marched in a slow circle, more frightening, somehow, in their silence. It seemed that one man was the leader, because when he suddenly halted, everyone else followed suit. He lifted a hand, and as one they closed the circle, torches pointed downward. Together, they dropped the torches to the ground.

Ethan didn't see it until it caught on fire: at the center of the circle, wrapped in black cloth, was a hulking cross. As they watched, flames clambered up the cross's base to consume the entire structure. Soon it was just a hazy mass of red and orange, blowing smoke into the sky. The Klansmen stood in a tighter circle now around the burning cross, heads bowed in reverence.

"Ethan." Juniper's nails in his arm pulled Ethan from his trance. She had the map and telescope tucked to her chest. "We need to go. Right now."

The men weren't close—the lake was at least a quarter mile away—but Ethan knew she was right. He cast one more glance at the white-clad figures in pointed hats, then nodded at Juniper. She gripped his hand and they ran down the hill.

Or tried—it wasn't long before the momentum sent them half running, half tumbling down the sloping grass. When they reached the bottom, both of their jeans were streaked with dirt. Neither seemed to notice.

Juniper sprinted toward their bikes, tossing the map and telescope into her basket before climbing into the seat. Ethan was slower to follow. "Where are we going?" he called. "Back to Aunt Cara's house?"

Juniper shook her head. "Not safe. We're going to the clearing. Follow me."

Ethan knew the way to the clearing from here, and so he knew that the path they needed to take ran dangerously close to the lake. But Juniper had other ideas. Instead of staying on the path, she suddenly veered her bike to the right and took off straight into the forest, dodging trees and rocks with quick flicks of her handlebars. Ethan maneuvered perilously behind her, his teeth rattling with every bump.

"June, are you sure about this?"

"Keep your voice down," she hissed over her shoulder, going airborne for a moment as she skimmed over a tree root. Ethan hunched over his handlebars and pedaled harder. Once they were deep enough that they could no longer see the path in any direction, Juniper ground to a halt. They were both panting.

Without saying a word, Juniper stepped off her bike and began walking to the left, kicking up dirt and leaves in her wake. Ethan followed. They walked in silence for several minutes, winding through the trees on a path that Ethan thought must be totally random. But then, suddenly, he heard the gentle trickle of water, and the clearing appeared through a break in the trees.

Juniper pushed her bike into a bush and motioned for

Ethan to follow suit. Then she circled the clearing until she found the tree with the largest hollow, the one in which they had hidden their invincible summer list, and crawled inside. Ethan ducked in after her. They squatted on the damp dirt, knee to knee, and shrank as far away from the gap of the hollow as they could.

The darkness was nearly absolute and only Juniper's soft breaths gave away that she was there at all. Ethan thought his heartbeat must be ricocheting off the bark around him, it was so loud in his ears. It wasn't until Juniper put a hand on his arm that Ethan realized he was shaking. When he put a hand to his forehead, sweat came off on his fingers. He squeezed his eyes shut and pressed his head against his knees.

"We're going to be okay," Juniper said. "They're just trying to scare us."

"What about what Noah said?" Ethan whispered. "About Cole Parker, and when they came for him?"

"That was different. Cole was a total stranger in town, and black as night to boot. No one gave a care about him or his family. But you have your dad, and more importantly, Mr. and Mrs. Shay. Sure, you don't look like them, but you're blood. And people 'round here like your aunt and uncle. They respect them. And that's enough. Just barely."

Ethan lifted a hand to his face as if he could see it, then pressed his palm to his cheek. He knew that the skin beneath his fingers was brown, but not like his mother's. Not like the girl on the bus who got arrested in Montgomery. Not, he was sure, like Cole Parker. He wondered if this shade of brown meant he got stares on the street but not assault; pushed down on the bus but not arrested. If it meant he was threatened by the Ku Klux Klan—but not killed.

He couldn't get his heart to slow down.

Juniper felt around for his hand, not saying a word but squeezing it tightly. He squeezed back. Outside, all they could hear was the murmur of the brook. They couldn't see the flames or smell the smoke, but Ethan felt as if the men were just outside. He closed his eyes and held tight to Juniper's hand, wishing he could disappear.

He wasn't sure how long they crouched there, squeezed into the tree trunk, but at some point, he drifted to sleep. When he woke up, there was a crick in his neck. Juniper, he could tell, was sitting straight up, her hand still wrapped around his.

"Are you awake?" she whispered.

"Yeah. How long has it been?"

"An hour and a half. I've been counting." Ethan's heart broke, thinking of Juniper sitting there in the darkness, ticking off the time second by second. He squeezed her hand a little tighter.

"Do you think it's safe now?" he asked.

She hesitated for a moment. "I don't know. But we can't stay here forever. And we'll be faster than them on our bikes, right?"

"Right," Ethan agreed but didn't move.

They sat there for a moment longer, staring at each other—though they couldn't tell in the darkness—before Juniper took a deep breath and slithered out of the hollow. Bracing himself for the worst, Ethan followed.

But it was empty in the clearing, peaceful even, with the moon a sliver through the trees and the brook reflecting branches on its surface. Standing here, no one could have guessed that there was a cross burning only a thicket away.

Ethan pulled their bikes from the bush and they walked, side by side, through the undergrowth, making another nonsensical winding path before finally emerging onto the path. He knew where they were—five minutes east and they'd be at Aunt Cara's—but out on the open road he felt like a moving target.

"Let's hurry," he urged, mounting his bike. They pedaled off as quietly as they could, leaving a shivering cloud of dust behind them.

Ethan didn't let himself look anywhere except straight ahead. Every sound made him start and then pedal faster. Juniper was just behind him, more silent than he thought she'd ever been. His heart was in his throat until they reached Aunt Cara's house, where they leapt off their bikes mid pedal and saw Uncle Robert and Aunt Cara huddled on the porch steps. They stood when they saw the kids, and even in the dim light, Ethan noticed their ashen faces.

Ethan tried to speak, but only a strangled sound came out. He stumbled up the steps and into their waiting arms. Juniper was right behind him.

"Thank God," Aunt Cara breathed, burying her head in Ethan's shoulder. "Oh, thank God."

Even Uncle Robert sounded teary as he said, "They walked by the house with their torches. Didn't say anything, just marched around and around the house. I'm glad you kids weren't here."

"We saw them," Ethan said. "By the lake. Burning a cross."

Aunt Cara made a pained sound and drew back from the embrace to swipe at her eyes. "I'm so sorry," she said. "Both of you. I'm so, so sorry."

Juniper struggled to smile. "It's okay, Mrs. Shay. We're all right."

Aunt Cara reached out and cupped Juniper's face in her hand, then nodded. "Well, you're staying here tonight,

Juniper. We'll make up the couch for you. Are you both hungry? I have some leftover biscuits."

"Come on," Uncle Robert said. "We'd better get inside."

Ethan lingered for a moment longer on the porch as his family made their way inside. The road was silent now, the trees dark. He looked up at the sky, still so clear and beautiful that it seemed like an insult. From where he stood, he could just barely make out the cross of stars that had seemed so magical from the top of Alligator Hill. It didn't look like a bird anymore.

TWENTY

Ethan had been swallowed by silence. He lay face up on his bed, his fingers laced over his stomach, trying to remember a time when the air hadn't felt like a building on his chest. Two days had passed since the monsters in white had marched through Ellison. His aunt and uncle had insisted, gently but firmly, that he was not to leave the house. Uncle Robert was covering his shifts at the Malt, and Aunt Cara, who was almost due, made up plenty of tasks to keep him busy around the house. And though the Shays both worried about her riding through the forest alone, Juniper came by every day, keeping watch from the arm of the couch as if ready for the men to come back at any moment. Ethan stayed in his room, playing music at top volume to drown out his thoughts. All he wanted was to sit with Juniper at the lake and stare so hard into the sun that he could no longer see or think anything at all.

On the evening of the second day, after Juniper had gone home, Aunt Cara knocked gently on Ethan's door. Groaning, Ethan turned down the volume.

"Hey," she said. "Dinner's ready."

Ethan nodded, pushing himself out of bed and following her into the kitchen. There was a pot of chicken soup laid out on the table and Uncle Robert was already waiting. Ethan mumbled a hello as he sat down. Dimly, he heard his aunt pull out the chair across from him, easing precariously into it with a hand on her stomach. She regarded Ethan silently as she ladled soup into the bowls, but he kept his eyes fiercely trained on the tablecloth. It was a moment before he realized he was clutching his spoon in a trembling grip.

"Honey," Aunt Cara said gently, and Ethan released the spoon. It bounced off the surface of the table and clattered to the floor.

"Sorry."

"It's all right," Uncle Robert said, bending to pick up the spoon. Already, Aunt Cara had set another one beside his bowl.

"Please eat something, Ethan," she said. Obligingly, Ethan lifted the spoon to his lips, tasting nothing as the soup went down. He felt his aunt and uncle share a concerned glance and he forced himself to take a few more bites. When they seemed satisfied, he cleared his throat.

"I was thinking. Maybe after dinner I could take a walk? I've been cooped up in here, and I just think it'd help me clear my head—" The stricken look on Aunt Cara's face stopped him. "Right," he said. "Okay. Never mind."

"I'm sorry, honey," she said. "I just don't know if it's safe out there. At least here, we know where you are."

"No, I get it. It's fine." He stirred his soup. His aunt and uncle ate in silence, but he couldn't bring himself to take more than a few bites. He'd felt sick to his stomach ever since that night.

"That all you're having?" Uncle Robert asked. He peered over Ethan's dish. Ethan nodded. "Suit yourself." He didn't pry further. Ethan sat there at the kitchen table, staring out the window, until the sun sank fully behind the trees and his soup, barely touched, went cold.

*

Late the next morning, Ethan woke to the sound of his aunt's voice, sharper than he'd ever heard it. She was in the living room, but he could make out her words even from beneath his covers.

"Andrew, you heard what I said," she was saying. "They came through town, just like last year with the Parker boy." She paused. "Why on *earth* would I exaggerate about something like this? If you don't want to admit you made a mistake, fine. But the fact is, your son isn't safe here."

At this, Ethan sat up, pulled on a T-shirt from a pile on the floor, and tiptoed into the hall. His aunt stood by the couch, phone to her ear, seething.

"Yes, actually, I think that's exactly what you need to do," she said. She looked up and noticed Ethan standing in the hallway. She mouthed, "It's your dad," and he nodded.

"Don't be like that, Andrew," Aunt Cara said, softer now. She sighed. "All right. I know. Do you want to speak to Ethan? He's up now."

His father must have said yes, because a moment later, Aunt Cara beckoned to him and held out the phone. She squeezed his shoulder as he pressed the receiver against his ear. His eyes were still heavy from sleep.

"Hi, Dad," he said hoarsely.

From the way Aunt Cara had been talking, Ethan expected

to find his dad cold and angry on the other line. He was braced for it. Instead, though, he seemed to be choking back tears.

"I had no idea," came his voice, soft and broken. He repeated the same words again and again. "I had no idea. I had no idea."

Ethan held still, unsure what to say. He imagined his father slumped against their kitchen counter, whispering into the phone so he wouldn't wake Anthony and Sadie. He would almost rather his dad be angry, the way he'd been after the fight with Samuel Hill. This sadness, this remorse, was almost too much to bear.

"I didn't know it would be like this," his dad said eventually, voice clearer now. There was such confusion in his tone that Ethan felt a shock of anger.

"I don't know if I believe that, Dad."

"I mean it. I mostly mean it," he amended. "I knew being in Ellison would be a little hard on you. I thought you needed that. But Cara told me about the march and I—I didn't know it would be like this."

Ethan closed his eyes and took a deep breath to keep from screaming. He could hear in his dad's voice that the man was serious—he really hadn't known. But ignorance was no excuse.

"Okay, well, it is bad," he said. "And I didn't need it."

"I know. I understand that now."

Ethan toed at the living room floor with his bare foot. He could hear Aunt Cara in the kitchen, rustling around but undoubtedly listening.

"I saw Mom, you know," Ethan said. "In Montgomery."

His dad was silent for a long moment. Ethan fiddled with the cord. "I know," his dad said finally. "She told me."

"It wasn't fair of you," Ethan went on, "not telling her about all of this."

"I know."

Ethan couldn't think of a time his dad had agreed with him so readily. He sounded tired, defeated. His voice was thick with regret.

"I know that there's a lot I don't understand about you," his father said now. "And some of it I'll maybe never understand. But I guess—I guess I haven't really been trying." Ethan said nothing. "I'm so sorry, Ethan. For making you go to Ellison, for not telling your mother—all of it."

"Okay," Ethan said.

His father took a breath. "Your aunt is right: it's not safe for you there anymore. Probably never was, really. I'm dropping off the twins at a neighbor's after breakfast and leaving for Ellison tonight."

Ethan blinked, registering his father's words. "Tonight?" he echoed.

"I'd leave right now if I could. But it shouldn't take me more than five days to get there. And then we'll come right back home. How does that sound?"

Ethan was frozen, staring at the floor with the phone at his ear. All summer, this was what he had wanted: to leave. And after everything that had just happened, he should have been thrilled. Instead, he just felt kind of ill.

His father's question still hung in the air and he screwed his eyes shut. After a moment, the words came out on their own. "You think that makes up for it?" he asked after a moment, very quietly.

"Sorry?"

"I said, do you think that makes up for it? Everything you've put me through, sending me here for the summer.

You think that deciding to come pick me up early makes up for it?"

"No, of course not, but—"

"Because it doesn't."

His father was silent. When he didn't say anything for several moments, Ethan went on, "I want to leave. I want you to come and get me. But it's going to take a long time for me to forgive you."

Another beat of silence, then his dad murmured, "I know." His voice was shaky, muffled. "I'm sorry. I know."

"I know you know. And I know you're sorry. But that's not enough."

Ethan could see his dad standing at the kitchen counter, hunched uncomfortably next to the phone. He sniffled, and Ethan imagined him rubbing at his eyes, trying to maintain his composure. It made his stomach twist, but he didn't take it back. Sorry wasn't enough. The hurt he felt was deep and heavy and tinged with betrayal. He didn't know when that would go away.

"You don't have to forgive me, Ethan," his dad said eventually, the words coming out strangled. "I'll try to be better—I'm going to be better. But you don't have to forgive me."

"Thanks, Dad," Ethan said quietly.

"You're a good kid, Ethan. You deserve better."

And now it was Ethan's turn, softly but with conviction, to say, "I know."

"I'll see you soon, okay? Five days."

Ethan thought about Juniper Jones and the incomplete bucket list taped to the inside of a hollow tree. He thought of how she was there for him, over and over, when she didn't need to be. How she tried so hard to see the best in people. But he also thought of Noah O'Neil, the men in white, the burning cross. He shuddered. Juniper, he knew, would understand.

"Five days," he said. "I'll see you then."

✳

When Juniper showed up that afternoon, Ethan was sprawled across the couch, staring blankly at the television. She came inside quietly when Aunt Cara opened the door and dropped into the love seat beside Ethan.

"No sign of them today," she said, updating him just as she had the two days before. "I think they're gone."

"Yeah," Ethan said, but it didn't make him feel much better. They watched TV in silence for a while, Juniper laughing every now and then at one of the actors' antics. Sun came through the windows, warming the room. Eventually the program ended and Ethan rolled off the couch to turn the set off.

"My dad called today," he said as he did, not looking at Juniper.

"He did?"

"Yeah."

"And?"

Ethan tapped at the TV knob, still squatting in front of it. "Well, Aunt Cara told him. About the Klan, and everything. He was pretty freaked." He saw Juniper nod out of the corner of his eye. She was still waiting. "And he decided—he decided he's leaving tonight. From Arcadia. And coming to get me."

"Oh," Juniper said softly, and he braced himself for her disappointment. Instead, she only said, "Thank God."

"What?" Ethan turned to her.

"Ethan," she said, leaning forward in the chair, "I'm *so* worried about you. Like, more than you could ever imagine, probably. I have been all along, but after the other night—" She shook her head. "I don't want you to leave, obviously. I wish you could stay forever. I wish summer could just go on and on and on."

Ethan imagined this: a life of biking through the forest, swimming in the lake, rolling down Alligator Hill. He wished it could be real.

"More than that, though, I want you to be happy," Juniper went on. "And safe. Especially safe. And you're not safe here. I don't really see another way."

Ethan looked at her across the room, her chin in her hands and her blue eyes wide. She looked sad, but certain, and he nodded.

"Yeah," he said quietly. "Me neither."

"When will he be here?"

"In five days."

She nodded slowly. "All right, then. Five days. We'll make the most of it."

"I can't." Ethan shook his head. "I'm not allowed to go outside." He looked past Juniper to Aunt Cara, who was in the kitchen, stirring a pot on the stove.

"We'll make the most of it," Juniper repeated firmly. "If you don't think I know how to have fun inside, I'll be seriously offended."

For what felt like the first time in days, Ethan cracked a smile. "All right, you've got me there."

"I'll start planning." She leaned back in the chair again, closing her eyes.

Ethan snorted. "What are you doing?"

"Be quiet! I'm planning."

And sure enough, Juniper opened her eyes several minutes later with a full list of activities. Card games, puzzles, painting lessons, handstand contests, dance parties — she had enough to fill a whole other summer. Ethan smiled, watching her rattle on. He couldn't wait to go; couldn't wait to breathe easy again. And yet — seeing Juniper, hair in her face, eyes bright, he wished that he could stay.

Twenty-One

It was the night of the fifth day after the cross burning. That was how Ethan counted time now—before and after the Klan came to town. In just three days, his dad would pull up outside in his Mercury. Ethan had packed his few belongings, which waited neatly on the floor of his room. Juniper had helped, in between orchestrating games and competitions in Aunt Cara's living room. She'd left that night, in fact, after staying for dinner and leading a lively game of charades that even his aunt and uncle had participated in.

The house was quiet now, with Juniper gone and Aunt Cara and Uncle Robert having retreated to their room. When Ethan went to brush his teeth, he thought they had gone to sleep. But as he opened the medicine cabinet in the bathroom that separated his room from theirs, he heard soft coughing and then, louder, his name. He froze, hand on his toothbrush, and strained to listen. Inching closer to their door, he realized that what he had thought was coughing was actually quiet sobs.

"—just want to know how we're supposed to raise a child in a place like this," Aunt Cara was saying between sniffles.

"It's not just here, Cara," Uncle Robert said.

"A *world* like this, then. I'm scared for our baby."

Uncle Robert laughed harshly. "Look at us. Our baby will be fine."

"That's not what I'm scared of," Aunt Cara said.

Uncle Robert was silent for a moment, and when he spoke again, his voice was barely audible. Ethan pressed his ear harder against the door.

"No child we raise will be anything like those monsters. We won't let that happen."

Aunt Cara seemed calmed by this, because she didn't say anything for a while. Then, in a stronger voice, she said, "I love that boy. Like he's our own son. But I wish Andy had never sent him here."

"I know," Uncle Robert said. "I know. But there's nothing we can do now. We just have to make it through these last few days."

Ethan heard a shuffling sound, then footsteps approaching the bathroom. He stumbled back from the door and back into his room without brushing his teeth, just barely managing to close the door behind him. His heart was racing. Just a couple of months earlier, to hear his aunt and uncle speak this way would have been a shock. And while he was comforted to know that it was on their minds, there was a strange, twisted feeling in his stomach.

Jealousy, he realized, sinking back onto his bed. Of Aunt Cara and Uncle Robert's child, who would grow up learning about race but could just as easily not. Their child would have no moment of rude awakening, of looking around a crowd of people and not seeing a single face that looked like his own.

He would never look in the mirror and feel his whiteness as a terrible shame.

Ethan remembered what his mother said, about how black kids were never allowed to be innocent. And yet he had been, for a time. Aunt Cara said she wished her brother had never sent him to Ellison—and he knew that things would have been much easier if that had been the case. But now, at least, he could see the world for what it was. He could see himself for who he was. And maybe, in time, he'd learn to look in the mirror and see his blackness as a precious gift.

*

Ethan must have fallen asleep at some point because he found himself opening his eyes sometime later to complete darkness and the gentle clicks of a finished record still spinning. His room was completely dark and no sounds came from the hall. Groaning, he rolled over and tried to fall back asleep. But after tossing and turning for what felt like hours, he finally accepted that he wouldn't be sleeping anytime soon.

The clock on his nightstand told him it was close to midnight. Aunt Cara and Uncle Robert had to be asleep now, and Ethan knew what would calm his nerves. With a quick glance at his bedroom door, just to be sure, he reached for his sneakers underneath the bed.

The window glided open smoothly, and Ethan dropped down onto the dust, just as he had so many times this summer. He didn't hesitate, just took off running, guided by the moonlight and accompanied by the song of cicadas. He was in his pajamas—a ratty T-shirt and sweats—and it wasn't long before he had sweated through both of them. Still, he continued jogging down the path, winding in the direction of the lake. He needed to see where it happened.

When he arrived on the quiet beach and skidded to a stop, it was empty. No figures in white robes, no flames, no cross. But in the sand, a few charred scraps of fabric were a reminder of what had happened here only a few days before.

Ethan turned in a slow circle where he was pretty sure the cross had stood, his arms out to his sides. The sand crunched beneath his feet. When he made it all the way around, he saw Juniper watching him from the edge of the woods, her face half shrouded by darkness.

"Hey," he said, dropping his arms.

"Hey." She stepped out of the shadows. "I've been coming here every night. I just felt like I needed to see it for myself."

"Me too."

They stood there, staring at the ashy sand, both imagining the heat of a burning cross on their faces. Ethan sighed. "Wanna sit on the dock?"

Juniper offered a small smile. "Always."

They sat on the very edge, as they always did, with the bottoms of their shoes just barely skimming the surface of the lake. Juniper glanced skyward. "Have you ever been in an airplane?" she asked.

Ethan shook his head. "I want to, someday. Sure seems cool."

"When I was little I used to be so scared of them." She laughed slightly. "I thought, there's no way anything can fly like that. It'd just explode in the air. But now, by gosh. What I wouldn't give to be up there." She paused then added, "I know this isn't how it works, but if I could reach out an airplane window, I think I'd borrow a few stars and bring them back home."

"What would you do with them?"

She paused for a moment, thinking. "I think I'd hang them on people's front doors," she decided. "So much sunshine here in the summer, but God knows this town could use a little light."

"I think that's a great idea," Ethan said, and meant it.

Juniper leaned forward, trailing her hand in the water. "You leave so soon."

"Yeah. Three more days. I'm really gonna miss you, Juniper."

Juniper nodded, chewing on her bottom lip. "Hey, wanna bike somewhere with me real quick?"

"I didn't bring my bike with me."

"That's okay. You can stand on my pegs, just like old times." She smiled at him sideways. "Anyway, we're not going far, just to the cove. I have something to show you. A piece I've been working on."

Ethan grinned despite himself. "I think that's exactly what I need," he said. "Let's go."

"Go where?" a voice asked, and Ethan turned to Juniper in confusion. But she was turning too, and they both saw Noah O'Neil at the same time. Alex stood beside him, smirking.

"Sorry," Noah said. "Go on. Didn't mean to interrupt."

"Go away, Noah." Juniper turned back toward the lake.

"But I haven't heard what you thought about my uncle's show the other night. You saw it, didn't you?"

"Go *away*, Noah," Juniper repeated.

Sighing, Ethan pushed himself to his feet and held a hand out to Juniper. "Come on, it's not worth it. Let's just go home." He tried to push past Noah and Alex, but the boys stood tall and blocked his way. "Move it, would you?"

"What's the rush?" Noah asked.

"Yeah, we're not done yet," Alex said.

Ethan stared up into Noah's eyes, his jaw tight. The thing was—for all he'd been afraid of what Noah and his friends represented, he'd never thought of Noah as a threat in and of himself. But now, standing toe to toe with him, Ethan realized that the other boy was bigger, likely stronger. And it was obvious from his easy smirk that Noah knew it too.

Still, Ethan managed to keep his voice level as he asked, "What do you want, Noah?"

The older boy shrugged. "Oh, nothing much. It's just that I've been hearing about these adventures y'all have been taking, and I thought it'd be fun if we did one all together. Whatcha say we take a little boat ride?"

"Yeah, I'll pass," Ethan said. He took Juniper's hand and tried to push past again. This time, Noah grabbed him by the shoulders.

"Sorry, might've confused you there," he said. "That wasn't a question."

Without hesitation, Juniper dropped Ethan's hand and tried to dodge around the boys, but Alex was faster. Though she kicked and flailed furiously, he managed to wrestle both of her arms behind her back. Ethan, who had just managed to slip past Noah, was stopped by a hand gripping his collar. The jarring halt sent him tumbling to the ground and he was breathless just long enough for Noah to get him in a headlock.

Seeing this, Juniper shrieked—but was cut off when Alex shoved a piece of cloth into her mouth and tied it clumsily behind her head. Her eyes went wide as she struggled in vain against his grip, unable to make more than a few unintelligible, muffled sounds.

Ethan swung his feet at Noah's shins, but he simply

laughed. Moments before Ethan, too, was gagged, he managed to let out a single, scathing syllable: "Why?"

And then a dirty strip of fabric was blocking his speech and Noah was stepping on his heels, forcing him to walk forward. "Because," Noah growled. "You don't belong here." He pulled out a length of rope from his back pocket, and Ethan saw Alex do the same. "There was only so much my uncle could do, but I didn't think it was enough to really teach you a lesson. So I thought I'd handle things myself."

Noah and Alex finished their knots and shoved their captives roughly forward. It quickly became clear to Ethan that neither he nor Juniper would be able to wrestle themselves away from Noah and Alex; both boys were tall and well built, and they were fueled by a malice that swelled above them like a storm cloud. He glanced back toward Gus's house, just visible a ways down the lake, but all the lights were out.

"Keep it moving," Noah barked, digging his knee into Ethan's shin. Unable to speak, he stumbled forward, nearly collapsing onto the sand.

All Ethan could think about was Cole Parker, hanging dead from a tree because he'd crossed a line that shouldn't have existed in the first place. Ethan had hardly done more than dare to breathe the same air as Noah O'Neil, but if he suffered the same fate, no one in Ellison would give a damn.

Except Juniper Jones, who, at this moment, was glaring unblinkingly at Alex as he hustled her along. Her stare seemed to make him uncomfortable, and he pointedly set his jaw and averted his eyes.

"Freak," he muttered under his breath. They continued away from Gus's house to where the lake curved slightly around a bend, until the beach gave way to grass and the forest closed in on the water's edge. They were far from the docks; here, rocks rose jaggedly from the water.

Noah and Alex stopped out of sight of the main beach, in a quiet inlet where the willows grew low on the shore. Ethan caught sight of a small wooden boat tethered to one of the trunks. He squinted at Noah, trying to determine how dire this was going to get, but the blond just leered at him. When he smiled like that, with all his teeth, he looked more shark than human.

"Get ready, Alex," Noah ordered, pointing to the boat. Dutifully, Alex stepped into the water in his jeans and tennis shoes, untying the boat and pushing it against the shore. Noah herded Ethan and Juniper into the craft and forced them to sit on the floor at the bow, facing each other. When their eyes met, Ethan's heart sank to see the fear in Juniper's eyes. He knew the same must be mirrored in his own.

"All right, freaks," Noah said, jumping roughly into the stern of the boat so that it shook. "Let's go."

"Got the oars." Alex climbed onto the center bench with one oar in each hand. He fitted them into the oarlocks and, with a hefty swing, began to row away from the shore.

"Hang on tight," he jeered.

Ethan shifted, trying to bring the feeling back into his arms. He was sitting with his legs pulled tightly up to his chest and his left shoulder was bent behind him at a painful angle. The ropes were chafing against his wrists. His shoulder throbbed and the cloth in his mouth tasted like sweat.

Breathing deeply through his nose, he glanced over at Juniper, who was sitting cross-legged with her head bowed. Only half of her face was illuminated by the moon, and her big blue eyes were filled with tears.

If only they hadn't come out to the lake, Ethan thought.

He was furious with himself—he could have lived without a run, even if he never got back to sleep. If he hadn't been here, he was sure Noah and Alex would have left Juniper alone. He looked at Juniper and tried to apologize with his eyes.

Alex grunted with the effort of rowing as Ethan looked around, hoping for some impossible savior. The lake was empty and dark. By the time they reached the center, and Alex stopped rowing, Ethan had given up hope.

The moon seemed suspended on a string. It should have been beautiful, but where it hung above Noah's head, it looked ominous.

"So, here's the deal," Noah said, standing again. "We're out here in the middle of the lake. You're gagged and bound. We could do anything we want to you right about now. But we're gonna be nice. See, in a few, Alex and I are gonna swim to shore. And you two, well, you're gonna stay out here in this boat until someone finds you. Maybe in the morning, but who knows where the drift will take you."

Noah was still talking, but Ethan had stopped listening. Over Noah and Alex's shoulders, on the other side of the lake, was Gus's house. And a light had just come on.

"Pay attention!" Alex snapped. He slapped an oar against the water, splashing chilly water onto Ethan and Juniper. Juniper shivered, blinking droplets of water out of her eyes.

"What're you staring at, anyway?" Ethan quickly averted his eyes, but it was too late. Noah had turned, rocking the boat back and forth. "Shit," Noah said. "We gotta go, Alex." In Gus's little house, all the lights had come on. Whether or not the man knew something was wrong, it was only a matter of time before he'd see the scene out his window and come to their rescue.

"Shit," Noah repeated, as Ethan thought, *We're saved*. "Alex, go!"

Alex scrambled to his feet, and both boys fumbled with their clothes. They managed to kick off their shirts and shoes, then Gus's front door swung open. Alex and Noah dove over the sides of the boat and into the lake. The force of their movement sent the boat tipping onto its side and then all the way over so that Ethan and Juniper were dumped into the lake.

Ethan let out a strangled gasp as he was hit in the face with a tongue of water, one of the benches catching him on the head. The force of it knocked the gag off his mouth. Beneath the boat, it was completely dark, and the weight of his clothes made it difficult to stay afloat, but he treaded water as best he could and tried to keep his head above the surface. Outside, he heard the sharp cuts of swimmers' strokes growing progressively softer, and then above it—splashing. Juniper.

"Tread!" he shouted, thrashing his arms in an attempt to get out of his bonds. He dunked his head underwater but couldn't tell which way was which—when he surfaced again, he was still beneath the boat.

"I'm trying!" came Juniper's muffled voice. "The ropes—" She fell silent, but Ethan could still hear the sounds of her kicking.

With a furious scream, Ethan strained harder against the ropes, the skin of his wrists crying out in protest. He hit his head on the side of the boat again, but finally, the sloppy knot came loose. Ethan shook his hands free, kicking furiously as he felt around for the end of the boat. Then, from outside, he heard the sound of a motor and the hiss of water being sliced by a motorboat.

"Gus," Ethan whispered, then louder, "I'm coming, Juniper!" He followed the sound of the motor as he dove beneath the surface again. Water flowed into his mouth and he hit his head again on the way up, then he was out at the bow of the boat, the moon above his head. At the very edge of the lake, he could see Noah and Alex just clambering to shore—but he didn't see Juniper anywhere.

Treading furiously, Ethan cried, "*June!*"

His wrists were raw and numb, but Ethan dove forward anyway, slicing through the water as he called her name again and again. He glanced in every direction and couldn't see her, but he called until his throat was sore and continued even then. Gus had nearly reached them now, and as Ethan searched desperately, he pointed to the other end of the boat and cried, "She's there!"

Ethan turned in the water, and sure enough, he saw a flash of blue in the moonlight and then, a spread of orange.

"No," he whispered, swimming quickly toward Juniper's motionless form. She was sinking, but Ethan caught hold of her shirt and pulled her toward him, gathering her to his chest as he swam, one armed, to Gus's motorboat.

"Hold on," he shouted at her, trying to keep her head above water. "Please, hold on!"

"Here, here, I got her!" The older man reached over the edge to pull Juniper into the boat, and Ethan clambered in after them. His hair was flattened into his eyes and his clothes were soaked, but he didn't notice. All he could see was Juniper, splayed out on the deck of the boat, eyes closed and lips blue. Gus knelt beside her, pushing at her chest and shouting curses and prayers to the sky.

"Please," Ethan breathed. "Please." After what felt like hours, Gus leaned back from Juniper's soaked body, turning to Ethan with haunted eyes. The whole world seemed to tilt then, as if Ethan was underwater all over again. He pushed past Gus, hearing the man's words through a fog as he crawled toward Juniper and took her by the shoulders, shaking her.

"Wake up!" he screamed. Gus was shouting something at him, and the boat began to move, but Ethan couldn't understand the words. He could hardly even see. His vision was tunneling and all he could register was Juniper's face in front of him, cold and still.

He shook her again and still she did not move. The boat rocketed toward the shore. He let out a primal shriek. "No, Juniper. You can't—you can't. No. Please—" His words dissolved into sobs and his entire body shook with them. Juniper had always been a hurricane, but now Ethan felt like a natural disaster slipping across the deck of Gus's boat. They had made it to shore. Gus leapt out to pull Juniper from the boat, but Ethan held her tight.

"Please," he whispered, pressing his head against her chest, where her heartbeat should have been. Nothing. He laid his ear against her mouth and felt no breath. All he could think was that she was supposed to be invincible.

TWENTY-TWO

Everything after was a blur. There were a few things Ethan knew for sure: he remembered that Gus got him out of the boat and handed him a blanket. He sat on the dock, shivering, and after some time, he heard sirens in the distance. Maybe he watched as the paramedics lifted Juniper onto a stretcher and rolled her into the ambulance—all he remembered were the lights, red and blue. He remembered hearing Gus's gruff voice talking to a policeman, and then the officer came to talk to him too. Ethan knew he spoke, but couldn't remember what he said.

When the police and paramedics left, it was just Ethan and Gus, alone on the dock. Gus barely seemed to be holding himself up. He asked Ethan if he wanted to go inside and Ethan shook his head. He remembered, very clearly, staring out at the lake then, and seeing that the water was still. Apart from the overturned boat still floating in the center, there was no sign of what had happened at all.

Ethan remembered that at some point Uncle Robert came.

Later, Ethan would learn that it was only minutes later, but it felt like days that he sat there on the dock, staring out at the lake and feeling as if he was being stabbed in the chest again and again. Uncle Robert said nothing about Ethan sneaking out. He just stepped onto the dock and pulled Ethan close, wet clothes and all, and said, "Let's go home."

The next thing he remembered after that was what he wished, and would wish for the rest of his life, that he could forget. He was sitting in Aunt Cara's kitchen, shell shocked but dry, staring into a cup of hot chocolate, when the phone rang. It was Gus calling from the hospital, where he had followed in his car after Ethan and Uncle Robert had gone. Aunt Cara answered, her face twisted in pain. When Ethan saw her stagger into the arm of the couch, he knew for sure.

"This can't be real," he said out loud, even as a voice in his head said *It is, it is, it is*. This wasn't supposed to happen, especially not to the most alive person he knew. But the way his heart constricted, he knew that it was true.

"I'm so sorry, Ethan," Aunt Cara said, coming into the kitchen with Uncle Robert a moment later. Tears streamed freely down both their faces. Ethan found that he wasn't crying, but everything felt like it was in slow motion. When his aunt and uncle moved in to hold him close, he could barely feel their touch.

For years after, when Ethan dreamt of this night, this was the way things played out. The blanket, the paramedics, the lake, Uncle Robert, Aunt Cara, the news. And it always ended the same way too: with a baby. Because the next day, in some cruel miracle, Ethan's cousin was born.

✶

It was nearly noon, but Ethan hadn't been able to get out of bed. His dad was supposed to be arriving tomorrow—he couldn't even think about it. He could hardly think of anything. He lay beneath the covers in silence, staring at the ceiling, thinking every now and then that he heard Juniper tapping at his window. It wasn't, of course. He'd never hear that sound, that way, again.

As the sun emerged from behind the clouds to shine bright through his window, he heard the tapping again. "Stop!" he cried to his window, pulling his pillow over his face. "Please."

"Ethan?" came Uncle Robert's voice from the hall. Ethan peered out from under the pillow as his uncle opened the door. He looked haggard and exhausted, wearing wrinkled clothes and with dark circles under his eyes. But there was an urgency in his voice that surprised Ethan. "We have to go," he said. "Your aunt's in labor."

"Oh," Ethan said. He couldn't feel excited—only numb. He didn't move. "Can't I just stay here?"

"I'm sorry, son. I know. But after last night—"

The pain washed over both of them and Uncle Robert winced. Ethan squeezed his eyes shut.

"Okay," he whispered. "I'm coming."

When he stood, his legs barely knew how to hold him. He stumbled across the room and into the hall, where Uncle Robert was helping Aunt Cara to the front door. Ethan followed them, his limbs feeling heavier by the second.

"Hi, sweetie," Aunt Cara said, her breath coming in spurts. "Your cousin's on his way."

Ethan stared at his aunt's stomach as his uncle helped her into the pickup truck. He tried to imagine a baby in there, coming out into the world crying, kicking its tiny feet, but couldn't. For all the movement happening around him, he couldn't see anything but stillness.

Uncle Robert sped to the hospital with Aunt Cara in the middle seat, taking deep breaths. Ethan stared out the window, watching the town blur past, and remembered when Juniper had sat in this very spot not so long ago. And there was his chest again, caving in.

They arrived in record time, Uncle Robert and Ethan both helping Aunt Cara from the car in the parking lot. At the hospital doors, Uncle Robert half carried Aunt Cara through without hesitation, but Ethan, noticing a sign above them, stopped. WHITE ENTRANCE, it said simply.

"Ethan!" Uncle Robert called from just inside, and Ethan gestured helplessly at the sign.

"It says I can't—"

"I don't give a damn what it says, just get in here." And he said it so fiercely that Ethan didn't hesitate another second, just pushed through the door that was like any other door and took up his spot supporting Aunt Cara's left arm. Once inside, no one seemed to notice him. His aunt was whisked away in a flurry of doctors and nurses, his uncle following, and Ethan was left standing in the empty waiting room, staring at the tile. He shuffled over to the hard metal seats, where only a couple of other people sat. They looked at him hard as he approached; he couldn't bring himself to care.

Uncle Robert came down after a while, his cheeks flushed. "She's in her room," he said. "Now just got to wait." Ethan nodded. "How are you doing?" Ethan shrugged. "Yeah. Well, I'm going to grab some chips from the vending machine. You want anything?" Ethan shook his head.

When Uncle Robert disappeared back around the corner, it occurred to Ethan that this was likely the hospital where

Juniper had been taken the night before. Maybe down that hallway, in one of those rooms, was where doctors had looked at her and realized they couldn't save her. And for the first time since it happened, the pain rushed up from his chest and into his face, and Ethan began to cry. His shoulders shook and he folded himself in half, face pressed against his knees. He wailed—he felt that no matter how loud he might scream, nothing could capture his anguish. He wanted to climb out of his own skin, squeeze the memories out of his brain, shrink to a pinprick, and then disappear.

Instead, he sat there, sobbing, and feeling no better for it. He didn't stop when he felt the other people in the waiting room staring at him, or when a nurse came over and asked, tentatively, if he was okay—and then came back a few minutes later to ask if he could please quiet down. He didn't do that either. He cried until no more sounds or tears came out. Until no more could. Then he sat on that cold metal seat, shaking, until Uncle Robert came bursting back into the room several minutes later.

Ethan knew what a mess he looked, his face red and smeared with snot, the front of his shirt entirely damp. He saw Uncle Robert notice this and slow down, his face softening. He reached out a rough hand to cup the side of Ethan's head. "Whatever you need to do, son," he said. Ethan leaned into his touch, squeezing his eyes shut. A few stray tears slipped out.

They sat in silence for a long time—hours, according to the clock on the wall. Uncle Robert dozed, snoring occasionally, but Ethan stayed wide awake. He counted the tiles on the floor to distract himself. Eventually, a nurse approached, waking Uncle Robert with a tap on the shoulder. She whispered something to him and he stood quickly, casting Ethan a brief glance before following her into the hall.

Ethan hardly registered his uncle's departure. He just kept counting, starting over at even the slightest mistake. When at last Uncle Robert returned, wide eyed and red faced, Ethan had just reached seventy-four.

"Hey," Uncle Robert breathed, sitting down beside him.

"Hi," Ethan replied hollowly.

Uncle Robert sat there for a moment, elbows on his knees, staring at the nurses' station across the room. There was something wild in his eyes, like mixed panic and wonder. Finally, he took a breath.

"Ethan," Uncle Robert said. "You don't have to right away, but—do you want to meet your cousin?"

Eyes closed, Ethan nodded. Uncle Robert helped him out of his seat and they made their way across the waiting room to the big double doors. Behind them was a long, white hallway, lined with doors on either side. They followed the signs marked DELIVERY. Uncle Robert was walking fast and Ethan stumbled to catch up.

"Excuse me!" a voice called as they rounded the corner to the delivery wing. Ethan and his uncle turned to see a doctor, all in white. "Sorry," he said, "but the delivery room is whites only. Hospital policy."

Ethan was surprised to see Uncle Robert's lip curl into a sneer. He stepped up to the doctor, getting right into the man's face. "This boy right here," he said, stabbing a finger in Ethan's direction, "is family. And our family has been through hell and back these past twenty-four hours. So I'm going to take him to meet his baby cousin—hospital policy be damned."

The doctor looked at him in shock and Uncle Robert didn't wait for a response. He grabbed Ethan by the hand and pulled him into the delivery wing and up to Aunt Cara's room. Inside, the nurses looked at Ethan in shock, but one glare from Uncle Robert and they looked pointedly away.

"Ethan," Aunt Cara said breathlessly. Her face was flushed, but she wore a clean hospital gown and her hair had been pulled back from her face. While her eyes were filled with tears, she wore an electrifying smile. "Do you want to meet him?"

Ethan crept carefully forward, looking down at the baby swaddled in his aunt's arms. The baby's eyes were closed, his little face red and fists clutched tight. "Hi," Ethan whispered, leaning down to see him closer. He couldn't believe anyone could be so small. The baby cooed softly.

"What's his name?" Ethan asked.

His aunt and uncle looked at each other with sad smiles. "Henry," Uncle Robert said. "Henry Juniper Shay."

Ethan looked down at the baby boy and felt his heart break in two.

"We were thinking about doing it anyway," Aunt Cara said. "But after last night—"

Ethan nodded. "She would have loved it." And he knew she would have. She would have shrieked at the sight of this tiny creature, almost small enough to hold in one hand. *By gosh,* she would have said, *he's the cutest baby I've ever seen. I mean, I haven't seen many babies. But I just* know *—Henry is the cutest.*

Ethan laughed at the thought, but it petered off into a strangled sob. At the sound, baby Henry suddenly opened his eyes, staring straight up at his older cousin. Ethan started. Henry looked at him, quiet and strangely calm, as if they were old friends. His eyes, big and heavy lashed, were blue.

TWENTY-THREE

His heart throbbing in his chest, Ethan trekked through the forest. He was making the trip that he and Juniper had never finished—the trip to her secret cove. He had left his bike at his aunt and uncle's house, because this time, he felt he needed to take it all in. He was leaving this afternoon, after all. It was his last day in this forest for the summer, and, he had decided, his last day for a long, long while. Once he left Ellison, he didn't know if he could ever come back.

His parents were at his aunt and uncle's house—his mom had made the drive down that morning, the soonest she could come after Uncle Robert had called to tell her what had happened. His dad had been in town for four days now, this time sticking around for more than a Coke and a quick hello.

When Ethan's mom had arrived, she and his father shared tense greetings, not meeting each other's eyes. Thankfully, Henry, brought home from the hospital just a couple of days before, was a welcome distraction. They both doted over the baby, which kept an easy peace. Still, as soon as the breakfast conversations were done, Ethan had slipped outside. He knew they were probably sitting around the kitchen table now in uncomfortable silence, but he tried to put that image out of his mind.

It wasn't hard. He pushed through the trees and into the secret cove — and there, all he could think of was Juniper. He fell to his knees beside the brook, his legs no longer able to hold him. His stomach twisted with longing and regret, and he squeezed his eyes shut. He reached out an arm and trailed it through the running water, thinking about how he had lain there all those weeks ago, watching Juniper paint.

She had been a whirlwind of movement, a paintbrush in each hand and a rainbow across her face — he remembered how she'd laughed for no reason other than that she was alive. Had been alive. His heart ached as he stared up at the canopy of trees, the patches of blue through the green. At her funeral the previous morning, he had been ill at the thought of her lying in the coffin, motionless — she was, by nature, never still. That feeling hadn't gone away.

Juniper's funeral had been a small affair, and Ethan resented it. She deserved a marching band, a ticker-tape parade, and a guest appearance by Elvis Presley. But Ellison, Alabama, didn't care about the strange girl who lived in a house in the woods, so there were seven people in attendance: Ethan, Gus, Cara, Robert, Henry, Abrams, and Juniper's aunt, Annabelle.

The latter was a wreck through the whole thing, standing between Abrams and Gus and sobbing loudly into her thick black veil. She couldn't even look at the casket.

"Poor woman," Aunt Cara remarked as they followed the short procession into the cemetery. "We'll have to find someone to take care of her."

Ethan, dressed in a suit borrowed from Uncle Robert that was two sizes too big, had sworn that he wouldn't lose his composure. He told himself that Juniper wouldn't want him to cry. Even after everything, and even through his pain, she would have wanted him to celebrate her.

But when they lowered the casket into the ground, he fell to his knees beside the grave and wailed.

Two men from the church filled the hole with dirt and Ethan wanted to tell them to stop, because she couldn't be dead, could she? She was in there, wondering what in the world was going on, and they were burying her alive. He waited to hear her cries, her fists banging against the lid, but there was nothing. Just Ethan's sobs, competing in volume with Aunt Annabelle's, and the sound of soil hitting wood.

When it was over, Uncle Robert put an arm around Annabelle and led her away from the grave. Aunt Cara stepped beside Ethan, who was still kneeling at the edge of the plot, and squeezed his shoulder.

"We're going to take Anna back home," she said, rocking Harry Juniper Shay in one arm. The baby blinked at Ethan. "Do you want to come?"

"Can I meet you guys at the house?" he whispered. "I just need some time."

"Of course, sweetie. Take as long as you need."

When she walked away to join Uncle Robert at the car, Ethan looked at the top of the grave, where the headstone would eventually sit. He had chosen the inscription himself. It would read IN MEMORY OF JUNIPER STARFISH JONES. ADVENTURER, NIECE, AND BEST FRIEND.

The finality of it all made his stomach churn.

With a shuddering breath, Ethan pushed himself to his feet and turned away from the grave. Gus was standing a few feet behind him, sporting a few days of stubble and a dusty old suit.

"Real sad," he said, even now a man of very few words. He stood with shoulders raised and fists clenched, but Ethan could see the tears pooling in his eyes.

"Yeah," he agreed. "Real sad."

Gus—tough, kind old Gus—clapped a gentle hand on Ethan's shoulder and stared at the freshly planted grave. "Awful, is what I mean. Terrible." He shrugged as if to ask, what more can I say? "Gonna miss her."

Ethan nodded, feeling new dampness on his cheeks. "Me too."

"You know." Gus sighed. "I know you didn't look at the casket, but they put her in her favorite dress. That yellow one, you know, with the polka dots. And they put a sunflower in her hair."

"Good," Ethan managed to murmur. "She would've wanted that, I think."

Gus dipped his head in agreement, then, unexpectedly, pulled Ethan into a tight embrace. "Anyway," he mumbled gruffly, turning away. "I'll leave you to it."

Juniper's grave was atop a small hill in the center of the cemetery, and Ethan watched Gus descend it with some difficulty. Meanwhile, Abrams was climbing back up, and the two men nodded as they passed each other.

Ethan had been surprised to see Abrams here—the man hardly seemed to leave his store. "Hi, Abrams," he said as the man approached.

"Hello, Ethan," Abrams replied, stroking his beard. "This is tragic, it really is. Juniper was one of my best vendors."

Ethan muttered, "Yeah, well, she was my best *friend*."

"Oh, don't get me wrong"—Abrams waved a hand in the

air—"she was a wonderful girl. Had the heart and wisdom of a child." He smiled, and for once it reached his eyes. "A wonderful girl, yes. And also wonderful at supplying fresh-cut flowers, as it were."

Ethan rolled his eyes.

After a moment of silence, Abrams continued, saying, "I hear the police went knocking on Noah O'Neil's door yesterday morning. Threw his mother into a fit, which I appreciate. Never met such an irritating woman in my life." Ethan, who had not heard this, raised an eyebrow. "Anyway, they questioned him, and that Alex kid as well. Everyone knows what they did. Not that it matters, of course."

Ethan felt his body tense at the thought of Noah and Alex. "Why not?"

"Ethan, don't be a fool. They're two young white boys from well-known families in town, and their victims were you, a half-Negro boy, and Juniper, the town loony. Even if the case makes it to court, which I doubt it will, they'll never be convicted. The whole thing will be written off as a terrible accident, and they'll go free."

"Whatever," Ethan snapped. He turned away from Juniper's grave and pushed past Abrams. His tears were gone now, replaced by fire. "See you around."

"Ethan," Abrams said, grabbing the boy's arm as he passed. Ethan glared over his shoulder, hot coals in his eyes. Abrams stared right back.

"Those pigs won't ever end up in jail," he said. "But that doesn't mean they don't deserve it. And the guilt of what they did will eat them alive until the day they die."

They do deserve it, Ethan thought now, pushing himself into a sitting position next to the brook. In his mind, they deserved to rot in prison for the rest of their lives. But in his heart, he knew that Juniper would not have felt the same way.

I know they're terrible, she would have said, *but I want to believe that they could become better. No one can be all bad, right?*

And Ethan would have shrugged, not agreeing with her but listening as she described, in elaborate fashion, her ten-part plan to fix them.

Add it to the list, she'd say.

Ethan shook his head, wishing, as he often had these past few days, that she were here.

Sighing heavily, he reached for a stone along the bank and skipped in across the brook. He wondered, picking up another stone, where Noah and Alex were. Probably in their houses, waiting for a trial and a guilty verdict that would never come.

He wondered, too, where Courtney was; he'd been thinking about her. He'd seen her just a few hours before, when he'd visited Juniper's grave, and he still wasn't sure why.

The late-August sun had been high in the sky as Ethan returned to the cemetery. He rode his bike to the church and left it leaning against the front steps. He took the small envelope and watering can from his basket and circled the building to the cemetery.

When he reached Juniper's grave, he dropped to his knees beside it and carefully opened the envelope. Soon grass would grow, but for now there was only fertilized soil. It was the perfect time.

He did it exactly as Juniper had taught him: he dragged his hand through the dirt, making three long rows; he shook the sunflower seeds carefully out of the envelope until they were all gone, then he covered them with dirt; he lifted the watering can and tipped it over, letting a gentle stream of water pour out.

When he was done, he stood up, brushed the dirt off his pants, and nodded. "There you go, June," he said. "Soon you'll have a garden." He was just turning to go when he saw a girl ascending the slope. His heart raced.

But squinting against the sun, Ethan realized that it was Courtney, her head bowed and a bouquet of seven pink roses in her fists. She stared down at the flowers and didn't seem to notice him.

"Sunflowers," Ethan said, as she approached. Courtney looked up quickly, a hand rising to her chest; when recognition registered in her eyes, she did not look at all relieved.

"Sorry?" she squeaked.

Ethan shook his head, suddenly wishing he hadn't spoken because now there was an ocean rising in his chest. "Sunflowers," he repeated softly. "Her favorite flowers are sunflowers."

"Oh." Courtney shifted uncomfortably. "I just grabbed the first ones I saw at the store, so . . ."

Her light hair, pulled into a bun, left her face bare, and etched into her features Ethan saw only sadness. Her eyes were puffy, her lips were chapped, and red splotches marred her cheeks. As Ethan watched, she moved awkwardly to the grave and laid down all the roses except one. She seemed to be holding back a sob. Perhaps he should have been angry; this grief was not hers to feel. Instead, Ethan felt only pity.

"She'd love them anyway," he said, for some reason wanting to ease her anguish. "She loved all flowers."

In response, Courtney flashed the slightest smile of gratitude—but it became a frown almost instantly. She opened her mouth to speak, her bottom lip trembling.

"I talked to Noah and Alex. They didn't realize—or, well, they didn't know . . . they thought she could swim," she finished emptily. "They didn't mean for her to, well. To die." She squeaked out the last word like a curse.

Ethan blinked at her. "That doesn't change the fact that it happened," he said. She nodded, agreeing, but didn't turn to leave.

There was something else; he could see it in her eyes. She swallowed hard, and he waited.

"I'm sorry," she said eventually, though the hollowness of her words made it clear that they were not the ones she wanted to say. "I know it's not my place, and I know that it will never be enough, but I am. I'm sorry."

And before Ethan could respond, she turned and hurried away through the cemetery.

Perhaps he should have let her go, but something urged him to follow her down the hill and through the gravestones. The cemetery wasn't large, and it wasn't long before, from several yards away, Ethan saw Courtney stop at a small grave near the edge of the forest and carefully place the last rose in front of the headstone. Straightening, she glanced quickly left and right and did not seem surprised to find Ethan standing there, watching her. Instead of speaking, she simply let out a breath that it seemed she had been holding for years and hurried away into the trees.

Once she had gone, Ethan walked slowly to the grave. The stone was small and unevenly cut, not nearly as elaborate as some of the others. The name looked as if it had been etched with a set of keys, and his heart sank for the boy who lay beneath the earth. Courtney's fresh rose seemed out of place beneath the jagged, familiar letters. Cole Parker.

He frowned at the grave, wondering why—and wondering, too, if there might be something good inside Courtney, after all.

Juniper would have loved that. Ethan knew she'd never really hated Courtney. The girl was friends with terrible people, but she'd left flowers for June—and for Cole.

The thought of them both, two people in Ellison who'd died far too young, made Ethan shake with anger. He hadn't known Cole, but he knew that the boy hadn't deserved to die. And Juniper, well, she deserved to live forever.

Now, in the clearing, Ethan was on his feet and seeing red. He kicked at the grass, leaving a brown smear across his sneakers. He kicked at the water, spraying the bank and himself. And then he screamed. Loudly, angrily, he screamed for Juniper and for Cole and for the girl arrested on the bus and for himself, because none of them deserved the cards they'd been dealt. He emptied his lungs of air and his voice of sound as he stomped blindly around the cove, kicking at the ground. This anger had been building all summer, and now that it was out, he felt like he could tear down the entire forest with his bare hands.

When the anger at last subsided, Ethan found himself standing in front of the largest hollow, his and Juniper's hiding place. The home of fairies, like in the very first painting she'd shown him. Choking back a sob, he crawled inside.

It was dark and cool in here, and Ethan sat cross-legged. If he focused, he could remember what it felt like to sit in here with Juniper, her knees against his, breathing together. As he stared up into the tree's hollow trunk, the light shifted, sun suddenly coming through a hole in the bark somewhere above him. Immediately, his hiding place was illuminated.

And all around him, he saw color.

I have something to show you, she'd said that night. *A piece I've been working on.*

This must have been what she meant, Ethan realized,

craning his neck to take it all in. All around him, painted straight onto the wood, were dozens of images. A redheaded girl drinking a vanilla milk shake; a dark-skinned boy running through the trees. A movie theater, a jukebox, fireworks. Ethan and Juniper on the lake, on Aunt Cara's couch, rolling down Alligator Hill.

She had painted their summer.

Ethan stared at it all, trying to memorize every single last brushstroke. Tears flowed freely down his face. In the center, right where their bucket list was still taped to the bark, were a few simple words.

To E. from J. Thank you for everything.

*

"She was my best friend," Ethan had said of Juniper, when his parents asked. Before they'd eaten breakfast that morning, Uncle Robert and Aunt Cara had been out of the room changing Henry and it was just Ethan and his parents. They hadn't sat around a table like this in years.

His father asked him, awkwardly, if he was okay. His mother told him, emphatically, that he didn't need to be. He sensed a fight brewing and looked desperately between.

"Please don't," he said. "Not now."

Chastened, his parents looked down at the table. Then, after a moment, his dad said, "Tell us about her."

Ethan had opened his mouth to respond, but realized it was an incredibly difficult question. There were so many things he could say about Juniper Jones—that she loved dancing to Elvis, that she had the best green thumb of everyone he'd ever known, that her heart was probably the size of the entire world—but none of them seemed like enough.

So: "She was my best friend," he began. He told them about their invincible summer. About meeting her in the malt shop that day, rowing at the lake, climbing the tallest tree in Alabama, planting a garden, going to Montgomery. His mom nodded, tears in her eyes, remembering her brief evening with Juniper. He told them about Juniper's compassion and patience and kindness; how she stood up for him and cared for him and saw the good in him even when no one else did. And he told them how, with every last fiber in her being, she wanted things to change.

"She's the reason," he had finished. He'd looked at his parents across the table, at the covered breakfast plates between them. "The whole reason I made it through this summer. She showed me that people can be good and there can be hope, even when it hurts."

And it was true, he thought now, taking one last look at the painted hollow as the sun moved again and eased him back into darkness. The images were seared into his memory, and would be forever. When he closed his eyes, he saw only color.

Ethan suddenly realized that he was crying, but for the first time since that night on the lake, he wasn't consumed by sorrow. He pressed a hand to his lips and his shoulders shook and tears ran down his cheeks, but he was also laughing, because Juniper was *here*. He felt her presence here, in this tiny cove, in this painted tree trunk, in the forest air. The brook babbled, and in the trickling sound, he swore he heard her laughter.

"I'll never stop missing you, Starfish," he promised, staring up into the hollow. He imagined her in here when the light was just right, painting furiously with a brush in each hand. "Never ever in my whole life." He was certain that she could hear every word. As an afterthought, he added, softly, "But thank you. This summer really was invincible."

Finally, he felt that he could leave. He had bags to load and a floor to sweep and a chicken sandwich to scarf down before he got into his dad's car for five days of driving. He had good-byes to say to his mom, who'd promised she would visit soon. He had a conversation to stumble through with his father about all the things he didn't understand about Ethan, and needed to. But he felt like he could do that now.

And so, with a deep breath, Ethan slipped out of the hollow. He gave it one last glance, seeing Juniper everywhere he looked. And then he ran. Over the brook, through the forest, past the lake, down the path—he ran. When Aunt Cara's house came into view down the road, he slowed to a stop, resting his hands on his knees. Juniper's smile burned behind his eyes as he turned and surveyed the cloud of dirt behind him. It lingered in the air for a moment, then, like a sigh, settled gently back down to the earth. All was still.

June 2015

In many ways, Ellison, Alabama has changed. The roads are paved, for one thing, and the population has risen to just over seventeen thousand. Downtown has more than one intersection and features both a McDonald's and a Starbucks. On the lake, a company rents out kayaks and paddleboards to summer tourists—because now there are tourists. Uncle Robert and Aunt Cara's house is different too: when they died, Ethan's cousin Henry moved in with his wife, Hannah, and they completely redecorated. Now, there's a sixty-four inch flat screen and stainless steel kitchen appliances.

The church, though, is just as Ethan remembers it: small, house shaped, and white, with a clapboard roof and a simple steeple topped with a cross. He arrives at the funeral several minutes late and sits in a pew near the back just as a man steps up to the podium and begins a eulogy. Ethan half listens, all the while keeping his eyes on the closed casket in front of the altar, which is topped by an elaborate flower arrangement and pictures of the deceased. It makes his heart contract. This is not a grand funeral by any means; it seems that most of the attendees are townspeople who hardly knew the man in the casket, and even the pastor looks disinterested. But it is far better than what Juniper had received.

"You don't have to go," were Henry's first words when he opened his front door and found his cousin standing on the porch, suitcase in hand. "You don't owe him anything."

Ethan replied, "I know." And smiled. "It's difficult to explain, but it's something I need to do."

He still feels that now, as the service ends and he rises on shaky legs. A lot was left unfinished sixty years ago. He watches as six men carry the casket down the nave and out the front doors. People begin to spill from the pews to join the procession, but Ethan lingers for a moment, watching them pass. A few do a double take when they see him, surprised even now by the shade of his skin. But then they just look away.

It's not that everything is fixed now—not here in Ellison, or at home in Arcadia, or anywhere else in the world. But it's better in so many ways, and always changing. And the fight that Ethan's mother instilled in him at her kitchen table all those years ago is the same fight he found in his wife, Eleanor, and the same that they passed down to their children, and then their grandchildren. The revolution is a fire set to burn for generations. Ethan feels this fire even now, as he follows the slow procession and his knees groan in protest. He can hardly believe that once he ran through this town with ease.

"Gets harder every year, doesn't it?" someone jokes, and it takes Ethan a moment to realize that the comment is directed at him. He looks up to see a woman with short gray hair and brown eyes set into wrinkled cheeks. She grips the arm of a middle-aged man in one hand and a handkerchief in the other—as Ethan examines her face, she dabs delicately at the corners of her eyes.

Rather than responding, Ethan tilts his head and frowns curiously at her. "Are you his wife?" he asks.

"Ex-wife," she corrects, smiling wryly. "We split up decades ago. This is our son, Robin." The man, who has his father's blond hair but not his beady eyes, murmurs a polite greeting.

"Nice to meet you." Ethan nods at them both. He continues walking, realizing only when the woman stares at him that he hasn't explained his own reason for being here. He purses his lips and says, after a pause, "I knew him in high school. I haven't seen him in sixty years."

It is enough of an answer for the woman and her son, and they say nothing more.

When they reach the grave, Ethan remains at the edge of the crowd and watches silently as the casket is lowered into the earth. There are few tears shed: no woman rushes forward, gasping for breath as her husband is put to rest; no grown children kneel beside the grave and wail a final good-bye to their father. Noah O'Neil's burial is grossly starved for love.

And though he has every reason not to, Ethan feels the slightest bit of pity for this man who, after seventy-seven years of life, was only human enough to earn some halfhearted eulogies and a few bouquets left on his grave. Juniper would have felt sorry for him. But then again, Juniper would have been here if not for him.

The last scoop of dirt is shoveled onto the grave, and, one by one, the apathetic mourners pay their final respects. Noah's ex-wife is one of the last people to walk back to the church, and she nods at Ethan as she passes. He remains where he is. Just as he did sixty years ago, he lingers beside the freshly dug grave. And just as she did sixty years ago, a woman passes the stragglers and makes her way toward Ethan. This time, he is expecting her. She is much older now—they both are—but her face is still familiar. There are no pink roses in her hands.

"Hi, Courtney," Ethan says. She looks tired; her shoulders slump beneath her black shawl and her gray-brown hair hangs limp around her face. Wire-framed glasses perch on her nose.

Still, she manages to smile.

"It's been a long time," she says. "I wasn't sure you'd come."

Ethan looks long and hard at the grave, letting himself accept that the monster who killed his best friend is finally gone. "Maybe I shouldn't have," he murmurs eventually. "But I think I needed to see this through."

Courtney nods. "Yeah. So did I." She sighs and steps next to Ethan, her eyes on the engraving. "It's so strange that he's gone," she says. "I haven't seen him in ten years, you know—not since our fiftieth high school reunion—and when I got the invitation to the funeral, I almost wanted to ignore it. But I knew I couldn't, there's too much history. And I thought you'd want to know too." She glances up at him, squinting slightly. "But, like I said, I wasn't sure you'd come."

Ethan says nothing. He looks away from Noah's grave and up the hill. Courtney's gaze follows his.

"I know it doesn't change anything," she says softly, "but he regretted it every day of his life. The doctors said it was a heart attack, but I think it was the guilt that killed him, in the end."

"Good," Ethan says, then sighs. "I came here thinking I might be able to forgive him. I don't think I can."

"I don't think you have to. Noah died a better man than

he was when you knew him, but that's not saying much. It doesn't excuse the things he did or said back then."

Ethan nods. For a long moment both are silent. Ethan wonders if Courtney, too, is thinking about that summer sixty years before.

Eventually, she takes a deep breath and tells him, "There are two reasons I told you about the funeral. The first was closure. The second was because, well — all those years ago there was something I wanted to tell you, but I was too scared."

Ethan glances at her, and for a moment he sees the seventeen-year-old Courtney, with her bright eyes and high ponytail, who watched uncomfortably as Noah harassed Ethan all those years ago.

"Noah said he told you about Cole Parker," she continues. "How he was a black boy who had a relationship with a white girl in town and ended up — ended up lynched in the woods. And maybe you guessed this already, when you saw me leaving flowers at his grave, if you even remember that day" — Ethan does — "but I was that girl. And no matter what anyone says, he didn't trick me into anything. I cared about him, and I knew everyone would think it was wrong, but I didn't give a damn."

When she says the words, it's as if she grows three inches: her back is straight and her jaw is set. Ethan did wonder, once, if she had been the girl, but he hasn't thought about it in years. The thought of it doesn't surprise him, but her honesty does.

"Noah and Alex didn't know it was me. No one did, besides my family. All anyone knew was that a nice white girl in town was tricked into sleeping with a black boy, and that was enough for them to think he deserved to die. My father covered it all up — he swore Noah's uncle and the other Klan members to secrecy.

"Afterward, he even insisted that I date Noah. He said no one could ever be suspicious if I was dating someone like Noah O'Neil." She smiles, wryly. "I broke up with him at the end of that summer, right after you left. Best decision I ever made."

Ethan shifts from foot to foot to keep the blood flowing in his legs as Courtney closes her eyes for several seconds. "I've been keeping that secret almost my whole life."

"Courtney," he begins, because he doesn't know what else to say.

She shakes her head to cut him off. "I know you're probably wondering why the hell I'm telling you this sixty years later. I promise, I'm not trying to make you think better of me. I was — and still am — on your side, but when I was young, I was a coward. I was too afraid of what the townspeople would think to stand up for what I knew was right, and that was wrong. I was part of everything that happened to you too. If you hate me, that's fine." She smiles slightly, then goes on, "Anyway. I'm telling you this because, for a long time after Cole died, I blamed myself for what had happened. I convinced myself that his death was all my fault. It took me decades to realize that wasn't true."

With troubled eyes, Courtney examines the line between grass and dirt on Noah's grave. "And I know you feel the same way about June. When I saw you that day, I could tell you were blaming yourself. Even now, I see it. You know that it was Noah's fault, but you hate yourself for it all the same."

Ethan turns to her sharply, startled because he knows that she is right. For sixty years he has been plagued by 'if onlys.' If only he had taught her how to swim. If only they hadn't gone out that night. If only he had never befriended her, maybe she would still be here.

"Sixty years is a long time to live with someone else's guilt," Courtney says quietly, looking Ethan in the eye. "At some point, you just have to let it go. It wasn't your fault. And you shouldn't regret letting people into your life who changed it for the better, even if they didn't stay."

This makes Ethan's heart hammer. He misses Juniper more right now than he has in years.

When the seconds tick past and he says nothing, Courtney turns away. "Anyway," she murmurs, "just wanted to put in my two cents."

She begins to walk away, but Ethan halts her in her tracks with a sharp, "Courtney, wait." She looks back at him, and he softens his voice. "Thank you," he says simply.

"Yeah." She smiles. "I hope it helps." She starts to turn again, then pauses, adding, "And hey—I'm sure you were planning on it already, but you should stop by her grave before you go. The sunflowers grew in beautifully."

*

They did, in fact. It takes Ethan several minutes and a lot of crackling joints to reach the top of the hill, but it's worth it when he sees the rows of tall yellow flowers standing guard over her gravestone.

He touches one of the petals and grins. Juniper would be proud.

Ethan says nothing as he stands there—he's never been one to talk to graves—and marvels at how strange it is that, after all these years, he is finally returning to Juniper Jones. He has spent so many summers without her, thinking that the emptiness would kill him. *People are funny that way*, he muses, examining the fading inscription in the stone. They find it in themselves to pick up and move on after the worst of tragedies. And so has he. Despite it all, people are quite invincible.

Ethan leaves the cemetery sometime later, as the sun brushes the treetops, and there is a lightness in his bones that he hasn't felt in years. He flies out tomorrow morning, back to Arcadia, and he knows that he will most likely never come back. But he doesn't mind. Of course he misses Juniper, but no matter how many miles he puts between himself and Ellison, Alabama, he'll never forget their summer.

Sometimes he dreams about riding his bike through the Ellison he knew in 1955. He stands up on his pedals and coasts down the forest paths, leaving a trail of dust behind him. Juniper is up ahead, biking so quickly that she doesn't seem to be touching the ground. Sunlight filters through the trees and sets her hair on fire. In his dream, he calls her name in a voice that is younger, lighter. She does not stop pedaling, just glances quickly over her shoulder with a wide smile. In her big blue eyes is the promise of an unbeatable adventure.

The end.

Acknowledgments

Thank you, first of all, to the team at Wattpad for this opportunity and all the others over the years. I couldn't have grown up in a better and more supportive writing community. Thank you especially to I-Yana Tucker for believing in this story from day one and being the strongest advocate for me and my writing. Because of you, I always knew Ethan and Juniper would be in good hands.

To my incomparable editor, Kortney Morrow, for reminding me with every draft that the editing process can be as rewarding as it is challenging. Thank you for dedicating so much time and care to this project, for getting to know my characters so well, and giving such valuable insights. I'm so proud of how the story has turned out, and I couldn't have gotten it here without you.

To the wonderful writing teachers and professors I've had over the years, from middle school to college: Gail Nowak, Sara Pearlman, Carlene Shultz, Tom Bailey, Joanna Howard, Meredith Steinbach, Stacy Kastner, Colin Channer, and Lori

Baker, among others. Thank you for teaching me to love writing and reminding me of that love again and again.

To my parents, Gina and Lloyd McQueen—you always said I would be a published author one day. Look, I did it! Thank you for your unwavering encouragement of my writing; I'm so lucky to have parents who support my craziest dreams and aren't surprised when they come true.

And finally, thank you to everyone who has read this story on Wattpad over the years. Thank you for loving it as it was and for spending time with it as it is now. I owe so much of my growth and confidence as a writer to this community, and I will always be grateful.

About the Author

Daven McQueen grew up outside of Los Angeles, California, and graduated from Brown University, where she earned a BA in literary arts and economics. Her works on Wattpad include *December*, *Beautiful Dreamer*, and *Superior*, which received a Watty Award for Science Fiction. When she's not writing, Daven can be found tap dancing, embroidering, cooking, and eating dessert. She lives in Boston, Massachusetts, with her cat, and works in education.

Want more? Why not try . . .

Want more? Why not try . . .

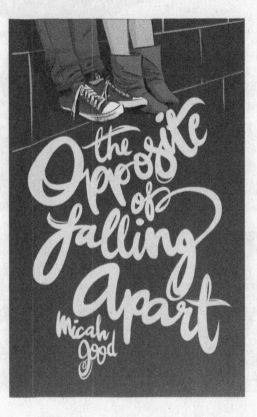

Can Jonas and Brennan help each other
to stop living in the past and start
dreaming about the future?

wattpad

Where stories live.

Discover millions of stories created by diverse writers from around the globe.

Download the app or visit
www.wattpad.com today.

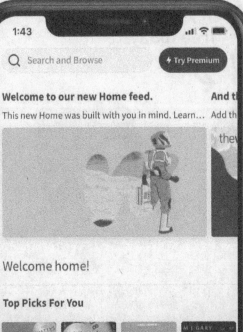

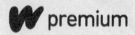